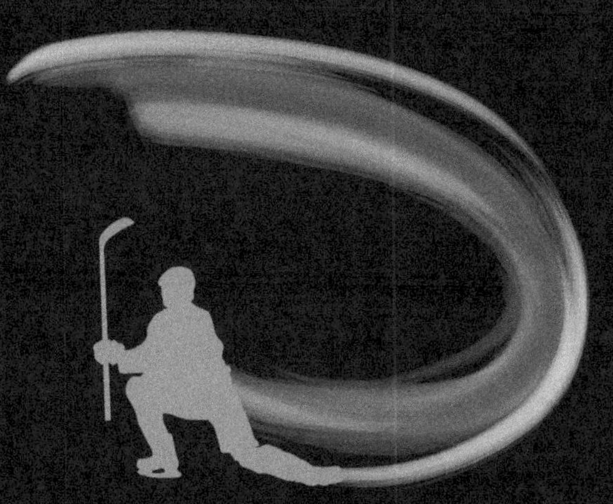

I0778465

THIS IS CRAZY

Zara Stone
All my life, I've said I will never date a hockey player. I know better because I've seen and lived it all. My father is a hockey god, my brother is the captain of the most successful NHL team in the world, and my brother-in-law also plays in the league. Their lives are complicated, so I went in the opposite direction.

I fell in love with a scholar. But instead of proposing marriage, he broke up with me.
Three months later, I saw his engagement picture on Instagram. I couldn't let him get away with that. No, it didn't matter what, I was going to make that man see that I did not need him.

Evan
I was in the running to pass my point record from last year, ready to claim the number one spot in the league. On top of my game, I was riding my career high wave.

Then, Hockey's Princess, Zara Stone tweeted me. She wanted me to crash her ex's wedding.

The worst that could happen? A PR nightmare. The best? A fun night with a beautiful woman.
It started out as a game—something I'm good at. Her crazy idea twisted into something I wasn't looking for, something neither of us wanted.

When push comes to shove, one thing runs through my mind:
This is Crazy.
This is Crazy. Also, this is crazy right.

Cover Design: Jay Aheer

Editing done by Jenny Sims Editing4Indies

Proofing Julie Deaton by Deaton Author Services

Interior Design CP Smith

To YOU the reader thank you for making my dreams come true!

THIS IS CRAZY

THE THIS IS SERIES

NATASHA MADISON

Special Edition

One

ZARA

"SO WHAT ARE your plans for winter break?" my twin sister, Zoe, asks me while we are on FaceTime. I lean back in the chair and look out the small window in my little home office at the raindrops lingering on the glass. We are both now in New York, but she lives in Soho in my brother-in-law Max's loft, and I live in Brooklyn in my sister-in-law Karrie's house.

It was no surprise we both ended up in New York. Our parents live in their house on Long Island, and my brother Matthew is the captain of the New York Stingers. My brother-in-law Max is the assistant of the team. Those two used to hate each other, but now they are always together.

"I have no idea. I have to ask Ed," I tell her of my boyfriend. We have been dating for over a year now, and I just met his parents, and he met mine. "I feel like something big is going to happen."

Her eyes go big. "No way. What kind of big? Like big, let's move in together, or big, let's buy a mansion and have your sister commission it?" she jokes, and it makes me laugh. As an up-and-coming real estate broker, she is slowly becoming the top player in the game.

"I don't know," I tell her. Sitting up, I cross my arms on the desk and lean toward the computer. I'm working from home today, but I will have to go into the office tomorrow morning. And by office, I mean Nordstrom. I have my dream job as personal shopper. I started at the bottom of the chain—sure, my family came in, and I dressed them all—but I finally got my name out there when Tyler Beckett came in one day with his then fiancée Jessica, and I dressed her for the red carpet event where her dress was ruined. They are Hollywood's royalty, and I dressed them. It was an honor, but what happened next was surreal. They say all it takes is one person, and that really is what it took. Soon, they were booking appointments just for me. Now I'm slowly building up my clientele so I can open my own company called Zara's Closet. The good news is that even the designers are reaching out to give me samples. It's a dream come true. "I just feel like something is coming, but I can't put my finger on it."

"Well, maybe he's finally going to propose," she says, and I open my eyes wide.

"Don't put it out there in the universe," I tell her. "It jinxes things. Remember when we put it in the universe about prom?"

She rolls her eyes. "It wasn't that bad. We both took the top ranked rookies of the year!" She smirks. "We also got a

Hummer stretch."

"We also didn't lose our virginity like we planned," I tell her. "Those rookies didn't even want to hold our hands."

"That's because Matthew gave them the dick shrinking talk before they got there," she reminds me. Since he's seventeen years older than us, our brother is always blocking the guys from us.

"This is what I'm talking about," I tell her.

"We were dumped two days before prom because you decided it would be a good idea to put a tracker on his phone." She shakes her head.

"That's because I had a feeling he was cheating on me, and you see I was right. I had a feeling in my gut." I slap my hand on the desk. I knew he was cheating. I felt it because he turned evasive and was all of a sudden always busy.

"You replaced his yearbook picture with picture of a pig." She laughs now and doesn't do it quietly.

"You helped me," I tell her. "You were the one who broke into student life and changed the picture." She just shakes her head, and I hear the doorbell. "I have to go. Ed is here, so I'll call you tomorrow."

"Unless you get engaged, then you call me ASAP," she tells me before I disconnect. Pushing away from the desk, I stand and walk down the steps to the front door. The doorbell rings again as soon as I get to the door, and I unlock it.

"Hey," I say, smiling at a frowning Ed.

"It's raining out here, and it took you forever to get to the door," he says, shaking off his jacket and spraying me with water.

"Well, hello to you too," I mumble, closing the door behind him as he takes off his shoes. "I didn't know you were on your way. You didn't send a text."

"I was in the area," he tells me. "I was visiting a client." I smile and walk to him. He matches my five-feet-eight height. If I wear heels, I'm taller than him—something that he hates—so I only wear heels when he isn't around. He is wearing a custom-made suit; I should know because I had it made for him. As a financial advisor at the top firm on Wall Street, he's making a name for himself. "I figured I would come by."

He doesn't make eye contact, and my stomach starts to turn over. "Do you have time to stay for lunch, or is this just a quickie?" I walk to him and put my hand on his stomach, throwing my arm around his shoulders.

"Actually," he says, walking out of my touch, "let's go sit on the couch and talk." Just the way he says that, I now know something is coming.

"What's going on?" I ask him, not moving from the door. "You are acting really weird."

He puts his hands in his pockets, and I look at him. "Listen." I cringe. Nothing good happens when someone starts with listen. "Things are just moving too fast." I cross my arms over my chest. "I'm under pressure at work to perform, and well, I think I just need to …"

"You're breaking up with me?" I ask him, not even sure I need to ask the question.

"Not so much breaking up, but maybe just stepping back and taking a break." His voice is soft, and I have the urge to cry, but I have the bigger urge to charge at him.

I put my hand up, and I point at him. "If you give me the

'it's not you, it's me' talk …" I stop talking before I threaten him.

"I'm sorry," he says softly. Grabbing his jacket in his hand, he walks to me, and I put my hand up to stop him. He just nods and walks out the door. I watch him through the frosted glass as he gets into his waiting Town Car. I walk to the stairs, turning around and sitting on the step. My phone pings in my hand, and I look down to see that is Zoe. I swear we feel each other's pain.

I dial her, and she answers with a low tone. "Don't tell me."

"He broke up with me," I say, putting my hand to my mouth to stop the sobs from ripping through me.

"I'll be there in ten," she says and disconnects, and I know that wherever she is, she will be here in ten minutes.

Two

Zara

"DO YOU WANT to car pool to Mom and Dad's after the game?" Zoe asks me, forcing me to look up from the salad I'm scooting around my plate.

I shrug. "I guess it would make the most sense." I drop my fork.

"It's been four months." She raises her voice to get my attention. "Four months, not weeks." She leans toward me to hiss the last part.

"I know ... it's just ..." I don't know how to explain it. "I really loved him."

Zoe leans back in her chair, and I look at her. We couldn't be more different in style. She is always dressed for business whereas I'm sitting here in my tight light blue jeans with a white tank top and a long gray knitted sweater. Sure, I have Louboutin on my feet and my tan Hermes purse, but other than that, my long blond hair is piled on top of my head while hers is long to her waist in loose curls. "We are going to leave here. We are going to go to your house, and then I'm going to choose an outfit for you." I raise an eyebrow, and she rolls her eyes. "Okay fine, you will help me pick out an outfit for you this Saturday. You are going to dress up and put on more than just mascara."

"I wear makeup. I'm just working from home today," I tell her. I mean, I put on some foundation and lip gloss yesterday when I had to meet a client. I even did my hair. Okay fine, there was half a bottle of dry shampoo in my hair, but it was sort of styled.

"I think it's safe to say the mourning of Ed is over." She picks up her water and raises her hand when she sees the waitress. "You've done the 'he left me, let's eat ice cream' for a week." I lean back in my chair, crossing my arms. "Then you did the 'why didn't he love me' song for two weeks."

"It was a day," I point out, and she now raises her eyebrow at me. "Okay fine, it was two weeks, but seriously, I loved him."

"Well, I think we are going in the right direction. You just used the past tense of love," she says, clapping her hands. I exhale a big breath I didn't know I was holding. "Anyway, the point is that you need to get back on that horse."

"What if all I'm riding are donkeys?" I ask. "What if I never fall in love again?"

"Are you kidding me?" she snaps, and I know her sympathy is out the window. In fact, it was out the window two days after the breakup. "Did you really love him?"

"Yes," I shriek.

"He didn't even know you were faking," she hisses, trying

to whisper, and I gasp. "*Every time.*"

"That was a secret." I reach for my bag and start to get up, and she tosses the napkin that was on her lap on the table. "A secret between twins."

"I know what a secret between twins means, jackass." She calls me the name I hate. "I've obviously kept it a secret because you don't have Vivienne blowing up your phone."

I don't say anything to her while we walk out, but she isn't wrong. Vivienne is my sister-in-law Karrie's best friend. She's originally from France but now calls New York home. She has one rule when it comes to dating—it's sex and nothing but sex—and she's very vocal about how many times she gets it and how good she gets it. So if she knew that I got it and didn't get it good, she would have rectified that. We walk out to the busy street, hearing the sound of honking everywhere.

"Where are you going now?" she asks me, and I look at the Town Car parked at the curb waiting for her. "I'm heading back to the office. Did you need a lift?" she says, walking to the car. The driver gets out to open her door for her, and she shakes her head. "Ricky, you don't need to open my door."

"Ms. Stone." He starts talking. "Your father gave me strict orders to make sure you were well taken care of."

I try to hide my laughter by rolling my lips. My parents are huge *Dateline* fans, and when they watched the one where the real estate agent was killed showing a house, they went a touch overboard by hiring him to drive and stay with her everywhere. That was two months ago, but she is the sensible one who will give in to them until she snaps.

Me, on the other hand, I would have squashed that idea the minute they mentioned it.

"It's finally a nice day, so I think I'm going to walk," I tell her, and she looks at me in surprise. "It's two blocks. I can survive." I laugh and blow her a kiss, then turn to walk down the sidewalk toward my brownstone. You can tell spring is in the air; the birds are chirping, and the trees are finally starting to get some green on them. I stop at the flower shop around the corner from my house and pick up some tulips. My feet finally start to hate me when I'm walking up the stairs to the brownstone. I unlock the door and slip my shoes off, then make my way to the kitchen to find a glass vase.

"Bring some sunshine to my day," I tell myself, placing the glass vase with pink tulips in the middle of the white counter. My phone pings, and when I walk back to my purse and pick it up, I see a couple of messages from a couple of clients. I walk up the stairs to my office when another one ping comes in. This time, it's from Vivi.

Vivi: I heard you are taking your vagina out for a walk again. See you Saturday.

I shake my head and immediately text Zoe.

Me: What did you tell Vivi?

She responds immediately.

Zoe: That you are finally ready to come out and social-ize.

I toss my phone down and block it all out while I work, only looking up when my stomach rumbles. I close my computer and walk downstairs, taking out a prepared meal that my mother had sent over. The rest of the week was uneventful. I was swamped at work with the summer season coming and people already arranging their summer wardrobe.

I'm bending down to zip up my suede black high heel bootie when the doorbell rings, but then the door opens. "Bonjour," I hear singsonged and know it's Vivienne.

"We're here," I hear Zoe yell from the stairs.

"Coming." I grab my black suede jacket and slip it on. I pull my hair out of the jacket and grab the gray knitted scarf to wrap around my neck. I walk down the stairs and look for them in the living room, but it's empty. I hear giggling and know that they are most likely in the kitchen. I walk in, and Vivienne is just toasting with her wine glass.

"Jesus, we get it," Vivi says. "You're in mourning." I look down at my outfit. Okay, the black jeans with matching shirt.

I throw my head back and laugh. "I swear, it wasn't what I was going for." I put my hand on my stomach. "I swear."

"Come, let's do a toast," Vivi says, and I walk to the counter as she pours me a glass of white wine. "To your brother and Max."

I throw my head back and moan. "How long are these retirement toasts going to go on for?" I ask, gulping down my wine.

"It's not every day they retire," Zoe says, and I glare at her.

" They aren't even retired. They are retiring"—I gulp more wine—"in three months. We've been toasting them since August when they announced it."

"I don't make the rules. I just live by them," Vivi says, wiggling her eyebrows. "Now, let's go before we get stuck in a shitload of traffic."

I finish my glass, then set the glasses in the sink and run out to meet them in the Town Car. "Well, this is surprising," I say, getting in and earning a punch in the arm from Zoe. "Ouch," I say, touching my arm. "I was just pointing out it's surprising Ed's working on Saturday." She winds up again, and I jump back. "Enough."

As we make our way to the arena, all three of us are on our phones instead of talking to each other. "Are you still following Ed?" my sister asks me, and I turn and look at her.

"No." I shake my head. "I blocked him. Why?"

"Um," she says, and I grab the phone from her. There on the screen in an Instagram picture is Ed with a brunette.

I look at her, and now Vivi is leaning over Zoe to see. "It could be a friend from work."

"Yes," Vivi says, "who he fucks." I open my mouth. "Her hand is on his stomach, and his is on her shoulder." I look down and see that she's right. "You only pose like that with someone you've been naked with."

"No, it's not," I say, looking at Zoe to help me out, and she shrugs her shoulders. "I have posed like that with Justin countless of times," I say, mentioning our little brother and then looking at Vivi who does a disgusted face.

"I don't really think you have." I grab my own phone now and scroll to the album that we have together. Standing at six foot five, my brother's a monster. With jet black hair and light blue eyes, he's my father's clone. "Okay, fine," I say when I finish looking at all the pictures and don't find any that support my claim. I grab Zoe's phone and go through his pictures now, and there is only one more with this woman. "Brenda."

"She sounds horrible," Zoe says and puts her hand around my arms.

"She looks like she doesn't give him anal," Vivi says, looking at her own phone, "and he looks like he hasn't had a good blow job since you left him."

"He didn't really like foreplay," I almost whisper, and Vivi's head snaps up. She's looking at me like I just told her Santa never really existed.

"What?" she whispers, and I swear she looks like she is going to cry.

"I mean, we did it, but every time I wanted to do it"—I look at Zoe who just shakes her head, telling me not to continue, but the words just come out—"he was not into it."

Vivi puts her hand to her mouth. "Are you sure you were doing it right?"

I throw my hands up. "Yes, I'm sure. I even watched porn before I did it to make sure I was, you know ..." I motion with my head up and down.

"But did he"—she looks down at my vagina and then looks up—"you know?"

"Stop," Zoe says, "you should stop there."

"Once," I tell her. "He didn't really enjoy it."

"Oh, my God." Vivienne slaps window. "How many times did you guys have sex?"

"A couple of times," I tell her.

"A week?" she questions.

"A month," I tell her. "He was busy and under stress."

She throws her had back and moans. "But the couple of times that you did it went on for hours, right? Like all night?"

Now, I'm the one shocked, and I gasp. "No, I mean it's

hard for men to get it up again after they …" I use my hands going big and small.

"This is worse than I thought," Vivi says, and then Zoe looks at her.

"Oh, trust me, it's worse," Zoe says, and then Vivi looks back at me. "There was only a happy ending for one of them."

"Shut the front door," Vivienne shrieks at the top of her lungs, and the car comes to a stop.

"I had happy endings." I glare at Zoe, who equally glares at me. "By myself." Vivienne doesn't have a chance to answer because her door is opened, and she has to get out.

I smack Zoe's arm, and she laughs, getting out of the car, and I follow. "This explains why you are always wearing black," Vivienne says, and then I look at her.

"Can we please not talk about this?" I tell her, and she just nods.

"My lips are sealed, but honey, you need to get laid," she says and turns to walk to the entrance used by the players and family members. "But tomorrow, that's another story."

"Oh my God," I say, looking up at the concrete ceiling and feeling Zoe put her arm around my shoulder.

"It could be worse," she says, and I look at her. "We could be at a male strip club right now, and you could be fighting off the baby oil." I close my eyes and picture it. "Don't close your eyes for too long."

I shake my head and make my way inside, not sure what tonight will hold.

THREE

ZARA

"YOU THINK SHE'S faking?" I hear whispering next to my ear, but my eyes stay closed.

"I don't know," the other little voice says, "but her breath stinks." And I can't even stop the laughter from coming out of my mouth, shocking my sister Allison's two kids, Michael and Alexandria, who are leaning against my bed. I try to grab them, but they run out of the room screaming.

"She's awake," Michael says. Tossing over the covers, I get out of bed. I'm in my old bedroom, and everything is pretty much the same as before I went to college. The walls are still a soft pink. My white desk sits in the corner with a huge cork board hanging over it with pictures from high school. I go to the walk-in closet and grab the robe that I keep there. The only thing I actually took from this closest were the cool clothes or at least what I thought were cool. walk out, going down the spiral staircase to the kitchen connected to the family room.

My mother is at the stove flipping pancakes, her auburn hair piled on top of her head.

"Who sent the rats to wake me up?" I ask. Walking to the coffee machine, I start my coffee and look over at my mother, who smiles at me.

"Good morning," she says. When my father comes in and goes straight to her, kissing her neck, I look out the window. He is always kissing her or touching her or holding her hand as far back as I can remember. The coffee machine stops, and I walk to the fridge and look at my parents. My father stands behind her, his hands on her hips while he looks over her head to watch *SportsCenter* on the television.

"Evan Richards is having the year of his life," my father says, not moving his hand but looking over at me and smiling. "Good morning, princess," he says, still using the nickname from when I was younger. I mean, I think Allison is thirty, and he still calls her princess.

"Morning," I say, going over to the table to sit and watch the television. I hate Evan Richards only because Ed loved him. Like worshiped him. I look at him on the screen while he celebrates a goal with his cocky smile. *His teeth are probably fake*, I think to myself.

"He needs to shave all that scruff," I say to the room, and my father just shakes his head. I feel bad for him. He was the biggest name in hockey, and he still is a legend, but Zara and I used to cry and scream as soon as he took out the skates. Luckily for us, he had Matthew and Justin.

"Honey, beards are sexy," my mother says, which earns her a glare from my clean-shaven father. "Well, not all beards are sexy."

"Babe," he growls and leans in to whisper something in her ear. Her eyes go wide, and she laughs.

"Go away." She pushes him away with her hip.

"Morning." I hear a grumble and watch Zoe dragging her feet as she walks in the room. "Those two gave me a heart attack." She walks to the coffee. "I opened my eyes and came face to face with Alex." I laugh. "She didn't even say anything. I thought she was possessed."

"Oh, good, you two are up," Allison says, coming into the room with her two kids behind her. My sister is seven years older than me. She was five when my dad came into the picture, but her father is a douche and slowly erased himself from their lives. "I owe them twenty dollars each," she says, turning to high-five her kids. She is dressed in jeans and a sweater, but she looks great in everything. It's why she landed her husband, Max. Or at least that's what I always say.

"Now go play in the basement. Aunt Karrie and Aunt Vivi are coming over in a bit." They turn and run toward the basement.

Great, I think to myself, *more kids.* My brother Matthew and Karrie have four kids, two boys and two girls, and I swear I call them the Duggars. Karrie says the factory is closed, but Matthew just shrugs when she says that. "Accidents happen," is his go-to saying.

"I want to play with the hockey sticks too," Alex says, going down the stairs to the basement. My parents love their kids, but they love their grandkids even more. The basement is literally a toy store.

"Why would you pay your kids to wake us up?" Zoe asks, sliding into a chair next to me. She is wearing almost the same thing as me without the robe, and her hair is also tied on top of her head.

"It's payback for all the times you woke me up when you were kids." She smirks and goes to kiss my dad's cheek.

"Suck-up," Zoe mumbles and just laughs at her while I just shake my head.

"We were kids," I tell her, and she just shrugs. Zoe opens her phone to scroll through her Instagram. "Are we having a family lunch?" I ask my parents and then turn when I hear Zoe gasp. Her eyes fly to mine, and when they go wide, I know something is up. And from the look of horror on her face, it's bad. Like tsunami bad.

"Oh. My. God," she says and puts her hand on the top of her phone to block what she's looking at. Her eyes fly to Allison. "I need backup," she says, and the way her voice comes out, Allison springs into action, getting on my other side. I look at both of them, and we are distracted when Karrie yells from the front door.

"We are here," she shouts, and the kids run in with a hurricane of kisses and hugs before they run off to the basement. They went traditional, and all their kids' names have to do with family members. Cooper is named after my dad and is the biggest honor that Matthew could have given him. Frances is named after Karrie's mom who passed away. There is Vivienne, who, thankfully, is nothing like her namesake. Then there is baby Allison, who is just starting to get her own sass, and she gets that from us apparently. She slashed Cooper in the mouth two months ago, and he needed five stitches. She looked at them with her big blue eyes, and said, "He's a puke ass bitch." We almost died when Matthew looked at us and glared.

"What's going on?" she asks innocently, stopping mid step into the kitchen to look at us. Vivi knocks into her from behind. My heart won't stop hammering in my chest.

"Things are about to go through the roof," Zoe says and then turns to me. "I need you to take a deep breath." Which makes everything so worse than before. Why would I need to take a deep breath? The worst-case scenarios are going through my mind. Wardrobe malfunction to one of the Hollywood stars, worst-dressed list. So many things.

"Holy shit, is there a paparazzi picture of one of my clients?" My hand goes to my chest, but she just shakes her head.

"It's worse," she whispers, and I see the tears forming in her eyes. I reach over and snatch the phone out of her hands. She tries to snatch it back, but she's too late. I see it there.

The picture is in color this time. Ed kissing his new girlfriend, but what my eyes fly to is the hand she is holding up with a diamond ring glistening on her finger. "Get my phone," she shouts, and they all spring into action, trying to get the phone from me, and I'm caught off guard.

Allison grabs my phone, Karrie grabs the remote to turn off the television, my mother rushes to my side, and Vivi rushes to the wine fridge and pulls out three bottles.

"What is going on?" My father just stands in the middle of the kitchen. Shocked and confused, he darts his eyes from one person to the other.

"MOTHERFUCKER," I yell at the top of my lungs, shooting out of my chair. Rage, anger, and hurt fill me.

"Oh my God," my father whispers, but he still doesn't move as he watches me start to pace. The women around the room spring into action. My mother comes to my side, but I can't stop walking. Zoe comes to stand next to her while Allison looks at the phone. Her eyes come to me when she finally reads what I just read.

"That motherfucker," she says and tosses the phone to Karrie who gasps out loud. She puts the phone down on the counter with more force than she should and then walks to the fridge for the bottle of tequila.

"What the hell is going on? Can someone please tell me what is going on?" my father asks, rubbing his hands through his hair.

No one answers him. Vivi pours the wine while Karrie pours a shot of tequila and brings it over to me. "This isn't going to help, but it can't hurt," she says. I take the shot from her and swallow it down, and it burns the whole way down.

"For the love of God, I need one of you women to tell me what is going on," he shouts. "Why am I the only man around here?"

"He's getting married," I tell my father after accepting another shot of tequila. Coughing after I swallow it down, I wipe my mouth with the back of my hand. "Ed is getting married." I shake my head. "That pencil dick lying motherfucker is getting married."

"Oh, honey," my mother says from beside me.

Vivienne now goes over to the cell phone and grabs it, reading the caption out loud. "When you find the one, you take the leap. Marry me." She rolls her eyes and pretends to gag. "*Le trou du cul.*" *Asshole,* she says in French.

"That pencil dick motherfucker," I say now angry again. "I knew he was a tool. You told me he was a tool." I point at Zoe who just nods.

"I did," she says, and I start to pace again, the heat from the tequila spreading through me.

"Oh no, baby, it's not you, it's me." I imitate him, sounding like a whiny baby. "I'm just tired, baby."

"She never even had a happy ending," Vivienne says from the counter while she drinks her glass of wine. Karrie walks up to her and grabs it from her, gulping it down.

"I don't want to hear this," my father says. "Are you going to be okay?" He comes to me and puts his hand on my arms, bringing me to his chest. My face rests in the middle of his chest, the safest place I can be.

"Of course, she's going to be okay," Zoe says, going to get her own shot of tequila. She winces when she swallows and then gags. "That's shit is fucking disgusting." She points at the bottle.

"I'm going to go down with the kids," my father says, kissing my mother's lips. "Love you."

"Ugh Dad, not now." I groan at him. He just laughs and walks out of the room.

"So what are you going to do?" Karrie asks me, and I look at her.

I shrug. "I have no fucking idea."

"We should send him a box of vibrators," Vivienne says, then looks at Karrie. "Remember when Matthew threw all yours out?"

We all groan now. "Right in the middle of the street."

Allison can't help but laugh and neither can I. "I need to see the picture again," I tell them and grab the phone from the counter where it was laid after making its way through everyone's hand. I look at the picture; his hands are on her face. "He's such an asshole."

"He is," Karrie says, "but you can't let him get to you."

"Well, you can let him get to you," Zoe says, and I look at her in shock. "But then you take all that energy, and we devise a plan to castrate him."

"Girls," my mother says, shaking her head. I am not going to lie, we are a handful, and no matter how many times we said we would be good, it would just go downhill and fast. The number of times they got pulled into the office at school was a record, and I swear the teachers let out a collective sigh of relief when we graduated.

"What?" Zoe puts her hands up. "I mean Allison"—she looks at her—"you watch *Game of Thrones*. Don't they do that, and the guy still lives, right?"

"It's true. You can survive without a penis," Allison says, then hears my mother groan. "But I don't suggest you guys cut off his penis."

"Thank you," my mother says.

"Fuck that," Vivienne says. "Hit him where it hurts."

"Yeah," Zoe says, nodding. "Hit him where it hurts, but will it hurt if he doesn't even use it?"

"Vivienne," Karrie hisses, "not helping."

My father walks back in the room. "Is everything okay in here?"

"We're talking castration, but it hasn't been decided," my

mother says, wringing her hands while my father's eyes go big.

"Oh, I know," I say, running upstairs and grabbing my phone. "That fucker wants to get married." I laugh bitterly, opening Twitter. "I'm crashing his fucking wedding."

"Oh dear God," Karrie says while Vivienne cheers me on, earning her another glare but this time from my parents also.

"What are you doing?" my father asks, and I smile, almost like a Cheshire cat with the mouse tail flipping my mouth.

"I am getting myself the hottest date out there, and we are going to go and congratulate that pencil dick asshole."

"What do you mean by getting yourself a date?" my father asks, his face going white. "Are you hiring an escort? Zara Stone," he hisses out my name.

"Not exactly," I say, smiling. "I'm going to do better."

"Why am I the only male in this house?" he yells and sits down on one of the stools, and my mother walks to him. "She is going to give me a heart attack."

"Oh my," I hear from Allison laughing on the side, "this is going to be so good."

"What is going on now?" my father asks, and then she hands him the phone and displays what I just did two seconds ago.

Zara Stone @ZaraStone

When your ex-boyfriend gets engaged, you ask his idol @EvanRichards to be your date to crash his wedding. What do you say? Wanna be my date?

#myexhasapencildick

Zoe reads it and turns to high-five me while Karrie rolls

her lips, trying not to laugh. Allison puts her hands in front of her mouth, and Vivienne just nods, drinking her wine. My phone beeps, and my father looks at me. "I think he answered."

I grab the phone from him just when I hear Karrie's cell phone ring. Her eyes look from the phone to me. "It's Matthew."

"Did he answer you?" Zoe asks, and I open my Twitter.

Evan Richards @EvanRichards

Sounds like a plan. DM me.

Zoe laughs out loud. "Yeah buddy, you better DM him right now."

"What does that even mean? Why is this happening?" My father just moans.

"It's happening because he is a pencil dick asshole who basically lied with the whole 'I have so much work, and I have to focus on that' bullshit. Well, guess what? I'm going to get the last laugh," I tell him, and he just shakes his head.

"Matthew is freaking out," Karrie says, trying not to laugh with the phone by her ear. "Hold on, let me put him on speaker."

"Zara." His voice fills the room. "Are you out of your mind?" he asks in one breath and then continues. "No, don't answer that. We all know you are out of your mind."

"Hey, Matthew," I say, and he stops talking. "Is it true you threw out Karrie's vibrator?"

"Who told her that?" he hisses. "I have to be on the ice in twenty minutes. I don't have time for this today."

"Who asked you to get involved?" Zoe says. "I mean, you won't even let your wife have a vibrator. She looks deprived."

"She isn't deprived," he says, "and the date with Evan is never going to happen."

"Matthew Grant," Karrie pipes in, "don't you dare. Your sister is brokenhearted."

"This is going to end up on SportsCenter," Matthew grumbles. "I have to go. Kiss the kids for me, and you twins ..." I look at Zara, and she looks at me. "I'll liquidate some stocks to make sure I have bail money." He laughs, but my father groans.

"I see this ending very badly." My mother laughs.

"For one of us anyway." I smirk at her.

FOUR

Evan

"LET'S GO." THE coach yells at me to start the drill. I skate from the corner of the rink to the blue line, looking slightly over my shoulder, and wait for the Corey, my defenseman, to pass me the puck. I skate a little to let the puck hit the back of my stick. I hustle it up now, pushing against the boards, the sound of ice crushing under my skates echoing in my ears. I skate past center ice all the way to the other blue line, looking over and seeing that line partner Denis a second behind me. This summer, I worked on my speed and my cardio, and it's paying off in one of my best seasons ever. I'm number one on the leaderboard for goals, number one for points, and if this continues, I'll be in the running for that Art Ross trophy.

It's so close I can taste it. "Skate harder," I yell to Denis. He tries, but I just go without him, shooting at the empty net and watching the puck drop in the back of the net. I skate around the net, laughing at Denis who is finally getting to the net. I now switch backward and look at him. "Guess having that doughnut before practice wasn't a good idea," I tell him, and he sticks his gloved hand up, telling me to fuck off. The sound of the whistle has me stopping.

"That's it," Coach says. "Rest for the night, boys. Tomorrow's practice ten a.m.," he says, skating off the ice, and we follow him. I get off the ice and walk down the red carpet to the dressing room. Unsnapping my helmet, I put my stick against the wall with the rest of them. I take off my glove and put it on the bench right under my name. I grab my phone and see that I have a couple of messages from my sister Candace who takes care of my social media. Well, she takes care of the Facebook and Twitter. I do my own Instagram, which is a pain in my ass.

I'm going to be dropping off fifty shirts for you to sign tonight.

Don't forget to call Mom.

I also fed your dogs.

Also you should check who just tweeted you? Might have to go undercover, brother.

I'm about to open my Twitter when I hear laughing behind me and look over to see Jari, our goalie, sitting down looking at his phone. He looks up at me. "Dude, did you check your Twitter?" I shake my head and open my phone.

Zara Stone @ZaraStone

When your ex-boyfriend gets engaged, you ask his idol @EvanRichards to be your date to crash his wedding. What do I say? Wanna be my date?

#myexhasapencildick

I chuckle at the hashtag and then look at the name again. Holy shit, Zara Stone. My fingers move across the keyboard before I think about it.

Evan Richards @EvanRichards
Sounds like a plan. DM me.

The minute I send it, my phone blows up, showing me Candace is calling.

"Yo," I answer, grabbing the bottle of Gatorade next to my gloves, then sitting and taking a drink.

"Are you out of your fucking mind?" she shouts, and I can so picture her in the Range Rover I bought her with her glasses on and her makeup and nails perfectly done. I shake my head. I'm the oldest of the three. Chloe is the middle child, and she stays out of my business unless she needs tickets or a reservation somewhere. But Candace is the one always up in my stuff. Okay fine, I pay her to take care of my things, but sometimes, she goes overboard. But she's knows hockey; I mean, our father played hockey, not pro level, but he played it in college, and then he took on the role of coaching. My uncle is also a huge hockey player, and he only played five games in the NHL.

You would think with a hockey family that I started playing hockey when I was a kid, but I didn't. When I was thirteen, my father forced me to go play with him and a couple of his friends, and the rest is history. I was drafted forty-fifth. I never thought I would actually play in the NHL, but the team gave me a shot, and at nineteen, I was raising the cup over my head. It was a dream come true. I was traded two years later, and now seven years later, I have a couple of months left on my contract before I'm a free agent.

"What are you talking about?" I try to act stupid, but I know the minute I sent out that tweet, she got a notification on her phone. Laughing, I lean down and untie my skates

"You really want to go on a date with Zara Stone?" She hisses out her name. "I heard she's a bitch."

"From who?" I ask her, knowing she doesn't even know who Zara is. But she has hated every single girlfriend I've had. The last one I had four years ago, she threw a party for me when we broke up and posted about it. It did not go over well with my mother, who was pissed at both of us.

"I know people," she says, and I laugh now loudly so she can hear me. "I'm serious, Evan." She stops taking. "I don't think it's a good idea. You are at the top of your game. You are like the most eligible bachelor out there."

"Cand, you can relax. It's just a date. If that even." I try to talk her off the ledge. My phone beeps, and I see I have an incoming call from an unknown number. "I have to go. Someone is calling me."

"Okay, are we still on for tacos?" she asks.

"Well, it's Tuesday, so yeah, pick it up and meet me at my house," I tell her and then accept the other call. "Hello?"

"Hey Evans," the male voice says, and I think I know who it is, but I'm not sure. "It's Grant, Matthew Grant." Holy shit. So Zara's father is *the* Cooper Stone—he's basically a hockey god or idol with more records than any other hockey player out there—and Matthew is her brother. From what I hear, you don't fuck with him, but apparently, his other sister dated his arch nemesis under his nose.

"Yeah," I say, trying not to laugh at how crazy my life has gotten in the past ten minutes.

"You know why I'm calling?" he says, and I hear guys talking in the back. He's probably at practice also.

"I have an idea," I tell him.

"So we are on the same page," he says, and I have no idea what book he's reading. "Yeah?"

"Yeah," I say, and he disconnects.

"What the fuck just happened?" I ask and don't expect anyone to answer, but Brett, my closest teammate and partner in crime on the ice, answers me.

"You just put another nail in your coffin." He laughs, and I get up, moving my skates out of the way, and pull my jersey off, tossing it in the big bin in the middle of the room.

"It's one date. Jesus," I tell him, and he just shakes his head.

"Have you seen her?" he asks me, and I shake my head.

"I mean, maybe in passing," I tell him and then grab my phone and go back to Twitter and click on Zara's picture. It fills my screen in the little circle, and I have to sit down. I swear I hold my breath when I see her. Her strawberry blond hair covers half her face and half her lips. Her gaze is aimed at the camera, and I swear it feels like she's staring straight at me. I zoom in and see her eyes look gray, and her lips are plump and half open. She isn't pretty, and she isn't beautiful. Exquisite is the only word that comes to mind.

I hear chuckling again, and I look at Brett. "So not really right."

"I …" I stutter, looking down at the picture and then up again, and he continues chuckling. "I didn't." It comes out lower now. He's shaking his head as he unwraps tape from his leg. "Do you know her?"

"Met her last year at the Max Horton Foundation event. She walked in and jaws dropped," he says. "Her date was this skinny dude who looked like a banker. Maybe that's the pencil dick."

I look down again, imprinting her picture into my brain. "It's just one date," I tell him, turning my phone off and putting it on the shelf. "One date." I don't know if I'm trying to tell him this, or if I'm trying to convince myself of it.

I get into the shower and then make my way over to the kitchen, grabbing a heaping plate of pasta and chicken. I look around and see it's almost empty, so I sit down and start eating while I scroll TSN to check the stats. I see my Twitter app is going nuts, and I'm about to open it when Candace calls.

"Hey," I say, putting the phone to my ear while grabbing another forkful.

"Hey so," she starts, and I know she is irritated. "In case you are wondering, you have about four thousand DMs with girl's numbers. There are actually fifty people who created fake Zara Stone accounts."

I shake my head. "But did Zara ever DM?" I ask.

"She did. She dropped her number," she says, and I go through them, stopping at the one I know is Zara's and see she put her number. "Are you going to call her?'

"Yes," I say, grabbing my drink and taking a sip.

"I think it's a mistake," she says.

"I'll remember that," I say and disconnect. I look down at the number, and for the first time ever, my palms are sweaty. This is stupid. I've called girls before. This isn't even me reaching out to her. She reached out to me first.

I don't have the balls to call her, so I text her instead.

Me: Hey, it's Evan. Is now good time to talk?

I press send and look at the text I should have sent with an emoji. While I'm looking down, I see the bubble with three dots at the bottom appear and then disappear, but no message is coming through. I watch it like a hawk, and finally, she answers back.

Zara: Getting ready to have family lunch. How is tonight?

I smile at the phone and then type out my answer

Me: Text me when you can talk.

I put the phone away and then get up and head to the gym. For two hours, I lift weights until I feel the burn everywhere. I take another quick shower before I leave and look at my phone. Grabbing my baseball cap, I put it on backward, then grab my phone, wallet, and keys. I look around and yell out a bye to whoever is left in the locker room. Today was not mandatory, but it's always good to get on the ice. I walk to my black BMW, pressing the button to unlock the door, and get in. I make my way home to my brand-new house. Well, it's not brand new because it's been six months. I know I shouldn't have bought it since I don't know where I will be at the end of the season, but I couldn't help myself. I pull through the gate to the community and make my way down the street. It's a new development, which is why I couldn't say no. I love huge properties. I don't really care how big the house is as long as I have my space.

I pull into the concrete drive that runs in front of the house and then turns into the driveway that leads to my house. The grass is green, but it's Dallas, so it's always green. After I park in front of the garage door, I get out, hearing the barking. I laugh and walk up the one step to the huge brown door. The tinted glass doesn't allow me to see inside, but if I know my dogs, they are at the door. I open the door, and Lilo and Stitch jump on me.

"Hey there," I say, walking into the huge foyer. A winding cast-iron staircase leads to upstairs, but the staircase is blocked off by a cast-iron gate to keep the dogs from going upstairs. I look to my left and see that the bedroom door is still closed, which is great, since two days ago, they got into there. Lilo is a golden lab and Stitch is a chocolate lab, and boy, do they get in trouble. I rub their heads and then walk through the foyer and straight into the family room.

This is where I spend most of the time. I had the brown couches custom made to be almost like you're are lying in bed. The eighty-inch television hangs over the sand-colored marble fireplace. A wooden bookcase sitting to one side contains photos of all my big moments in my career. A couple are also of my family at functions or at Christmas. On the other side is the hallway to my bedroom, which sits in the back of everything, and another gate stops them from going in there. I walk past the kitchen that sits on my right to the back door, and I open them to let the dogs run outside. I close the door, going straight to the kitchen to grab some water.

I grab the television remote that sits on the counter separating the family room from the kitchen. I turn it on to *SportsCenter* and then walk to my stainless-steel double fridge, opening it to grab a water bottle. I turn and grab an apple that sits in the middle of the island. The huge bowl sits on a marble countertop, the same marble counters all around the kitchen. The color is on the dark brown side, but the cabinets are a light brown, so the counters pop more. It came with a six-burner built-in range that I cook on sometimes—okay, maybe not that much—but my mother has cooked some delicious meals on there when she visits.

I grab my phone and order the stuff for the taco party that I'm having tonight with Candace. Hearing the dogs bark, I look out the window and make my way outside, seeing them running after each other at full speed. This, right here, is why I bought the house. I don't even see my neighbor, or if I do, it's far away. I walk to the end of the concrete patio covered by a wooden lanai. I have a fireplace on one side with the dog beds right in front of it. Two rocking chairs sit in front of the window by the door. My mother loves sitting in them and rocking in front of the fire at night. A grill sits on the other side of the patio, next to the outside bathroom I had installed. A white hammock hangs right at the end of the patio.

The pool in the middle of the yard surrounded by palm trees gives it a tropical feel. The dogs finally look up and see me and charge straight for me. Lilo drops the ball at my feet, and I bend over, picking it up and throwing it as far as I can and see them take off.

I play catch with them for about thirty minutes before they both lie at my feet panting. I turn around and pick up their water bowls to fill them with the outside hose. They get up right away, coming to the bowls. I leave them outside when my phone beeps, telling me someone just punched in my code at the gate, alerting me that my order has arrived. Walking inside, I go to the door right as he was about to ring the doorbell.

"Hey, Senor Evan," Manual says, handing me a huge bag. "This is everything for you," he says, and I nod at him. "Have a good night and keep up the scoring." He tips his hat to me and walks back to his car. I bring the big heavy bag back into the kitchen and put it on the island and start taking out the containers. I take the plastic bag of homemade tortillas out first. Then the round container of queso is next. I open it up and smell it.

I grab the big bag of homemade chips, dipping one in and letting it melt on my tongue. I unload the three containers of taco stuff. One is beef, one pork, and the other shrimp. A bowl of Spanish rice is on the bottom. The door slams shut, and I know it's Candace.

"Oh good, I'm just in time," she says, dumping her purse on the table right off the kitchen. She comes over and starts opening the containers. "I'm starving," she says, walking to the cupboard and taking out three plates. We get our tacos, and she tells me what needs to be done in the next week as we eat our dinner.

"Did you see Twitter?" she asks me when I finish my last bite of queso.

I shake my head. "No." I pick up my plate and bring it to the kitchen. "I only keep Instagram so I can do the stories."

She gets up from her chair and comes over, putting her own plate in the sink and rinsing it off just before she puts it in the dishwasher. She walks over to the counter and grabs the dish towel to wipe her wet hands.

"Your DMs were blowing up. I had to charge my phone

five times since that tweet this morning." I shrug, not sure what I'm supposed to say. "Are you really going to do this?"

"I honestly don't know what you mean." I lean back against the counter and cross my arms over my chest and watch her. "Are you asking me if I'm going to go on a date with her? Yes, I said I would."

"You don't even know this girl. I heard she's drama rolled up in her five-foot-ten body," she says, not missing a beat.

"It's one date, Can. I'm not getting married," I tell her, and she just nods.

"Fine, but when it blows up, and it will blow up, I'm not helping you clean up the mess," she tells me, walking to the table and grabbing her purse.

"I pay you to clean up the mess," I tell her. "Don't forget that."

"Yeah well, you don't pay me enough. I'll be demanding a raise," she says. Turning and walking out of the house, she slams the door behind her. I shake my head and rub my hands over my face.

The dogs follow me, and as soon as we get to my room, they run and jump up onto my king-size bed. My feet sink into the light gray carpet as I walk to the bed and scold them, pointing at their two beds at the end of the bed. They look at me and then walk out of the room to no doubt go lie on the couch. I walk to the dark gray side tables, taking the remote and turning on the television that hangs in front of the bed over the fireplace. I didn't want anything fancy in my bedroom, but then I came home and found my mother had gone against everything I wanted.

It's masculine, I will say that, but with a softer touch, according to her. The gray fabric headboard is comfortable when I sit up and watch television, so that is all that matters. The covers are a light gray and look fluffy as fuck, but I don't make my bed every morning either. I just throw the covers over. I fall into bed when the phone in my pocket buzzes. I see it's from Zara, and a smile comes over my face, but I have no idea why.

Zara: I'm free to talk if you are.

"Here goes nothing," I say to myself, pressing her name and listening to the phone ring.

FIVE

ZARA

WITH SHAKY HANDS, I type out a text I've been thinking about since this morning.

Me: I'm free to talk if you are.

I got home from my parents' house an hour ago, and for the last hour, I kept going over in my head what the hell I did. When he texted me if I was free to talk, I went into the bathroom so Zoe didn't know I regretted sending out the tweet. It was in the moment, and I'm totally blaming the te-quila.

The phone ringing makes me look at the bed where I tossed it when I sent him the text, not even thinking he would be by his phone. I pick it up, and my heart starts to speed up a touch—okay, a lot—and I finally press the green connect button.

"Hello," I say to him, trying to get my voice to sound as calm as possible, but it so doesn't.

"Zara," he says. I sit on the bed, listening to his gruff and deep voice. I'm not going to lie; I spent the whole drive home googling him. I can't say that I was surprised he was good looking, but he's honestly the hottest guy I've ever seen. His face has a scruff that I like—no, scratch that, that I love. His hair is cut short on the side and long on top, and I could see running my hand through it. When I looked into his brown eyes, and it looked like he was actually looking at me, I knew I was way out of my league with this guy. I mean, the man had a hundred Pinterest boards already dedicated to him. So I might have flipped through them. Okay, I did.

"Hey," I say, trying to sound casual. "What's up?"

He chuckles, and I swear my stomach flips. "Not much really," he says, and I hear the ruffling of sheets and wonder if he's at home or on the road. "Just getting into bed."

I look at the clock and see it's nine p.m. my time, so I ask him. "What time is it there?"

"Just after eight," he says, taking a deep breath.

"Is it almost your bedtime?" I joke with him.

"Gotta save my energy for you," he jokes. "Did you have a good day?"

I shake my head and chuckle. "Oh, you know, the normal. Found out my ex is engaged four months after breaking up with me so he can focus on work." I get into bed and sink down on the pillows and look up at the ceiling. "When if I found out, I kind of went ballistic and flew off the handle."

"Is that so?" he says, and I swear I could picture him smiling. A smile I've looked at for an hour now. Fucking Pinterest.

"I mean, I usually fly off the handle, but this one was a bit more than anything else." I laugh. "It didn't help that I had two shots of tequila in me, and it was nine a.m."

"So you drunk tweeted me?" He laughs now. "Interesting."

The way he says that word makes me sit up. "Why is that interesting?"

"It's just if you didn't have the tequila in you, you wouldn't have tweeted me?" he asks me, and I lie back down, thinking.

"Probably," I tell him the truth. "He loves you so hard. At first, I thought he did it just to get a rise out of Matthew and Max when he used to throw out your stats, but …"

"Yeah, your brother isn't my biggest fan, especially now," he tells me, and I turn over in the bed.

"Jesus, did he call you?" I ask him, holding my breath. This is so embarrassing.

"Yeah, he did," he says. "I mean, the conversation lasted maybe five seconds, and he said maybe four words. I heard Max in the background throwing clout." He chuckles. "But—"

I stop him from talking. "I am so sorry you got dragged into this. I totally understand if you don't want to come with me."

"I've never crashed a wedding before, but it's on my bucket list." I laugh now when he says that. "Do you even know when he's getting married?"

"According to his latest Instagram post, he can't wait to make her his wife, and he said beginning of June," I tell him. I don't tell him that after that happened, I had a couple more shots of tequila, but everyone held my phone hostage. They also hid their own phones.

"If you can get me the date, I can check my schedule

and see if I'm available," he tells me. "It should be the play-offs by that point," he says.

"I didn't even think," I say, and I turn over again. "Listen, Evan, I get that you probably think this is the stupidest thing that has ever been done, but if you knew me, you would know it's probably not, and I'll probably do something to top this." He laughs. "But I don't want to blow up your life."

"I got a thousand phone numbers today," he tells me. "My DMs were blowing up."

"Fuck," I whisper. "I'm so sorry."

"Why? It's not every day a gorgeous woman takes a stand for herself and, in return, asks me out."

"We've never even met," I tell him, waiting for him to answer.

"No, we haven't," he starts telling me, and his voice goes softer, "but after I agreed to be your wedding crasher date, I checked out your picture on Twitter." My heart starts picking up, and I put him on speakerphone while I go on Twitter and check the picture. It was taken on the beach when our family went to St. Barts.

"Do you know that you have hundreds of Pinterest boards dedicated to you?" I tell him. He laughs now but not just a small chuckle like he did before. This one is deep, and I can picture him leaning over and laughing. "What? It's true."

"You were checking me out," he says between the fits of laughter.

"Well, I knew what you looked like. Sort of," I tell him. "I mean with a helmet on and a visor."

I have seen him play before.

"Where do you live?" he asks me when he finally stops

laughing.

"New York," I tell him, and I know he lives in Dallas. He plays for Dallas.

"I leave tomorrow night for Jersey," he says, and I literally hold my breath. "I'm there for two days."

"Okay," I say.

"Zara, can I take you out?" he asks me. "I mean, I think it's good if we meet before we just crash a wedding."

"You want to drive into the city and take me out?" I ask him in shock, not expecting this at all. I expected a couple of texts, and then we would just mutually show up at the wedding and pretend we like each other and then go our separate ways.

"Yeah, we actually have the whole day free. We are flying up at night so we can rest," he tells me.

"I have a couple of appointments that day," I tell him, "but I'm free late afternoon." This is another bad idea.

"Well then," he says heavily, "it's a date."

"So a date before a date." I make sure I understand what's going on. "Or is it a meeting before a date?"

"What?" He chuckles again. "I don't even know what that means."

"So a date is wine and dine," I tell him, "and a meeting is sitting down and getting things on paper so there is no confusion on what is going to come."

"Zara," he says my name, and my stomach flips. "I'm coming into New York. I'm picking you up, and I'm taking you out for dinner." He doesn't stop there. "You can call it whatever you want to call it."

"That doesn't answer my question," I tell him, my hands

getting clammy.

"Well then, I guess we'll find out," he says. "What is your favorite food?"

"Um …" I say, not sure I can put a sentence together. What is going on with me? I think the tequila was spiked. Fucking Justin probably put moonshine in there.

"I'll surprise you," he says, and I want to tell him I hate surprises. I loathe them. I would water board a person to know. "So can you text me your address?"

"I can meet you," I tell him. "I mean, I'll already be in the city at work," I say.

"You can either give me your address, or I can call in a couple of favors and get it." If he was sitting in front of me, I would glare at him. "Fine. Challenge accepted."

"That wasn't a challenge," I tell him. "It was me thinking. Give a woman a second to think."

"Sleep tight, Zara," he says, ignoring me. "I'll see you soon." It's the last thing he says before hanging up. I look down at the phone and see that it's the screensaver of Zoe and me in Paris standing in front of the Eiffel Tower. When a text comes in, I see it's from Evan.

Sweet Dreams, Zara.

I think about answering it, but I don't. Tossing the phone on the bed, I get up and walk into the bathroom, flipping on the light to the small en suite. Well, it's big for New York but small for me. The huge deep white tub sits in front of the door next to the glass shower. The tiled floor cold on my feet as I walk toward the tub and turn on the water. I turn to the two hanging shelves that I had added when I moved in, lighting the four candles on each. I undress, turning off the light and taking in the glow of the candles. I get into the hot tub and lean back, closing my eyes. This usually relaxes me. I usually just let it wash over me, but all I can see are the different pictures of Evan going through my mind. The one with him in a Batman shirt. The one of him in a suit. The one without a shirt. My face starts to get hotter and hotter, and I give up on the bath. I get out, drying myself off, and I slip into bed.

The next day goes by so fast I don't even notice the time, nor do I stop to eat. But when the door opens and slams shut, I get up from my desk and go to check.

"I've been trying to call you all day long." I see Zoe kicking off her shoes and coming in with a brown bag. "Why haven't you picked up?" she asks me, and I walk downstairs.

"I am going nuts," I tell her. "Not only is there the gala for the Horton Foundation that everyone wants to get fitted for, but people are also starting to get ready for the NHL awards. Then there are two red carpet events coming up," I say, reaching out and grabbing the bag from her. "Did you get me Chinese?" I ask hopeful, and she looks at me.

"It's Monday. Of course, I got you Chinese. Go set up in the living room, and I'll get the plates," she says, going to the kitchen while I walk into the living room. I haven't really done anything to it since Karrie and Matthew lived here. It looks like it's been in a magazine ad. I walk into the room, looking out the bay windows at the night sky. A hidden bench where I've curled up with a book more than once sits under the window. The room has one color, all white, but the couch is a huge U-shaped deep brown. A million throw pillows are placed all over, but what gets me is the fireplace right in front of the couch. It's old school and hand-carved in white marble. A huge screen television sits on top of the fireplace. The coffee table is a huge square. I have a tray on there where I put all the remotes and glasses and stuff.

I turn on the television and find the Dallas game playing again. I don't change the channel, and I sit, opening the bag to take the food out. "Oh, you got so much food," I say over my shoulder as I take out the fried rice, lo mein, beef and broccoli, sweet and sour chicken, and kung pao shrimp. A bag of wonton and some egg rolls. "Jesus, how many people are we expecting?" I ask her when she comes into the room.

"I ordered when I was hungry," she says, coming over and grabbing an egg roll to pop into her mouth. I open the containers and grab the spoons she brought and put them in each each one. "I swear I don't think I've ever been this hungry."

"Did you not eat lunch?" I ask her, grabbing my own plate and putting food in it. "Did you work today?" I ask her, taking in her yoga pants and top. She's always dressed up.

"Yeah, I had a meeting this morning but then worked from home," she tells me, grabbing her own plate and then looking up at the television.

"Why are you watching this?" she asks me, and I just shrug. We don't like hockey. It's a known fact we go to the games for the food and to drink. We watch it only when forced to and only if our family is on the ice.

"I just turned it on, and it was this," I tell her between bites. I look at the screen when I hear Evan's last name. Seeing him skating on the ice, I follow him with my eyes as he skates over the blue line. It looks like it's two on two. He passes over to the guy on the other side, and the goalie follows the puck sliding across. Except the guy just slaps it back to Evan. He is already winding up for a one timer, and the goalie doesn't have enough time to get back before it sails past him.

"Whoa, that was a nice play," I say and watch him skate to the board and point at his teammate with a huge smile on his face. My sister is looking at me with her mouth opened.

"What the fuck did you just say?" she asks me, almost whispering. "Were you watching hockey and liking it?" She puts her plate down, and I just smile. "Oh my God. What's going on?" she says, getting up and looking around the room. "Am I being punked? Is that it?"

"I was just saying it was a good play." I pick up the remote and turn it while he skates to the bench and high-fives his teammates. "What do you want to watch?"

"Have you spoken to him?" she asks me and puts her hands on her hips. I try to lie to her, or at least, I attempt to by just shaking my head. But she knows me because she is half of me. "Pinky?"

Since we were four, we always said pinky if we were telling the truth. "What?"

"Don't play dumb with me, Zar. Have you spoken to him?" I put my plate down and turn to her.

"I called him yesterday, or he called me, actually," I tell her the truth. "But it was to talk about the wedding." It's a half-truth, and she sees it because now her hands go from her hips to cross over her chest. At times like these, I really hate that she knows me so well. "He's taking me out tomorrow."

"What?" she shrieks. "Spill."

I throw my hands up in the air. "There really isn't anything to say. He said I'm going to Jersey, so let's go out and talk about the wedding."

"So it's a date?" she asks me the same question I've been asking myself all day long.

"No," I say, and my tongue almost feels heavier. "It's a meeting!"

"Where are you meeting him?" she asks me, and I just shrug.

"I have no idea. I'm assuming he is going to text me tomorrow with the details." I pick up my plate again.

"He's driving in from Jersey to have dinner with you?" She comes back over. "What are you going to wear?"

"I have no idea," I tell her honestly. "Can we just talk about something else?"

"For now," she says, "but all bets are off tomorrow night."

I don't say anything. I just watch the television, and for the rest of the night, the only thing going through my head is this meeting/date I have tomorrow night.

Evan

*T*HE BUZZER RINGS, letting us know that the third period is over. I jump over the board from the bench and skate over to Jari to get in line to congratulate him on the victory.

"Good game." I knock my helmet to his goalie one.

"Nice one timer," he says, and I laugh and skate to the center ice, and the team raises their sticks to the applause of the fans who remain. I get off the ice, and the celebration is already underway when I sit down at my spot. Unsnapping my helmet, I take it off and set it next to me.

The door closes, and the coach comes in. "You guys did good out there," he starts, and I am already taking off my skates and grabbing my slides. Everyone else is also undressing. "You guys are getting caught up in the neutral zone, and I don't like it." No one says anything because he's right. "The bus leaves for the airport in one hour. We'll land at two a.m. local time. Tomorrow is an off day, so rest up."

He nods to us and walks out of the room, leaving the door open and giving the journalists time to come in and ask questions.

I'm about to peel off my jersey when I see Scott, the reporter with *SportsCenter,* approach me.

"Hey there, Evan. Good game tonight," he says. Taking out his phone, he presses the red button and takes out his little square notepad with questions. "Tonight's goal is for sure going to end up as one of the best plays of the night," he starts off saying, and I smile thinking about it. "Was that something you guys practiced?"

"No," I say. "It is just the chemistry that we have with each other on the ice. We play very similar."

"There were a couple of turnovers in the zone tonight. How crucial is it to stop that from happening?" he asks into his phone and then puts it in front of my mouth.

"I think we really have to tighten it up on our end. Mistakes happen and it's just part of the game. We learn from it and move on."

"You were trending on Twitter last night," he starts, and I force myself not to smile. "Zara Stone reached out to you for a date." He looks at me, raising his eyebrows. The reporters standing around us hear the question and look over with interest. "Is that date going to happen?"

I laugh now. "Come on, Scott. A gentleman never kisses and tells," I say then nod at him. "Thanks for the questions." I walk away from him and go into the shower area where I know they can't follow us. I wait there for ten minutes until I hear the music start playing, which means the reporters have left. I walk back out, stripping off my jersey and tossing it in the big bin. I find my skates and helmet packed away for our trip. I take off my pants and hang them on the hook. The sound of the Velcro echoes in the room once I take off my chest protector and also hang that. The only thing that comes on the road with me is my helmet and skates. Other than that, I have one I travel with and another that stays here. I'm one of the last ones in the shower, and when I finally slip on my black suit jacket, it's almost time to go.

I grab my overnight bag and head out to the waiting bus. I sit at the front of the bus since I'm one of the last ones on, and when Coach finally gets on, you hear the hiss of the bus as it finally pulls out of the parking garage. I grab my phone and go through my messages. I have a couple from my mother about my game tonight.

My father also sends me a couple, but his are harsher. He points out every single mistake I made, which are on point, and he isn't wrong. I guess that's why he's going for a head coach job next year.

The last one is from Candace.

Me: Good news is you're still trending on Twitter. This time because of that goal and not the stupid date.

I roll my eyes at the last comment and then go on Instagram. I scroll through the stories and, then I search Zara Stone. She is private, so I request to follow her. I see that she has her name and a website, so I click it and it takes me to Zara'a Closet.

I don't have time to search anything because the bus comes to a stop and I get up. I take a picture of the plane for my Instagram story. As soon as the plane takes off, the food starts coming out. The sound of plates clinking fills the air, and I open my phone again. I sat by myself this time, and when I look around, everyone seems to be in their own world. That is what happens when you travel late at night. I scan her website and see that she works for Nordstrom, and I set a plan in motion in my head.

When we finally land, it looks like everyone is ready to crash, and no one really says anything as we get our key cards. Dumping my bag right inside the door, I undress and finally lay my head down at almost three thirty. I close off my phone completely, and when I wake up in the morning, I'm shocked to see it's almost noon.

I pick up the phone and call the front desk to request a car. I get up, washing off my face and grabbing my black jeans and a black T-shirt. I run my fingers through my hair and then slide on my black leather jacket. With my wallet in my hand and my phone tucked into my back pocket, I make my way downstairs. I spot some of the guys and just nod at them while I walk to the front desk. I put on my dark Ray-Bans so no one really notices me.

I grab the keys to the car waiting at the front door and punch in the address on the GPS. It says I will arrive at my destination in forty minutes. I add twenty minutes for traffic, but I'm surprised when I make it there in under an hour. Finding parking is a nightmare, but I just park at the first underground garage I can find. When I walk out of the car and make my way to the store, I get all these butterflies in my stomach. I start to wonder if maybe this wasn't the best plan I've ever had.

I pull open the door to Nordstrom and take a look around. I walk through the cosmetic area and then spot a woman dressed in black. "Excuse me," I say, and she turns to look at me, a smile plastered on to her face. "I was wondering where the service counter was."

"Third floor," she says, pointing at the escalator. Nodding at her and smiling, I turn and make my way over to the service counter. The woman sitting behind the desk has a headset on as she fields calls.

"Good afternoon," she says, smiling. "How may I help you?"

"Hi," I start to say, and my heart beats so fast I swear it's going to come out of my chest. "I was wondering if I could have an appointment with Zara Stone."

The woman looks at me. "I don't know if she is taking any other clients today," she says and then looks down. "I know she is with someone now."

"If you can ask her, I would really appreciate it, and I will pay double if that helps." I smile at her, and she just nods.

"Let me see if I can reach her," she says.

"Sure thing," I say and walk over to the two chairs on my right. I sit down and take out my phone, and my head is down when I hear the sound of heels clicking.

My head comes up the second she walks into the room, and it's a good thing I'm sitting down because I think I would fall. She doesn't see me there, so it gives me time to get myself under control. Her strawberry blond hair hangs loose to her waist, and she is wearing loose blue pants that stop hallway down her calf. Her white long-sleeve sweater just makes her elegant and classy. The sleeves cut open at her wrist, and those fucking sky-high heels make her even hotter.

"Hey, Zara," she says, smiling at her. "This is the gentleman who asked for you," the receptionist says and points at me. Zara finally notices that I'm in the room, and if I thought she was breathtaking walking in, it's nothing compared to when she faces me. I see that her eyes are almost emerald and her lips a perfect shade of pink. Her eyes land on me, and surprise fills her face.

"Evan," she whispers, and my cock springs up for a salute. "What are you doing here?"

I get up, smiling now. "I need a suit. Figured I could kill two birds with one stone," I say as I walk up to her, and I'm not sure if I should go in for a hug or a kiss on the cheek or what, so I just stand in front of her. I breathe in her scent, and if my cock wasn't being strangled enough, it definitely is now.

"A suit?" she says, laughing. I see that her sweater goes off one shoulder, and I have this sudden urge to cover her with my jacket. I also have the sudden need to lean in and kiss her bare shoulder. I wonder if it's as soft as it looks. I wonder if she would get goose bumps. I wonder if she would lean into me. "Um, hello," she says. My eyes fly to hers, and I know I'm so not ready for her.

"Every year, we have our casino night," I start telling her, "and well, I need a suit."

She folds her arms over her chest, pushing up her perfect tits. Tits that would fit perfectly in my palm. "Interesting."

"Nothing interesting about it," I say with a chuckle as I push my hands into the back pockets of my jeans. "Can you help me out?"

She shakes her head, and her smile lights up her whole

face. "Fine," she says and turns to the girl. "Can you check me out please? I'll be leaving after this appointment."

"Sure thing, Zara. I also have five emails and twenty-five voicemails for you. I will forward them to you." She nods at her and then turns to me.

"Okay, Mr. Richards, let's get this appointment going." She holds out her hand to lead the way, and we walk side by side. "So tell me about your style. What's your favorite color?"

As we walk toward the suits, I see how everyone turns to watch her. Not me, just her, yet she doesn't see any of this. "Black."

"How many black suits do you have?" she asks, and I look at her.

"I have no idea," I answer her because I don't. I don't even need a suit, but I wanted to surprise her.

"What about blue?" she says, grabbing a blue suit and picking it up. "It's Hugo Boss."

I nod. "Are you opposed to prints?" she asks me, and I can see she is playing with me now. "Like a black with a gold tailoring?" she asks, picking up a suit that is too avant-garde for me.

I glare at her. "I like the blue one and that one," I say, pointing at a light gray suit.

"That's Gucci," she says, walking over to it. Then she turns to me. "Follow me," she says and brings me in the back to a private fitting room. There are mirrors on three walls with a solid door to the right. She walks to the door on the right and hangs the suits up. "Try this on, and I will get you a dress shirt. I think you're a sixteen, right?"

"Um, I have no idea," I tell her and then turn to see her with her hand on the door handle. "I don't usually go into stores."

"Well, aren't I special?" she says and then looks at the suits. "Get the pants on, and I'll be back in a minute with shirts. I'm assuming slim fit, right, to show off the guns and stuff?" She laughs and closes the door behind her. I kick off my shoes and take off my pants, grabbing the dress pants off the hanger and slipping them on. I pull off my shirt when I hear a knock on the door. I open the door and see her there with two shirts in her hand; one is light blue, and the other is a light pink. I smile when her eyes take in my chest, and now it's my turn. "Um, here, try the pink one with the gray, and this with the blue pants." She hands them to me and then turns to walk away, and I watch her hips swaying. I would love to have her bent over with the shoes still on. She looks over her shoulder and catches me staring. "You are paying me by the hour, so chop-chop."

I close the door and put the shirt on. When I walk out of the room, she is leaning against the wall with her phone in her hand. "Did you request to follow me on Instagram?"

"Yeah, last night," I say, getting on the platform and watching her in the mirror.

"I can't accept it," she says, and I turn around now to look at her face or more like down at her.

"Why the fuck not?" I ask her.

"It's my personal Instagram, and you're a client, so it crosses a certain line," she tells me, putting her phone back in her pocket.

"Fine, you're fired. Get me someone else," I tell her, and

she throws her head back and lets out a loud laugh, causing something in me to shift into place.

"You're a funny guy," she says when she finally stops laughing. "Now let me see the suit."

"I'll show you whatever you want to see," I tell her while I look at her in the mirror. Her eyes fly up to mine, and her cheeks get a touch pink. I am so fucked.

SEVEN

ZARA

"I'LL SHOW YOU whatever you want to see," he says to me. It's almost like he's challenging me, and I swear my stomach flutters.

When I got a call from Bernadette telling me someone requested to see me, I had just wrapped up a fitting with a new client. I almost didn't take it, and when I walked into the room and my eyes landed on his, I was shocked. I knew what he looked like from the hours I spent on Pinterest searching him, but I will deny that to my last dying breath.

Seeing him in person, though, made this whole thing more real. I will also say he was so much hotter than in his pictures. And I was totally fucked. I needed to get away from him ASAP. So I put him in a room and took off, but then he opened the door, and he was shirtless, and that feel-ing came back. Except now, my mouth was dry, my palms clammy, and my stomach was doing this butterfly thing.

"Calm down there, big boy," I tell him, going up to him and smoothing the back of the jacket. I swear it takes everything in me not to let my hand linger. "The fit is good," I tell him, walking in front of him and seeing I reach his nose. It took everything in me not to step a touch closer to feel his heat. "I mean, we have to get it fixed a bit since your arms are a bit bigger than this size."

I look up, and his eyes are looking down at me, and he puts his hands on my hips. If it were anyone else, I would step out of his hold. If I were smart, I would step out of his grasp, but I am not that smart. "Did you eat lunch?" he asks softly, and I just shake my head.

"I had back-to-back appointments," I tell him and step back when I hear steps approaching.

"Oh, there you are," Roman says, walking into the dressing room. Roman and I work side by side. He works full time and has an extensive client list. "I was wondering if you would leave without saying goodbye," he says, coming closer. He's six foot two and lean with a megawatt smile. He used to work at Abercrombie before starting here.

I laugh at him. "Nope still here. I had a last-minute addition." He turns to look at Evan now.

"Oh, sorry. For some reason, I thought it was someone from your brother's team," he says. He isn't a sports guy, so he has no idea what sport he plays, let alone what the team name is.

"Nope, he's a new client," I say, holding my hands in front of myself. "But he does play hockey. Roman, this is Evan Richards. He plays for Dallas." Evan looks about to burst out of his suit. "Evan, this is Roman. We work together."

Evan reaches out his hand for a handshake. "Nice to meet you, Roman," he says, and I think I see Roman flinch before Evan finally lets go of his hand.

"I was wondering if you wanted to catch up after work?" he asks me, and I'm about to tell him no when Evan speaks.

"She's busy," he says with a tight voice. I look at him, and the smile on Roman's face goes away.

"I'm sorry. I had no idea," he says, holding up his hand. "I'll see you next week," he says, nodding to me and walking away.

"What in the world was that?" I ask him, pointing my finger at Roman walking away.

"That was me getting you out of a date you didn't want to go on," he informs me, then looks at himself in the mirror, buttoning the jacket. "I like the fit of this suit."

"Don't you change the subject," I tell him. "What if I wanted to go on a date with him?"

He shrugs his shoulders. "Then you should have tweeted him instead of me," he says. "Should I try on the next one?" he says, and I don't know what to say. I've never been on the receiving end of this. I've seen it with Matthew and Max and my father, but I've never had anyone act like that for me. "I think I'm just going to take it," he says, ignoring the fact he just laid claim to me. "Can I have this shipped to me, or do I have to take it right now?"

"I can have it shipped to you," I say, "but that was not okay."

"What wasn't okay, Zara?" he asks. He steps closer to me, and I'm suddenly at a loss for words, again.

"You coming in here and just throwing down for me," I

tell him.

"What do you feel like? Italian?" he says, walking back to the room and shrugging off his jacket. "We can have whatever you feel like."

"I feel like kicking you right now," I tell him, and he looks up and smirks. It just makes me want to kick him even more. I mean, kick him and then kiss it better.

"Okay, I'll surprise you," he says and shuts the door before I say anything.

When I walked into work this morning, I had no idea I would be walking out with Evan by my side, let alone with his hand resting firmly on my lower back while he ushers me to where his car is parked. "Do you want to go home and change?" he asks me once we get to the car. I walk to the passenger door, and I'm about to reach for the door when his hand comes out of nowhere and opens the door for me. "Whatever you want." He stands there with the door open, and I get into the car and lean out to grab the door to close it, but he's standing in front of it. "So what do you think?"

"Um," I say, my brain literally on overdrive right now.

"Do you live alone?" he asks me, and I nod. "We can always pick up some food and eat it at your house."

"Yeah," I say, thinking that might be better than going out to a restaurant and risking someone taking a picture of us. "It might be better, so no one gets a picture."

"I don't care about that. I care that you were working all day, and you might be tired," he says, turning and shutting the door. I watch him walk around the car, putting on his glasses, and it takes everything in me not to call Zoe or text her or something.

He gets into the car. "Are you going to give me the address, or do you want to guide me there?" Starting the car, he looks over at me. He takes his phone out and enters the address I give him. I know my father would not be okay about this, but either way, he would know where I lived. I watch the road while he drives to my house and finds a parking spot right in front. He shuts off the car and then looks at me. "Don't get out," he says, getting out of the car and walking around to my side. He opens my door and holds out a hand for me. I look around, and he laughs. "Come on, it's getting chilly outside, and your jacket is thin," he says. I take his hand to step out of the car and he doesn't let my hand go while he shuts the door. My hand is almost lost in his, our palms together, and when I walk toward the house, he intertwines his fingers with mine. I have to release his hand to get my keys out of my purse, and I miss it the minute I do.

After opening the door, I turn one the light in the entrance. I put my keys and my purse on the mirrored table with fresh white roses in the middle. I turn to look at him come into my house, and he shuts the door behind him, sliding the deadbolt. When I slip off the Louboutins that I've been wearing all day, I think tomorrow will be a flip-flop kind of day. "Come in," I say, walking to the two big doors that load us into the house. We come face to face with a white staircase with a dark chestnut brown railing against the wall. The flooring is a glossy green almost black marble flooring. "Let me take your jacket," I tell him, and he takes off his glasses and places them with his keys by my stuff. He shrugs his jacket off, and I see that his shirt is tight on him, but I'm still picturing him shirtless in my head. He hands me his jacket, and I take it, walking to the living room and placing it over the back of the couch. "Do you want something to drink?" I ask him.

"Water would be great," he says. I nod, turning to get him water, and he follows me. I turn left and head down a narrow hallway. Various frames line the wall from top to bottom with personal pictures of the places I've traveled. When I look over my shoulder, he's looking at the pictures, but I'm already at the end of the hallway that opens to a huge kitchen. The middle counter is white and gray marble. A white vase with pink flowers brings out the light in the house, so I always keep them fresh. Skylights let in more light. The range against the wall is black. White cabinets line two walls while my huge ass fridge is against the wall on the other side. This was all here when I moved in. "Do you want sparkling or still?" I ask him, and he just laughs.

"Still is good," he says. I don't know why I'm nervous having him in my space. I open the fridge to grab the water bottle and hand it to him. He walks to me and stands in front of me. He twists open the bottle and takes a long sip, resting his hip against the counter. "Do you cook?" he asks me, looking at the range, and I cross my arms over my chest.

"I'm not cooking for you," I tell him. "I mean, I can cook, but I'm not cooking for you." I tilt my head to the side. "Do you have tools in your garage?"

"Yeah," he says, and he looks confused, setting his water on the counter.

"Do you build houses?" I cross my ankles, and he looks down at my feet. I'm suddenly happy I got that pedicure yesterday. He puts his head back and laughs. His laughter pulls his shirt tighter across his chest. "Touché."

"Yeah, exactly," I tell him. "Now, what do you want to eat?"

"I'm good with anything," he tells me. "I'm pretty hungry."

"So pizza?" I say. "Can you have pizza?" When he nods, I walk out of the room and grab my phone. When I turn around, I shriek 'cause he's right behind me. The hallway's dark with only the light from the front door and kitchen. "You scared me."

He puts his hands on my hips and brings me closer to him, my hand still holding my phone. "I didn't mean to scare you," he whispers, and I feel his hot breath on me. My heart speeds up, and my stomach feels all tingly. "I just didn't want to leave you alone." He takes one hand off my hips and brings it up to tuck my hair behind my ear. "You have to be the most beautiful woman I have ever met in my whole life." His voice is soft, and I swear I'm inching closer to him. All my words are stuck in my throat, and nothing seems to be coming out. "It's a dangerous place."

"What is?" I ask when I'm finally able to speak some words.

"Your eyes," he says. "I can get lost in your eyes." And just when I think he is going to lean in and kiss me, just when I can literally taste his lips on mine, the door swings open, and Zoe steps inside. I jump away from him and out of his reach, an action Zoe doesn't miss.

"Holy shit, I didn't know you were home," she says from the front door and then looks at Evan. "I thought you were going out."

"Change of plans," I tell her. "Come in."

"What the fuck?" I hear whispered from beside me, and I

look at him. "There are two of you?"

I shake my head and laugh. "This is my twin sister, Zoe." Zoe puts her purse down next to mine and slips off her jacket, tossing it on top of everything. This is the professional Zoe. She is wearing a maroon-colored pants suit with a white button-down silk shirt. I know exactly what brand her Yves St-Laurent shoes are because she stole them from my closet.

"I'm the pretty one," Zoe says, walking up to him and putting her hand out. "I'm also the funny one."

"She isn't the funny one at all," I finally pipe in. "She's the annoying one who has the worst timing of life."

She laughs now. "She didn't say that when I pulled the fire alarm at school and got her out of detention." I look over at Evan who just stands there laughing. "Anyway, I thought you guys were going out. I came by to borrow a dress for a function I have to attend this weekend."

"And you weren't going to ask me?" She shrugs after I ask her the question.

"We were just going to order pizza," Evan says and puts his arms around my shoulders. Zoe's eyes watch his every move. "You should join us."

"Oh, there is an us now is there?" she teases, and I don't know who I'm going to kill first.

Evan

I LOOK ACROSS the dining room table at her as she takes a bite of her pizza. Not with a knife and fork, not even with a plate in front of her. Straight out of the box, she's folded the piece in half and taken a bite.

"This has to be the best pizza of life," Zoe says, and my head turns to her. When we were standing in the hallway, and I was so close to tasting her, I would have made a deal with the devil for just one kiss. Just one. But no one was taking bets that day because the door opened and shut, and I thought I was going lightheaded when I saw the woman at the door. All the blood had left my head and traveled south.

"It's my favorite," I say, grabbing another slice out of one of the three boxes. We were going to eat in the living room, but Zara brought the pizza into the dining room. I'm now sitting in one of the brown chairs with the square marble table between us. She moved the vase of flowers to the other side. She sits at the head of the square table, I sit on her left, and Zoe sits on her right. "I have it every single time I'm here," I tell them, folding my own pizza except pieces of sausage fall out. I ordered a large pie for each of us since we couldn't decide on the same toppings. Zara was a just cheese girl, but Zoe added pineapples, and there was no way in fuck I was eating that one. Besides, I was going to finish this whole pie.

"So Evan," Zoe starts, and I look up mid chew. "What did you think of the tweet?"

"I thought it was funny." I look over at Zara who smiles and nods. "But I think the funniest part was the hashtag at the end."

"I think she should have put his picture with it so if you googled that hashtag, his picture would show up," Zoe said, and I almost choke now.

"I don't know the law all that well, but I think he could sue for defamation of character?" I tell her, grabbing the water bottle and taking a drink.

"But then he would have to prove he doesn't have a pencil dick. And well," Zoe says, lifting her hand open, "he's going to lose."

"Can we talk about something else?" Zara says.

"Yes, we can," Zoe says. "Let's talk about your date."

"No," Zara says at the same time I say, "Sure." And she turns and glares at me.

"Perfect," Zoe says, clapping her hands together and rubbing them. Zara drops the crust of her pizza in front of her and gets up.

"Eat." I look at her, pointing at the pizza, and Zoe stops

rubbing her hands together. "You didn't eat all day."

Zara puts her piece of pizza down and pushes away from the table. Zoe looks at her. "Where are you going?"

"I'm going to hide all the knives and maybe the serving forks," Zoe says, and I laugh at her. "She does not take well to being told what to do." She points at Zara who just shakes her head as she turns to walk away.

"What are your last wishes?" Zoe whispers when we hear drawers slamming shut in the kitchen. "Anyone you want me to mention in your eulogy?"

"She isn't really going to stab me?" I ask shocked and a touch scared. I look over her shoulder and see Zara come back in with a pizza cutter in one hand.

"It's going to be a slow death," Zoe says, sitting down. "The blade is dull."

Zara bursts out laughing, and I look over at her. She tied her hair on top of her head, which gives me full access to her neck. I picture my teeth marks there and want to bury my face there. "It's to cut his pizza," she points out. The rest of the meal goes by so fast, and my stomach hurts from laughing.

"Okay, lovebirds," Zoe says, coming back from upstairs while we were cleaning up the pizza boxes and everything. "I'm going to head out."

"What did you take?" Zara asks, wiping her hands on a rag while Zoe holds up what looks like a long shirt. It's a pinkish color with sequins all over it. "Are you sure you want to go with that outfit?"

"Outfit?" I ask puzzled. "Where is the rest of it?" I look at it, and the most material it has is on the long sleeves. "You need to wear pants with that."

Zara looks over at me while Zoe tries to hide her laughter by rolling her lips. "It's a dress."

She grabs the hanger from Zoe and holds it up to her chest, and I see it barely goes to her mid thigh. "See."

"Yeah," I say, crossing my arms over my chest. "You can keep it, Zoe," I tell her, and Zara stands there with her mouth open.

"Oh, this is going to be so good. I'm going to get a whole new wardrobe from this," she says, grabbing the dress from Zara, and I see now that it is all open in the back.

"There isn't even a back to this dress," I point out.

"It's sexy chic," Zara says.

"It's also mine now." Zoe turns and walks out of the kitchen.

"That dress cost me six hundred dollars." She turns to look at me. "And I got it at cost."

"I'm not sure, but I think you overpaid. There is no material on that dress." I wipe my own hands now. "Do you want to go into the living room and talk?"

"No." She glares at me, and I walk over to her, grab her hand, and lead her to the living room. I walk to the couch and sit down, bringing her down with me. She sits next to me, and I turn to face her as she gets comfortable. She tucks her feet under her and then puts her arm across the back of the couch. I put my own arm across the back of the couch behind hers, and my hand is close to her exposed shoulder.

"What are you doing tomorrow night?" I ask her, and I'm not sure why.

"I'm not sure. I have to fly out to Chicago on Thursday to meet with a client," she tells me, and my mind is suddenly spinning.

"Do you want to come watch the game tomorrow?" I ask her. I know it's not a good idea because it will get back to her family, but I don't really care. "I can get you tickets, and you can bring Zoe."

"Um." She starts saying and then smiles. "I don't really like hockey," she says, and I gasp in shock. "I mean, I go for the food and the drinks, and I get to see my family, but other than that …" She shrugs.

"Okay, what about this weekend?" I ask her. "What are you doing this weekend?"

"I'll have to check my schedule," she tells me. "I'm gone most of the next two weeks."

"Gone?" I ask her, my thumb now rubbing her arm slowly.

"I have five client meetings, so I'm flying out West for a week." Maybe it's a sign that this is going to just be a one wedding date, and I should move on.

"Do you want to be my date to the casino night?" I ask her, and I'm suddenly scared she is going to say no. "It's in Dallas in two weeks. I have four days off."

"I don't know," she says softly, and I suddenly wish that the lights were on bright so I could see her face and her eyes.

"I'd really like it," I tell her softly. Her tongue comes out to lick her lip and then she pulls the whole bottom lip into her mouth, her teeth biting it. My mind starts playing tricks on me because all I can see is me advancing on her, taking her face in my hands, and kissing the shit out of her. "I should get going," I say, getting up. I don't want to leave but know that I should really, really go before I do something stupid that I can't take back.

"Oh, yeah," she says, getting up and standing in front of me. My hand reaches out before I have a chance to take it back. Taking her cheek in my palm, I move it down to her neck and then her shoulder. I turn and walk away from her, my hand falling like a lead weight. She follows me to the door, and the light's on from when Zoe left.

"I really had fun today," I say, grabbing my keys and glasses, then turn and look at her, trying to take her all in. "Let me know about the game or the casino night." I try not to make a big deal about it, but my stomach is in knots.

"I will," she finally says, nodding.

Leaning in, I swear I hear her breath hitch. I'm so tempted to kiss her open mouth, but instead, I kiss her on the cheek softly. "Lock up after me," I tell her and walk out of the house and make my way to the car. I get in the car, starting it up, and pull away even though I have no idea where I'm going. The only thing I knew was that I needed to get away from her before I turned back around and begged her until she said yes.

I turn the corner and take out my phone. It's almost nine p.m., and I have forty-seven missed calls and over one hundred text messages. "Fuck," I say to myself and call my sister since she is the majority of the calls. She picks up after one ring.

"Where the hell have you been?" she shouts into the phone.

"I met up with some friends in New York. Why?" I say,

checking the texts to make sure I didn't miss anything urgent. Mostly, it's the guys discussing dinner.

"Friends in New York?" she asks. "What friends?"

"What difference does it make?" I open my maps and punch in the address to the hotel, following the directions while I connect the Bluetooth. "What were all the missed calls?"

"I was calling to ask you if I could go to Mexico for the four days when you guys are on break," she tells me. "Then you didn't answer me, and it pissed me off, so I booked it anyway."

"Why do I need to give you permission?" I ask her, getting on the bridge out of New York. Suddenly, I feel like I'm forgetting something.

"You don't need to give me permission. It's just during the casino night thing, and well, four of my friends are going, so I just booked it."

"It's fine, Cand," I tell her. "I didn't even think you were coming to the casino night. You hate those events."

"Yeah," she says. "Anyway, what did you do today?"

"Not much. Is everything good there? How are the dogs?" I change the subject, and she fills me in about everything that has been going on, which isn't much. I hang up with her just before I get to the hotel and park the car in front of the door, giving the valet the keys and telling him I borrowed it from the hotel. He nods his head and hands me a ticket to give the front desk.

By the time I make it to my room, I'm ready to crash, but I undress and take a shower. My body feels tense as fuck, and I let the hot water wash over my neck while I stand there playing over the day in my head. When I finally walk out of the bathroom, I check my phone and have one notification from Instagram.

Zara Stone has accepted your follow request.

NINE

ZARA

I FEEL HIS kiss linger on my cheek the whole time I'm locking the door after he left. My hands shake while I walk around the house, turning off the lights and heading upstairs to my bedroom. I'm exhausted and tense. Tense because I want to go watch his hockey game but know that I can't without it getting back to my brother. Tense because I want to be his date to that casino night and tense because all I wanted was for him to kiss me before he left.

I start the bath before I undress and light the candle. Slowly sinking into the hot water, I wait for the tension to leave my body. I'm usually good with closing off my mind and just letting it go but not tonight. Tonight, the only thing I see when I close my eyes is him. Smiling, laughing, looking into my eyes. I give up on relaxing and get out the bath, wrapping in a huge white plush towel. I walk to my bedroom and slide into bed, grabbing my phone and checking my messages. I can't even deal with the messages from Zoe right now or the fact that she started a group chat. Instead, I go on Instagram and see I still have it open to Evan's page.

I click on my own Instagram and go back to my follow requests, and right there on the top is Evan's name. I don't know if I should or not, but my finger has other plans, and I click confirm.

I put my phone down and turn off the nightlight I have beside my bed. My phone rings, and I see that it's Evan.

"Hello," I say softly.

"Does this mean we crossed a certain line?" he says, and I can see him smiling in my head.

"Don't celebrate yet. I just accepted for now, and then tomorrow, I'll block you," I say, rolling my lips when I hear him scoff.

"What are you doing?" he asks, and I hear his moving around.

"I just got out of the bath, and now I'm lying in bed. You?" I ask him and hear what sounds like him getting into bed.

"I was just getting out of the shower when I got the notification." I listen to his voice and wonder what he sleeps in. "Now, I'm sliding into bed. I have to be at the rink at nine for practice."

"You should get to bed," I tell him, looking at the clock.

"Have you thought about it?" he asks his voice soft, and I close my eyes, imagining him here. "Come visit me, sweet Zara."

"I'll think about it," I tell him, "but I'll let you go for now so you can get some sleep."

"Sweet dreams, sweet Zara," he says barely above a

whisper.

"Night," I say and hang up before I shout that I'll come to the game, and I'll come to his house. I'll give him anything he wants. What the hell is happening to me? I am never ever like this. It took Ed five dates for me to miss him or at least want to miss him. I raise my hand and put it to my forehead. Maybe I should call Denise, Max's sister, and see if she can check me out to see if I'm okay.

Closing my eyes, I spend the night tossing and turning. I have weird, vivid dreams that Evan is here or I'm somewhere with a huge ass lawn. It is so weird that when my alarm rings at eight, I groan and press snooze. But soon, the smell of coffee lingers in the air, and I sit up in bed, the covers falling off my naked body.

"Hello?" I shout.

"Seriously?" Zoe says as she comes up the stairs. "You hear a noise, and you shout instead of getting up and calling 911?" She comes into the room holding two cups of coffee. She is wearing yoga pants and a T-shirt with her hair tied on top of her head.

"I don't know many burglars who come into your house and make coffee," I tell her, sitting up and holding the blanket to my chest. "Give me," I say, reaching out for a cup and then hearing the front door open and slam.

"I brought bagels," Vivienne shouts, and I look at Zoe.

The door opens again, and this time, I hear more voices. "Did you just get here?"

I look at Zoe. "What's going on?" I ask her and then hear a stampede of feet coming up the stairs.

"Hey," Zoe says as Vivienne, Karrie, and Allison walk into

the room, wearing pretty much the same as Zoe.

"I didn't know this party was clothing optional," Vivienne says, and I just shake my head as Allison comes to sit on the bed.

"This bed is comfy. Did you replace the mattress?" she asks me, and I look at her.

"Of course, I did," I tell her. "I don't know if you and Max had sex on the other one."

"We didn't," she says. "He refused to come into the house in case Matthew had installed cameras." She laughs. "But I did replace the one that Karrie had when she was living here with Matthew because, well, we all know they were doing naked Twister in that bed." We look at Karrie who just shrugs her shoulders.

"He handcuffed me to this bed once," she says, smiling, "for three days." She sits on the bed also. "God, those were the days."

Allison, Zara, and I all fake gag when we see her getting all dreamy. "What is everyone doing here?" I finally ask.

"Zoe called an emergency meeting," Allison says, grabbing the coffee from my hand. "We had to get up at six thirty to be here. And all I heard was Max moaning since they just got home last night."

"Okay, you get dressed," Zoe says to me, "and we will go make breakfast."

"Why are we having an emergency meeting?" I ask even though I shouldn't since I know what Zoe is going to say.

"Evan came over for dinner last night," she says, and everyone gasps.

"He flew in from Dallas to have dinner with you?" Allison

asks when Vivienne starts looking around the room.

"Is he still here?" Vivienne says, her mouth and eyes both opened. "I was checking him out. He looks like he has a good one." She puts both hands to her crotch area.

"Oh my God, is he here?" Alison gets off the bed and runs into the bathroom while Karrie starts running upstairs to where my office is.

"He's not here," I shout at them and then look at Zoe. "Dude, twin secret."

"Sorry." She shrugs. "I don't think I can do this one alone."

"Get out," I say, getting out of bed naked and then having Allison look at me. "What I wouldn't give for your legs."

"I'd kill for her ass," Karrie says. Walking into the walk-in closet, I grab a thong, then slide on yoga pants and a camisole with a built-in bra.

When I come back out of the closet, they are still there talking about their bodies as they stand side by side. "I thought you guys were starting breakfast?"

"Oh shit, yeah," Karrie said. "I forgot." She turns and walks out of the room, but now we all follow. And just when she hits the last step, the doorbell rings.

"Seriously, it's like Grand Central Station in here," I say, and Karrie goes to the door. When I get to the bottom, I look around the corner and gasp out in shock.

"What is that?" I ask while she comes into the house with the largest bouquet I've ever seen in my whole life.

"Are those Fleur de Venus?" Vivienne asks of the flowers in the round cardboard box; the light blush pink roses look like a dome.

"Where is the card?" I ask, and they all look at me. Karrie

goes to the living room and places the flowers on the center table, and I walk to it, grabbing the white card tucked behind the side.

I open it up, and I can't help the smile that comes over my face.

Have a great day, sweet Zara

E

"What does it say?" Zoe asks.

Vivienne jumps up. "We need a drink for this," she says, running to the kitchen and then coming back with the bottle of prosecco and four glasses.

Karrie walks to the front door and brings in five boxes of food. "We stopped on the way here."

"We have Danishes, muffins, scones, croissants, and doughnuts," Allison says, taking a box and opening it, and then opening the rest and placing them around the huge bouquet.

"He paid over a thousand dollars for those flowers," Zoe says, and I look at her when she turns her phone around. "A thousand."

"Oh fuck," Vivienne says mid pour.

"You need to start at the beginning," Allison says, grabbing a glass from Vivienne, then going to the couch and sitting down. "And don't leave anything out."

I shrug. "There really isn't anything to say. He was in Jersey for his game tonight," I start. Sitting down on the carpet in front of the fireplace, I wait for the four girls to sit on the couch and give me their attention. "He showed up at my work and bought two suits I'm sure he didn't need."

"Did you charge him?" Vivienne asks.

"He paid for the suits," I tell her, and she cocks her head, "but I didn't charge him for my time."

"You charge Matthew double," Karrie says.

"That's because he is the worst person to shop for. He returned five suits I bought him last year. Five," I tell her, holding up my hand.

"Anyway," Allison says, "go on."

"So he shows up and then he about lost his shit with Roman." I remember that part.

"What do you mean by lost his shit?" Allison asks. "Like 'dude, watch it' or 'dude, you best fuck off.'"

"More like the second one," I answer and see her eyes widen. "Anyway, after he held the door open for me and helped me get in his car," I say shocked, "then when we got here, he told me to stay seated so he could help me out."

"Wait, what?" Vienne says. "Like holding the door open for you?"

"Asshole," Zoe says sarcastically, and I glare at her.

I don't bother answering her. Instead, I just continue. "Then we came here, and he was all like can you cook, and I was like can you build a house."

"I walked in, and I think they were about to kiss," Zoe says almost with glee in her voice.

"Shut up," Karrie says, grabbing the bottle to fill her glass up.

"We were talking about what we were going to eat," I tell her, and I'm not lying.

"He had his arm around her shoulder the whole time." I roll my eyes now when Allison snickers. "And was like join us for dinner." Karrie slaps her leg, laughing. "Wait, wait, it gets better," Zoe says, laughing. "He told her to sit down and eat."

Karrie and Allison both sit up straight. "So fucked."

"He wants me to go watch the game tonight."

"You hate hockey," Zoe says.

"Then he wants me to visit him and attend the casino night his team is hosting," I tell them, and the doorbell rings again. I get up and go to the door and unlock it, and I'm shocked when I see two people at the door, and one is carrying a huge fruit basket.

"Oh, my God," someone says from behind me. I reach for the fruit basket and then hand it to Zoe so I can take the big white box that is handed to me.

I thank them and close the door, walking into the living room. "If you don't want to date him, I will," Vivienne says. "Well, not really date. I don't date. I will have sex with him for you."

I know she is joking, and I know this because that is what she does, but it bothers me. Zoe places the fruit basket down and hands me the card. "There is no room for anything on this table anymore."

I open the card and everything in me flips—my heart, my stomach, everything.

For my sweet Zara.

I hand the card to Zoe 'cause I don't think I would be able to talk without it sounding all giddy. I open the box and let out a huge laugh. There is a Dallas jersey, a T-shirt, a sweater, and a baseball hat. The card has my name on the top, and I know he wrote this one himself.

Just in case you venture out tonight, here are four tick-

ets. Also, it might be bad luck if you don't wear my jersey!

E.

"Oh dear," I say out loud and then hand the card over to the girls while I go get my phone from upstairs. I pull up his name, but I don't know if I should call him or text him, so I walk downstairs. "Should I text him or call him?"

"He sent you flowers that cost a thousand dollars, a fruit basket, and seven hundred dollars' worth of merchandise," Vivienne says. "You need to go and see him naked."

"NO," Karrie and Allison both shout.

"I'll go with you tonight." Zoe comes to me, and I know she is trying to support me. "I can work while the game is on."

"What if Matthew and Max find out?" I look at Karrie and Allison.

"Well, rumor is you're a couple, so let's just go with that. It's a rumor," Alison says, looking at Karrie.

"Yeah, totally," Karrie says, and I look at her. "But what if it had nothing to do with Matthew and Max? What if he was just a normal guy who asked you out on a date? What would you do?"

"I would go," I answer truthfully. Hands down, without a doubt, I would go.

"Then fuck what the guys have to say," Allison says.

"For the record, I'm a hundred percent against this whole dating thing," Vivienne says. "Off the record, I think you should fuck his brains out."

"Call him and tell him you'll be there tonight."

"Or ..." Karrie says, "you show up and surprise him."

"That is so good," Allison says. "I remember when I wore

Max's jersey for the first time. He about lost his mind."

"Guys, isn't this too soon?" I look at them. "I mean, two days ago I sent this man a tweet to make my ex jealous."

"No," Zoe says. "You sent him a tweet because you were angry he lied to you." I think about it. "And then you thought maybe he cheated on you."

I look at the women in the room who all nod in agreement. My head spins with everything going on, but my gut is looking at the box with his jersey in it and telling me to go to that game.

Ten

Evan

"**W**ARM-UP STARTS in ten minutes," one of the guys say, and I stand to put on my chest protector. I really need to focus on the game, but the whole day, my mind has been absent. Last night after she told me good night, I ordered her flowers that apparently last a year. I have no idea if it's really true, but for the price I paid for them, they better.

I expected her to text me at least a thank you, but I got nothing. Not even a phone call. I even sent her four tickets to the game tonight and nothing.

"You look crabby," Denis says to me, putting on his jersey. "Did you not sleep okay?"

"Yeah," I say gruffly, "I'm fine." I grab my jersey and then pull it over my head. I finish getting ready to go and stand in the hallway, waiting for the signal to go on the ice. They usually let the home team skate for a minute or so before they let us take the ice.

I stand there leaning against the concrete wall, debating whether I should call her. I mean, maybe she's sick, or maybe she got busy. I have no idea, and when the guys start moving, I turn my neck right and left and then run till I glide on the ice. I look around while I skate in the out zone, and I see the spectators are still trickling into the arena. I skate to the corner, grab a puck, and then wait in line for my turn to skate and shoot on the net when I hear a soft knock on the glass. Usually, I never look up because there are always home team fans knocking away, but this time when I look up, I'm shocked to say the least.

There, dressed like she threw up Dallas merchandise, stands the woman who has taken over me. Standing there in tight jeans, wearing my jersey and the baseball hat with her hair in a ponytail, she looks so fucking beautiful. She smiles at me, and I want to get off the ice and ask her why she didn't call me or text me. I want to ask her if she is okay and if she is staying for the game. I'm about to mouth something to her when I get nudged in the back. "Dibs," Corey says from behind me, and I turn and put my whole glove in his face, pushing him.

"What? There are two of them. You aren't going to date both of them," he says, and I look over Zara's shoulder and see that Zoe is sitting in the chair behind her typing away on her phone. They are dressed the same, and if you didn't know better, you probably wouldn't be able to tell them apart, but I'd know Zara anywhere. Her eyes light up a different color when she is really happy, whereas Zoe's stays the same. I skate and do my turn, and I shoot it to the back of the net. Jari doesn't even try to stop it. I skate the bench and see her walk over. Everything that I went through all day—the worry and everything—made this moment so much better. I see that the reporters are looking over, so I only look at her and shake my head just a touch, so she sees it. She looks behind me and then looks down and turns around, going back to sit next to Zoe in the seats I got them.

I skate off the ice and go into the back to look for Tristan, our public relations guy. I see him in the corner in his suit as he types away on his phone. I walk to him, and he looks up. "What did you do?"

I look at him, pulling my eyebrows together. "There are two girls outside."

"I'm not your pimp, and this isn't a rock concert where we bring groupies in the back," he says, and I push him as he laughs. "You know those tickets you got me this morning?"

"You mean the reason for my six a.m. phone call?" he asks me, and I shrug.

"Yeah, that," I say. "I want you to bring them in the back when the game is over."

"What aren't you telling me?" he says, and I look left and right to make sure no one can hear.

"It's Zara Stone," I say, and he puts his head back and moans.

"I've been dodging reporters since Sunday," he hisses, and now he sees all the guys coming back from the ice. "Why can't you date a nice girl?"

"She is a nice girl," I tell him.

"Why can't you date a girl who isn't going to end up with you in the hospital?" he says. "Matthew, I think you can take, but Max? Dude, that guy is a beast."

"No one is going to be beating anyone. Jesus," I say, shaking my head. "It's just a hockey game. Then a date to her ex's wedding." When he folds his arms over his chest, I don't tell him she might be coming to Dallas for the casino night because I think he might literally lose his shit. "Can you just please make sure she comes back after the game?" I lean in. "Undercover."

"Why do I suddenly feel like a pimp?" he says to me, and I laugh, looking him up and down.

"Might be the suit, man." I look him up and down and see he has a velour suit this time.

"You shouldn't insult the man you need something from," he says, turning and walking away from me. I go back into the room, and I sit down and listen to Coach's speech, forcing myself to focus on the game at hand.

We get up and head for the ice now. "Ready, boys?" Paul, the captain of the team, shouts to pump up the guys. "Let's take their home away from them," he shouts. The music starts playing, and the boys head to the ice. I skate on the ice with the lights off to get in our zone. The lights flicker, and we head for the bench. I take a sip of water and then go and line up on the ice for the national anthem.

I take my helmet off and stand on the blue line with my guys. The spotlight comes on when a lady comes out and starts singing. I force myself not to look where I know she is sitting, so I don't make a fool of myself. I don't even know when the singing stops until I hear claps and then put my helmet on. I skate to center ice and look to the side. Denis is on one side, and Paul is on the other.

I stand there with my stick down, waiting for the ref to

come over with the puck. Mav, the center for the Jersey Chiefs, is there. "Look who it is," he says, smiling. "The bachelor."

I roll my eyes at him. "Will you accept this stick up your ass?" I ask him, and he throws his head back and laughs.

"When do you play New York again?" he asks me, and I don't answer him. "I need to get tickets for that game. My money is on Horton," he says. The ref comes over, and the music in the arena gets louder.

"Okay, boys, let's get this game on the road," he says. I get into position, bending a little and holding my stick in front of me.

I look at Mav and smile at him, throwing him off a bit. The ref looks at both of us, and he drops the puck. My stick flies out, and I win the face-off and skate past Mav. Paul gets the puck and passes it to Corey who skates it up and sees us waiting at the blue line for the pass. Once he passes the puck to Paul, Mav tries to block me, but I'm a touch faster than he is. I get in front of the goalie and try to block his view of the puck and the play. Their top defenseman tries to push me out of the way, but I don't budge, and when the shot comes, I move out of the way a touch to see if it'll make it behind the net, and it doesn't. The goalie makes a glove save, and the whistles blows. My line skates off the ice for a change. As I sit there catching my breath, I make the mistake of looking up at the seats.

Zoe is still on her phone, but Zara sits with her legs crossed and her elbows on her knees, resting her chin in the palm of her hand. She watches the play, and I swear she couldn't look more beautiful. The music in the arena turns off again, so I know the play is starting, and I shut my mind again and focus on the game. The rush is coming from both sides, and at the end of twenty minutes, it's still a non-scoring game.

When I get on the ice for the second period, I'm ready to turn things around. I skate in a circle while waiting for everyone to get into position, and the referee is skating over. He gets between Mav and I, and he drops the puck. I lose the face-off, and I'm pissed about it, so I start skating backward, keeping my eyes on the puck as the defense passes it among themselves. Once, twice, and then passing to the right wingers who take it into the zone. I play close to the blue line, and I wait for the pass I know is going to come. They box us in, but I skate a touch out of place, and then I see my opening. They try to pass it to the defenseman, but I intercept it. I poke it out of the zone, and I pick up speed. The defenseman is so close on my ass I can feel it, but no one else is beside me. I skate past center ice and hear everyone hustling behind me, but I'm in the zone. I watch the goalie come out of his crease and then back up. I suddenly feel someone at my feet, and he trips me. I lose my balance and end up in the boards, but when I look at the ref, he already has his arm up and is blowing the whistle. Paul goes to the defenseman who is getting up from the ice and pushes him while he tells him to fuck his mother.

I watch the referee take his arm and point at center ice and see that it's a penalty shot. I raise one foot and get up with my back to the board. The crowd starts booing, and I skate to the middle of the ice, looking up at the replay on the jumbotron.

I watch as everyone else goes to their respective benches and then the referee comes over and puts the puck in
the middle of the ice. The goalie skates left and right. The
linesman stands in the middle of the ice, and the referee
stands to the right. He turns and looks at the scorekeeper,
then gives him a nod. He turns back and points at the puck
while the linesman now points at the goalie. I skate around,
going to the blue line, and then start skating the puck. I pick
up the puck on the blade of my stick and skate to the right
and then bring it back to the left. I skate straight down the
middle, seeing that the goalie is coming out of his crease
a touch and then backing up a bit when I get closer. I know
the exact spot where I'm going to score. He hunches down
and that gives me an even bigger window. He's expecting
me to come in and try to deke him, but I'm not. Instead, I
flick my wrist and raise the puck a bit, and it flies right over
his shoulder and falls in the back of the net. I raise my stick
in the air and skate back to the bench, but while doing that,
I glance over and see Zara standing on her feet. She is the
only one in her section, and she is clapping. I smile and then
go up to the bench and high-five everyone.

The game ends with us winning by one point, and I honestly don't care. I rush to the dressing room and am the
first one in the shower. When I'm finally dressed in my suit,
I walk out of the room and look for her. I spot Tristan talking
to someone, and all he does is point at a room. I walk to the
closed door, and I knock before opening it.

When the door finally opens, I see Zara sitting on a chair
in front of a brown wooden desk. When she looks up from
her phone and sees me, her whole face lights up. The base-

ball cap gone now leaving her hair in just a ponytail.

"There he is, the man of the hour," she says, getting up, and I look around looking for Zoe.

"Where is your sister?" I ask her, walking into the room and closing the door.

"She went to the bathroom," she says, using quotation marks. "I think she just wanted to give us privacy."

"Did she now?" I say, the smile not leaving my face. "That color looks good on you."

"Does it?" she asks, and she turns around. Seeing her wearing my jersey makes me want to go all hulk—rip off my shirt, puff out my chest, and roar. I put my hands in my pockets before I yank her to me. "Thank you," she says, her voice going soft, "for the flowers and the fruit and the merchandise."

"It's the least I can do. That tweet put me in running for bachelor of the year." She laughs, shaking her head, and covers her face with her hands. "Don't do that." I close the distance between us and reach out, pulling her hands away from her face. "Don't hide your face from me."

"This is crazy," she says, and I turn to sit on the chair in front of her. "You live in Dallas."

"You live in New York," I tell her. The same thought was running through my mind all day long.

"You travel all over the place." I look up at her.

"You do too," I remind her, and I can't sit any more while she tries to talk herself out of whatever this is. She stands there in front of me, and my hand reaches up to cup her face, my thumb rubbing her cheek. "Why don't we play this day by day?" She looks up at me, her eyes a shade of crystal green with blue inside them. I hear the racket coming from the hallway and know that my team is getting ready to leave. "I can't kiss you right now," I tell her, and her mouth opens a touch. "And it's not 'cause I don't want to. I've never wanted anything more in my life." She looks down now and then up at me. "It's because one kiss won't be good enough. I know if I kiss you, I won't stop kissing you."

"Okay, people, time to load the bus," someone shouts from the hallway.

"You have to go," she says, and her hand comes out to hold the wrist cupping her cheek.

"Sweet Zara," I say softly. "Sweet, sweet Zara," I finally say and lean in and kiss her on the cheek. When I lift my face, I'm so close to her lips, so very close. I look into her eyes, and I swear it's more dangerous than swimming in shark-infested waters.

There is a soft knock on the door, but I don't move. I don't drop my hand from her face. I do nothing but get lost in her. "Sorry to interrupt," Zoe says, sticking her head in the door, "but ..."

"You have to go," she says again. My heart sinks while I nod my head because I know I won't see her tomorrow. I know I won't even see her the day after that. I let my hand drop from her face, and her own hand drops like lead to her side.

"Good job out there tonight," Zoe says. "Great time on the ice," she says, and I shake my head and laugh. How are these two so oblivious to hockey when their whole family is the face of hockey?

"Take care of her, Zoe," I tell her, and she nods. I step out of the room, pick up my bag that I put down before I went in, and walk out of the arena, never once looking back.

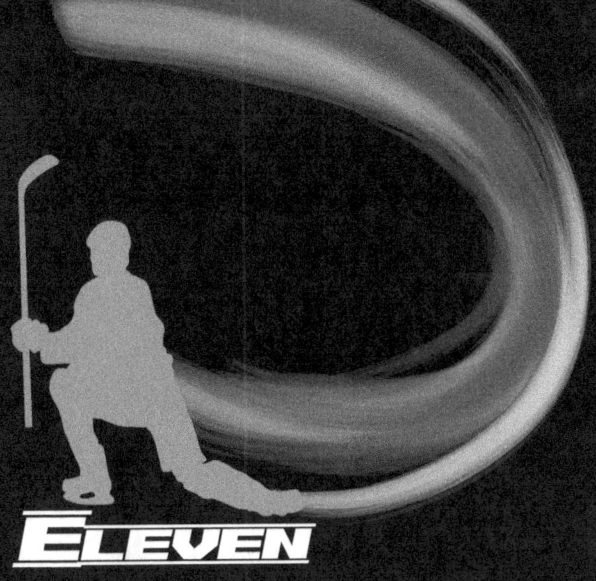

ELEVEN

ZARA

I WATCH HIM walk away from me. The black suit molding him with his leather backpack slung over his shoulder.

"I knew I shouldn't have come tonight." I look at Zoe once I can't see him anymore, yet I can still feel his hand on my face. When he walked into the room, I knew I was fucked. And not even in a good way. His suit was on point, his hair still wet from the shower, and I know he just ran his fingers through it because you could see it. But then he smiled, and I literally forgot my own fucking name.

"There is nothing wrong with liking him," Zoe says, and I grab the baseball hat and put it back on my head.

"I don't like him. He's just a friend," I lie, and we walk out, making our way down to the underground parking garage where the driver waits for us. There is almost no one here. I see some of the players walking out with their wives or girlfriends, but we don't make eye contact. The driver sees us and gets out of the car to open the door. I get in first and then Zoe.

"Want company tonight?" she asks me, and I just shake my head.

"No, I have to pack for Chicago," I tell her, and I just look out the window. I don't bother looking at my phone. My head is a fucking mess, and I just don't get it. I look over at her.

"I've known him three fucking days," I tell her, and she knows this is the how we work things out. I just do all the talking. "Three days. I can't like him." I shake my head. "It's crazy. Three days. I have food in my fridge older than that."

"Why?" she finally says. "If it's in the fridge longer than two days, chuck that shit out. It starts to smell." Her face grimaces.

"He lives in a different time zone." I keep the list going. "In a different state."

"It could never work," she says and then looks at me. "I have a friend in Dallas. I could maybe play matchmaker." I turn and glare at her. "Well, that answers that question."

"How do I know he doesn't have a chick waiting in Dallas?" I tell her. "Or puck bunnies all around the United States?"

"Don't forget Canada," she says. "United States and Can-ada."

"Yeah, there too," I point out.

"He's got a great smile," she says, and I look over at her. I don't have to agree with her because it's obvious. "He has great sense of style that he had before you." I nod. "He opens your door for you." I roll my eyes. "And sends you one hundred roses."

"He lives five hours from here by plane," I tell her.

"What if this was me?" she asks me. "What if I were in your situation? What would you tell me to do?"

I cross my arms over my chest, not answering. "Exactly. You would be like fucking YOLO, Zoe."

"I would not say that," I tell her.

"Really? What about that biker I dated?" she says. "Zoe, YOLO. Zoe, who cares that he has a warrant for his arrest. Pretend he's Charlie Hunnam."

"I didn't tell you to marry him," I point out. "And didn't you have good sex?"

"I woke up to his old lady coming in with their kid," she points out. "She didn't even blink that I was naked in his bed."

I shrug. "I mean, I guess it's a win."

"Why don't you just stop overthinking it and just go with it? Call him, don't call him. Answer his calls, text him when you feel like it," she says. "Just don't shut it down before it even starts. Worst case, you have a great story to tell your kids."

I look out the window, and she doesn't say anything when the car pulls up to my house. I kiss my sister and tell her I'll call her tomorrow. I walk up the steps to the house and unlock the door. My phone rings, and it's Matthew.

"Hello," I say, looking at the clock and seeing it's almost eleven.

"Hey," he says, and then I hear Karrie in the background. "Don't answer anything."

"Is something wrong?" I ask him, thinking the worst.

"I don't know. Did you go to a hockey game tonight?" he

asks, and I stop mid step. "You see, my sister hates hockey. She hates hockey like I hate going shopping."

"I don't hate hockey," I tell him and start walking up the steps. "I attend most of your games."

"So imagine my surprise when I turn on the game tonight and see a dipshit taking a penalty shot." I try not to laugh at the nickname. "Then the camera zooms in on this woman who looks like my sister," he says.

"Would you leave her alone, Matthew," Karrie says in the background.

"Babe," he hisses at her, "I'm talking to my sister." Then he comes back to me. "I mean, she looks like my sister, but she's wearing the ugliest green jersey of I've ever seen in my life."

Now, I laugh. "Don't laugh, Zara. What the hell is going on?"

"Nothing. I got tickets from a friend."

"A friend?" he hisses. "You know he comes to town in three weeks, right?"

"And?" I ask him, turning on the light in my room and kicking off my shoes.

"And I'm going to kick his ass."

"You will not," Karrie hisses.

"Okay fine, I won't, but I think Max needs to visit the penalty box."

"Is this all you called for?" I ask him.

"No," he says. "I also called to tell you that I don't like him."

"Duly noted." I roll my lips.

"Rumors are going around that you two are dating," he asks quietly.

"Don't listen to rumors, Matthew," I tell him. "Rumors were going around that you are too old to be on the ice." I know he hates that rumor.

"I am not too old, dammit." He raises his voice. "I don't like him."

"Why?" I ask him. "Why don't you like him?"

"Because he's sly, and he's trying to date my sister," he says, and I throw my head back and laugh. "Fuckers. I have to go. Karrie is winking at me."

"Gross," I say, and he disconnects. I look down at my phone, and I see that I'm tagged in a picture on Twitter. I click to open the app, and there it is.

Me standing clapping after his goal.

Caught @ZaraStone cheering on her man @EvanRichards.

I smile till I see what Evan commented on the post.

@ZaraStone thanks for coming. Maybe next time we can actually meet.

What the fuck? I'm so tempted to answer back not to flatter yourself, but I don't. Instead, I do the grown-up thing and take a screenshot and send it to him via text. I don't even know what to write, so I write nothing and just toss my phone aside.

I take off his jersey and toss it in the basket, making a mental note to add bleach to the wash that day. I take my luggage out of the hallway closet and start filling it. I will be in Chicago for three days, a max of four, so I pack and obviously overpack, thinking about all the places I'm going to go but knowing I'll probably be curled up in a ball at the end of the night.

I'm on my way to Chicago to meet with Hollywood's Princess Kellie. She releases a new album in a couple of months, and she wants me to work with her on her video shots and also to go over her interview outfits. I love working with her, and it helps that her husband is fine to look at.

I finish packing and have my bag ready by the door. She is sending her private plane for me, so there are no long lines. The car will be here at eight to get me, so I set my alarm for six thirty. I ignore all the tags from Twitter, and I put my phone on airplane mode so the notifications don't keep me up.

I slide into bed once I wash off my makeup, and I turn off the light. The clock shows me it's almost one a.m. Tomorrow is going to be a rough one.

"Welcome aboard, Ms. Stone. We will be taking off in about five minutes," the flight attendant tells me once I walk up the five stairs to the plane. "You will have Wi-Fi on the plane, so you can go ahead and log on."

"Perfect. Thank you," I say to her, shrugging off my Burberry jacket and placing it on the seat beside me. Since I'm going straight to work after the plan lands, I dressed for it. I'm wearing tight white pants topped with a lace crocheted button-down beige short-sleeved shirt. I paired it with strappy Jimmy Choo gold high heels. I place the cream-colored Celine purse with my jacket and grab my phone out of my bag.

I fasten my seat belt and finally turn my phone back on. The phone doesn't stop with the notifications coming in, and I see I have fifteen missed phone calls.

I see that Evan answered me back, and all he said is:

Evan: I'll speak to you in the morning.

"Really," I say to myself. "Or not," I answer him and then check the messages from Zoe.

Zoe: Where the fuck are you?

Zoe: You need to call me back ASAP

I text her.

Me: I'm on the plane. Sorry, my phone was on airplane mode.

Not more than three seconds after I press send does the phone light up in my hands.

"What the fuck?" she hisses. "I've been trying to get in touch with you all night and this morning."

"Why?" I say and feel the plane moving.

"Um, have you not been on Twitter?" she asks me, and I put her on speakerphone and then go to Twitter. "People are going nuts."

"Why?" I ask and go on Twitter.

I have over a hundred notification. "What is going on?"

"I'm not sure you caught the photo from last night be-cause you didn't comment on it and knowing you, you would have been 'Bye, Felicia.'"

"I saw it, but I just texted him a picture of it," I tell her.

"Well, the comment is gone, and in its place is a new one. I think he just threw down." She snickers. I go back to the picture.

Doesn't my girl @zarastone look great in my jersey?

"Oh my God," I say and then see that it's being retweeted over a hundred times.

"Yeah," Zoe says. "Anyway, I have to go. I have a client on the phone, but call me." She disconnects, and I go through the comments. One of them even tags Matthew and Max, and I have to put my hand over my mouth when I see Max's response.

@EvanRichards, define your girl.

I text Allison.

Me: Is Max okay?

She answers me right away.

Allison: Matthew called him this morning. They are going over plays for when Evan comes to town. This is funny as shit.

Me: They aren't really going to hurt him, right?

I have to ask her since I'm actually scared.

Allison: Good news is that they have a couple of games to calm down.

I scan the texts and finally open the ones from Evan.

Evan: Can you call me in the morning? I tried calling you, and I'm going straight to voicemail.

Evan: Sweet Zara, please call me.

Evan: I can't sleep.

I'm about to call him when my phone rings, and I see it's him.

"Hello," I say, looking out the windows at the clouds.

"Hey," he mumbles, and I can hear sleep in his voice. "I've been trying to call you all night."

"I put my phone on airplane mode," I tell him, and the phone sounds like it's ringing. "Are you FaceTiming me?"

"Yes," he says, and I accept the call. The little circle goes round and round, and then his face fills the screen, and I see he is in bed. He in on his stomach, and the phone is in front of him. I see his head. "Fuck, you're beautiful," he says, and I look down. "I don't take care of my Twitter account."

I look at him confused. "My sister Candace does, and she is the one who wrote that comment," he says, and I hear barking, and then the phone flies out of his hand when the dog jumps on the bed. "Lilo, off," he says and picks up the phone again. "Sorry, the dog jumped on the bed."

I laugh, looking at the dog look at the camera his nose coming to the screen and sniffing it. "Go away, she's mine."

"Were you the one who wrote the comment about me being your girl?" I ask him. "Or was that your sister?"

"No," he says, "she was sleeping. I deleted her comment and added my own."

"You know that Max replied, right?" I tell him, and he just smirks. "From what my sister-in-law said, he's fired up."

He just shrugs. "Whatever," he says. "Where are you?"

"I'm on a plane going to Chicago," I tell him. "I'll be there for four days."

"When are you going home?" he asks.

"Saturday and then I'm out again on Sunday to LA." I look at him, and he looks so tired. "Why don't you go back to bed and call me later?"

"I'm going to sleep better now knowing you're okay," he says and tries to hide his yawn. "I'll talk to you later, sweet Zara."

I smile at the nickname he keeps using. "Talk to you later." I hang up the phone, and the flight attendant comes out with my breakfast. I smile at her, eating the fruit and going over the designs I'm going to show Kellie. My phone rings again, and I look down, seeing it's from my mom.

"Hey, Mom," I say, putting it on speaker while I put every-thing back together.

"Hi, princess, you are on speakerphone. I'm here with your father," she says and then, "Cooper, you said you would behave."

"Oh dear," I say. "I haven't even done anything."

"Why the hell is Evan calling you his girl?" my father says, and I swear I could see him coming closer and closer to the phone while he asks that question. "And why were you wearing that jersey?"

"Oh that," I say, and I hear my mother laugh. "He invited me to watch his game."

"How many minutes in a game?" my father asks me.

"A lot?" I answer.

"Parker," he hisses at my mother.

"Honey, your father just got off the phone with your brother, and they are a little bit worried."

"That I went to a hockey game? I've survived before, so I'll survive now."

"This isn't a joke, Zara," my father says. "He said you were his. You know what that means."

"Um," I say, and my father continues.

"There are certain men out there …" he starts.

"Like your father," my mother says, "and your brother and Max and Zack."

"Parker, this is not funny," he says, and I can see them. "These men. Once they say you're theirs, you're theirs."

"Dad," I say. "I love you, I really do, but it was a joke."

"You don't joke about things like this," he says.

"Dad, I have to go. We are landing right now," I tell him. "Mom, can you calm him and the others please?"

"Will do, honey. Call me later," she says, and I disconnect the call the minute the wheels touch down.

I put my jacket on and grab my purse, walking down the steps and seeing that a car waits for me. The driver puts my luggage in the trunk. "Welcome to Chicago," he says, walking to the back door and opening it.

I get in and see a huge bouquet of red roses. "Those were delivered five minutes ago," he says. I look at them and grab the white card.

To MY sweet Zara

E.

I smile a smile I don't think I've ever worn. It's a smile that can't be erased. It's a smile that even if you want to erase it, you can't. It's a smile that fills your heart, it fills you with warmth and makes your stomach do that little flip.

"Dad was right," I say to myself as soon as the driver gets into the car.

TWELVE

EVAN

"COME ON, YOU two, let's get you outside." I roll out of bed, grabbing a pair of shorts and rubbing my face. I walk out of my bedroom and open the back door, letting the dogs free.

Turning, I go back and start my coffee and turn on the television when the front door opens, and I hear heels click-ing on the floor. I walk to the fridge and grab the orange juice, shaking it. I see that there is just a bit left, so I bring it to my mouth and swallow the rest of it.

"That's so gross," Candace says, and I turn to watch her put her bag down and shrug off her jacket. She looks at me. "You don't remember?" I look at her confused. "We are go-ing to go over your schedule for the next couple of months," she says. Going to the coffee machine, she takes my cup out, placing her own cup there, and makes her coffee. "I literally texted you last night."

I finish off the juice and recycle the container. I open the fridge, taking out the milk and dumping some in mine, then hold it out to Candace in question, and she nods. I place it on the counter and walk over to the door, opening it for the dogs to come in, and they both run to my sister. "Hello, little ones." Her voice changes to a baby voice. They sit in front of her, their tails wagging while they wait for their turn. I hear my name from the television and look up to see the replays from last night.

The first one is the tripping call, and I laugh, looking at how I tried not to fall on my ass but failed miserably. Then the camera cuts to me skating and replays my penalty shot. I'm watching the screen, and it cuts to Zara when I was celebrating.

"That was a shitshow," Candace says next to me, and I wait to hear what the commentary says.

"So what do you think, Jim?" one of the reporters says. "You think this is the start of a love story?"

Jim laughs. "I have no idea, but I'm sure everyone will be watching the meetup between Richards and her family."

"No doubt," the other reporter says, and I turn the television off.

"It's ridiculous that your love life is even a topic on *SportsCenter*," she says, going to the table and pulling out a chair. Grabbing her purse, she starts taking her stuff out. "I must have seen that replay fifty times since last night, and they always switch from you to that girl." I keep my anger at bay with that comment.

"That girl," I say, going to the table, "has a name." I look at her. "It's Zara."

"Yeah, I know. I keep having to fucking tag her in my posts," she says, and I wait for her to settle all her things. Once she has the laptop opened and is writing on the yellow legal pad in front of her, she looks up at me. "What?"

"How about I help you with that?" I tell her. "If it has to do with Zara and me, let me answer it."

"You haven't answered your Twitter since you opened it." She sits back, folding her arms over her chest.

"Yeah except when she asked me out, and I commented," I tell her, taking a sip of my coffee. "That reply was low and rude."

She shrugs her shoulders. "How was I supposed to know you met her?"

"I did meet her. I was the one who gave her the tickets," I tell her, and the doorbell rings. "This isn't over," I say. Getting up and going to the door, I see that it's the suits I bought in New York.

I walk back into the house, going to get a knife to open the boxes. "What did you buy?" she asks me, looking over at me

"I bought a couple of suits," I say to her. I get the suits out and see a whole bag of stuff under it. I take the bag out and find five pairs of jeans, really nice jeans, two sweaters, and a couple of shirts. There is a white envelope with my name on it.

Evan

It was great working with you. I saw these and knew you would look good in them.

Zara.

I smile, knowing she was thinking about me.

"You have these same suits hanging in your closet," Candace says, "and this sweater." She laughs. "I also bought you these jeans at Christmas."

I grab the stuff and take it to my room. Grabbing my phone, I send her a text.

Evan: Sweet Zara, nothing better than getting a note that you're thinking of me.

I press send and bring my phone with me to the kitchen. "She's shopping for you now?"

"What's the problem exactly?" I finally ask her. "Like what has she ever done to you?"

"What has she done to me? That fucking tweet flooded my phone. I've heard she's immature and fake."

"By who?" I ask her

"A couple of the wives who have met her." She mentions the wives of the players. They all get together to go over fundraising ideas, and Candace has always been in the clique.

"Well, I've met her, and she isn't immature, and she is nothing but real," I tell her, and she rolls her eyes.

"I am not going to fight with you about a woman who is going to be a distant memory in four months," she says and sits down. "Now let's get to work. I have a meeting in two hours."

I let it slide for now, but I know we will have this conversation again in the near future. For the next two hours, we go over all the things she wants me to do. I make a list of things I will do and things I won't do.

"The NHL awards are in late June," she starts saying. "I'm going to book the rooms this week. Mom and Dad said they are flying in and so is Chloe."

"Cool," I tell her, and she starts packing up her things.

"Don't forget I leave on Thursday, and I'm back the week after," she says. "I will check your account in the morning and at night. Can you lay off the girl shit, please?"

"I invited her to casino night," I tell her, and she stops packing her stuff.

"You did not," she hisses. "Are you crazy?"

"Why?" I ask her. "It's a fundraiser. Besides, she didn't say she would."

"Well, here's hoping that she doesn't." She fake smiles. "If you want to have sex, call Tina or even Karina. She's in town and would love to have dinner with you."

I push my chair away from the table, and it scratches the floor. "Enough, Cand."

She shakes her head. "Use your brain, Evan," she says and storms out of the house. I look up and close my eyes, counting to ten, but it doesn't seem to help. I'm pissed that she is being like this, and I have no idea what to do about it. When the phone rings, I don't even look to see who it is.

"What?" I snap.

"Okay." I hear her voice, and I'm suddenly calm. "How about you call me back after ..." she says. "Or not. That is good also," she mumbles and then hangs up.

I call her right back, and she answers. "Yes," she says, and I have to laugh.

"I'm sorry. I was just ..." I take a deep breath. "I didn't look to see who was calling me."

"Do you not have caller ID?" she asks me, and I hear a car door slamming.

"Where are you?" I ask her, and then I hear cars honking in the distance.

"I just got to my hotel," she tells me. "I was calling to one, thank you for the flowers again. And two, to tell you that if you want to return any of the items, you can do so just using my name. It's in the system."

"You didn't have to send me all that stuff," I tell her and go to sit on the couch. "But …"

"But?" she says. "I may lose you. I'm stepping into the elevator," she says. I hear a ding, and sure enough, the call drops.

I wait by the phone for her to call me back, and she does. "Sorry," she says, out of breath, and I press the FaceTime button and hear the phone ring. "Are you trying to FaceTime me?"

"Yeah," I say, and then I look at my phone and see the little circle go around, and then I finally see her. She's looking down at the phone with one side of her hair tucked behind her ear. She isn't wearing any makeup, or if she is, I can't even tell. Her smile fills the screen. "Hi," she says softly.

"Hi," I say back, and I want to see her. "How far is Chicago to Dallas?" I ask her, and she laughs.

"I have no idea," she says, and I see that she is sitting on the bed now. "Why?"

"I wonder if there is a flight out," I tell her the truth.

"Are you crazy?" she says, laughing. "You can't just come here."

"Why not?" I ask her. "Don't you want to see me?" I joke with her.

"What were you saying about the clothes?" she asks me.

"Oh that," I tell her. "I really liked the fact that I was on your mind so much you got me clothes."

She rolls her eyes. "How bad was your Twitter account?" she asks me, and I shrug.

"Did you know I was on *SportsCenter* five times last night," she tells me and now lies down on her side while looking at me. She is so beautiful, she takes my breath away. "My sister texted me each time she saw it."

"Yeah, I saw it too," I tell her. "Now the question is whose jersey are you going to wear when I come to town?"

She giggles. "I don't usually wear jerseys," she says, and I frown at her.

"Did you think about the casino night?" I ask her.

"I did" she says softly. "Do you think it's a good idea?"

"Yes." I don't even think about it. "I think it's the best idea I've had in a long time."

"Okay," she finally agrees. "I'll book myself a hotel."

"No," I tell her. "I have three bedrooms."

"Um," she says. "I'm not really ..."

"Okay, book a hotel," I say. If this is the only way she will come, then she can have her hotel room.

"I have a call coming in from a client. Let me call you back," she says. I nod at her, and the phone disconnects.

I get off the couch in search of some food when my phone rings again, and I think it's her, but see it's my mother.

"Hey, Mom," I say, picking up the phone and putting one of my prepared meal in the microwave.

"Evan," she says. "I was thinking about you." Her voice getting tight.

"You saw the news?" I ask her with a laugh, knowing she

saw the news.

"If you're asking me if I saw your penalty shot from last night, I did," she says. "It was a great shot." She pauses. "She's very pretty."

I laugh now. "Have you spoken to Candace?"

"I have," she says. "She isn't happy about this."

"Yeah well, she needs to get used to it," I tell her.

"It's just that …" she says and trails off.

"Yeah, I get it, Mom. I date a lot," I tell her. "I get that I've had lots of woman. But," I say, trailing off, "I like her."

"Okay," she says quietly and waits for me to continue.

"I really like her," I tell her. "It just feels different."

"Your sister doesn't want you to get hurt," she tries to defend her.

"I don't want to get hurt either." I look up. "But I want to get to know her."

"Then you get to know her," she says. "Just tread lightly."

"I will, Mom," I say, and she changes the subject. We speak for about ten minutes, and then I let her go.

I'm cleaning up the kitchen when the phone rings, and I suddenly smile. She isn't just calling me; she's FaceTiming me. I prop the phone up while I wash my dish and see her face come into the picture.

"Are you washing the dishes?" she asks, and I see she is sitting at the desk now with her own phone propped up.

"I am. I just finished eating," I tell her.

"I just ordered room service," she says. "What did you eat?"

"Chicken and veggies," I tell her.

"Did you cook that yourself?" She raises her eyebrows.

"Nope," I say turning off the water and walking to grab a hand towel. "I have meals brought in. What did you order?"

"A kale salad and some grilled salmon," she says. "I'm going to hit the gym tomorrow morning before work."

"I have to be on the ice at nine," I tell her. "We have two away games on Tuesday and Thursday but then come right back and have a Friday game."

"Where are you going?" she asks me.

"First Philly and then Boston," I tell her.

"Oh, you have to have a cheesesteak for me," she moans. "The one with the Cheez Whiz."

When her meal gets there, she doesn't let me go. Instead, she eats, and we chat the whole time. She tells me about getting kicked off her school bus when she was six for telling the bus driver he was a douche canoe. Then Zoe also did because she just did what Zara did. The stories had me in stitches, and it makes me like her even more. She loves her family fiercely, and she will fight tooth and nail for them. She reminds me of Candace.

When she hides her fifth yawn, I look at her. "How do you get more beautiful?" I ask her as she lies in the bed with a soft light in the background. Her eyes look down shyly when I say that.

"I'm not beautiful," she says, and her voice is soft, almost as though she's embarrassed.

"You are so much more than beautiful," I say, and suddenly, I wish I could reach out and push the hair behind her ear and lean over and kiss her. Softly. "I'm going to get to bed."

"Me too," she says. "Sweet dreams, Evan."

"Sweet dreams, my sweet Zara," I tell her. She looks at me with that sly smile again and then disconnects. I turn off the lights in my bedroom, and I fall asleep with her smile on my mind.

THIRTEEN

ZARA

"**T**HANK YOU SO, so much," Kellie says, hugging me when the car arrives to bring me to the airport. It's been a whirlwind of four days filled with fittings and design changes. We hit up a couple of designers who bent over backward to design what she needed. I even picked up a little something in case I went to the casino night with Evan.

Every single night, we've spent hours and hours on the phone talking. He makes me laugh at the stupidest things. He also is hands down the hottest guy I've ever seen. When he traveled and FaceTimed me wearing his cashmere Burberry jacket and beanie, I swear I had drool dribble out of my mouth. His scruff makes it that much hotter. I'm usually drawn to a clean-shaven man, but something about Evan just makes it.

"I want you to promise me you'll go to that casino party," Kellie says to me, rubbing my back. I usually never bring my private life into anything, but she saw me on *SportsCenter* and had to ask me about it. When I told her the story, she was bent over laughing. "Even if I have to send the plane to LA and drag you to Dallas myself."

I laugh at her and go to hug her husband, Brian. "I would listen to her if I were you," he says, and I just shake my head.

"Thank you guys so much for having me," I tell them both and watch the driver load my bag into the car. I get into the car and text my sister that I am on my way home.

I don't bother texting Evan because I know he got in last night close to two a.m. They have their game tonight at home, and then he's off again for another two games road trip. I jog up the steps to get on the plane and smile at the flight attendant when she asks to take my jacket. I shrug it off and give it to her and walk to the table and see a square white box on it.

"Those were delivered less than two minutes ago," she says, and I turn and take off the curled ribbon. When I open the box, I laugh because there are four cupcakes in the box. With a little note on the side.

A sweet treat for my sweet Zara.

E.

I shake my head and sit on the chair, taking a picture of it and adding it to my Instagram.

A sweet treat for a sweet Zara. I don't tag him, but I know he'll see it. He's been all over my Instagram these past couple of days. Liking pictures. Sending me DMs about my pictures. And they come at all hours of the night. Probably when he's on the bus or the plane.

They look too good to eat, but I reach in and grab a red

velvet one, which is my favorite. I bite into it, and I swear it's the best cupcake of life. The cream cheese frosting is whipped, which makes it so much lighter.

I'm taking my second bite when I see that Justin, my younger brother, commented on my picture. I open it up.

You have never been called sweet in your WHOLE LIFE.

I laugh and answer him back.

It just depends for who.

I click on his name and see that he has just one picture up, which I know is a freaking lie. I know he has a secret Instagram that is not for family members. I also know that Snapchat is his social media of choice. He's going to turn eighteen in a couple of months, and from what I've been told, he's a hot one on the ice, and his extra activities off ice have him nicknamed "Sly Stone."

The flight goes by faster than I thought, and by the time I'm finished checking my email and responding, the flight attendant is opening the door for me. I walk out, and I'm met by Zoe who stands by her Town Car. Her phone in her hand as her fingers fly over the keyboard.

"Well, well," I say when I finally get close enough to her. "To what do I owe this surprise?"

She looks up and smiles. "I saw your cupcakes on Instagram." She winks at me. "Sweet Zara." She makes fun of the nickname.

"I already ate two," I tell her, and I wish I was lying. "The red velvet and the carrot cake."

"Ugh," she says. Turning and opening the back door for me, she holds out her hands for the white box. "What's left?"

"I think chocolate and vanilla," I say, scooting over so she can get in.

"Ugh, those suck," she says and opens the box and then glares at me. "That is not funny. This is a Reese's peanut butter cupcake," she says with a smile. She reaches into the box and takes it out and bites into it and some of the frosting gets on her nose. "This is the best thing I've ever tasted in my life," she says between bites. "It's so good."

"Yeah, the other one is smores," I tell her, and then the phone beeps in my pocket. I see it's a text from Evan.

Evan: Don't watch the game tonight.

I look over to see what Zoe is doing, and she is chewing the cupcake with her eyes closed.

Me: And why is that.

He answers right away.

Evan: Because I'm going to suck, and I don't want you to see it.

Me: Doubt it.

I don't tell him that I've watched every single game he's played in the hotel room. I don't tell him I've cheered so loud when he's scored that the front desk called to check and see if I was okay.

I get home and walk into the house, seeing the mountain of mail that Zoe picked up while I was gone. I carry the suitcase upstairs and start a load of wash. Zoe comes back up carrying two glasses of wine.

"What time is your flight tomorrow?" she asks me, handing me one glass.

"My flight is at noon," I tell her. "I get in at two." Putting my glass of wine down, I go to grab my other luggage.

"How long are you there for?" she asks, grabbing her phone and lying on my bed.

"I swear, I thought I would get a little bit of a break after award season was over," I tell her, looking at the closet and packing things. "Instead, it's even more busy."

"They all want to shop at Zara's Closet." She smiles at me.

For the next two hours, I show her the different outfits that I am packing, and she also takes a couple home to "spice them up," as she says. When it's close to seven, the doorbell rings. We look at each other and then walk downstairs. The man at the door holds two pizzas.

"Delivery for Ms. Stone," he says and hands me both pies and then turns and walks away.

"I think your man is trying to get you to like him. You know the saying the way to a man's heart is through his stomach?" she says, grabbing one box and bringing it to her nose and smelling it. "I'm starving."

She walks into the living room, and I turn on the television and go to the guide. When I turn on his game, my sister moans.

"The least we can do is watch his hockey game."

She looks over at me and glares. "He isn't trying to get me to like him," she says, and then I turn the volume up and see that the game has already started. I grab a slice of pizza and watch the game. Finally, when it's the third period, Zoe gets up and stretches. "I'm bringing the pizza home since you are leaving tomorrow." She puts the leftover slices into one box. "When are you going to be home?" she asks, looking over her shoulder.

"I don't know," I tell her the truth, and I stand. "I was thinking of going to the casino night and staying for a couple of days." I try to avoid her stare by looking at the television.

She smiles at me. "Going to get the D."

I shake my head. "Maybe not the D, but I am going to see him."

"Does he know?" she asks me, and I shake my head

"I want to surprise him," I say with my own sly smile. I hear the announcer say his name, and I look up to see the other team has scored.

"What a horrible turnover from Richards," he says, and I watch the replay. "That is just a horrible, horrible turnover." You see that he was trying to pass it to his line mate, and the defense got a touch of the puck, and the other team went out to score. "It's a rookie mistake I don't think he'll make again." The cameraman goes to Evan where he's sitting on the bench. His hands are in front of him, and he is just watching the play. I turn off the game and walk Zoe out and then walk upstairs.

I close the luggage and grab my phone. I don't know if I should text him or not. I text him anyway.

Me: Thank you for the pizza.

I sit in bed, waiting for his reply. I try not to let it get to me when I know the game is over, yet he doesn't answer me. When I finally turn off the lights, it's after one a.m. and still nothing.

Nothing during my coffee, nothing while I'm waiting for my flight, and nothing when I land. It's like he's gone off the grid, and it bothers me. Or pisses me off. I'm not sure yet which one I am. I think I'm more aggravated.

When I'm standing there waiting for my luggage to come out, my phone finally rings.

"What," I snap.

"Whoa there," he says, laughing. "I take it that it wasn't a good flight."

"The flight was fine." My tone doesn't change, and then I'm too stubborn to even listen to myself. "Where have you been?'

"I've been at T-Mobile all day," he says. "I kind of got a bit aggravated after the game last night. And well, apparently a concrete wall can totally win against an iPhone." When he laughs, everything that I've been feeling is out the window. I'm not mad at him anymore or aggravated with him. I'm sad I'm not there to tell him that it's just a game.

"It's just a game," I tell him softly, "and everyone has bad games."

"I know that, sweet Zara," he says softly. "I just ... my head wasn't in the game, and it should have been."

"Well, what were you thinking about?" I ask him, my stomach tight and my heart speeding up.

"I was thinking about this strawberry blond, green-eyed sweet woman who has taken over all my thoughts," he says softly, and I smile. "She has me tied up in knots, and I don't know what to do about it."

"Have you told her?" I ask him, spotting my bag and not even moving.

"I'm thinking about it," he says. "I'm just scared that she isn't ready for it yet."

"Oh, I don't know about that," I say, and finally, all the stress from the day suddenly leaves me.

"I have to get my bag," I tell him. "I'll call you when I get to the hotel."

"Okay, sweet Zara," he says.

"If I were you, I would think about telling this girl how you feel," I joke with him, and he laughs.

"I'll keep that in mind, sweet Zara." And I hang up to the sound of his laughter.

Between his games on the road and my clients and the different time zones, we've spoken maybe twice. Many texts going back and forth, and although I've decided to go to the casino night, and I even have a ticket and a hotel reservation, he hasn't asked me about it.

I'm zipping up my bag when my phone rings, and I see it's him. "Hello," I answer and hold the phone with my shoulder while I get my other bag ready.

"Hey," he says, and I can hear sleep in his voice. "Sorry I didn't call earlier."

"It's okay," I say, looking at the clock. "It's ten a.m. there."

"Yeah, I honestly am looking forward to not traveling for the next eight days," he says. "What time is your flight?" he asks, and he doesn't even ask if I'm coming or not.

"Eleven," I tell him. "The car is picking me up in fifteen minutes."

"Um," he says, and he gets quiet. "Did you think about coming to see me?"

"I did," I tell him, and then my phone beeps, telling me that my driver is downstairs, but also, he is trying to Face-Time me.

"Hey," he says when his face finally fills the screen, and I know I should be walking out of my hotel room, but I just watch him.

"Hey," I answer him.

"So?" he says, and I just watch him as he turns to his side in his bed.

"I land at 4 p.m. your time," I tell him. He shoots up in bed, his eyes big and his smile huge. The sleep now gone from his features.

"You're coming to Dallas?" he asks, his voice shrieking so much the dogs start barking and jumping in the bed.

"I'm coming to Dallas," I say to him. "But if I don't leave right now, I might miss my flight."

"Text me all the details," he says. "Why are you sitting down? Get up and get going." I laugh when he says this and follow his lead. When I'm in the car, I text him all the details. He doesn't call me before I take off nor do I see a text from him when I land either. I get out of my first class seat and grab my brown beige suede jacket and my black purse.

I look down at my outfit and wonder if it is good enough, if it is sexy enough. My tight black pants fit like a glove, and I paired it with a loose white V-neck silk shirt and my black Louboutins. My hair is hanging down loose, and I walk out of the plane and follow the signs to my luggage. Walking through the airport, I turn right and finally get on the escalator going toward the exit and the luggage.

Halfway down, I see him. He stands there wearing black jeans and a white T-shirt. His eyes watch the escalator, and I see them light up as soon as he sees me. My eyes lock on his, and when I finally make it to the bottom, I walk to him and see that he has flowers in his hand.

"Welcome, my sweet Zara," he says, holding the flowers

out for me. I reach out and grab them, and he walks closer to me, so close I can smell him finally. I look up at him and wait for him to finally kiss me. My heart beating, my palms sweaty, my stomach making that little flip as the butterflies fly around. I look down at the flowers in my hand and then look up at him, and he comes close and kisses me softly on the cheek. "Beautiful, sweet Zara," he whispers, and my heart sinks.

FOURTEEN

EVAN

I DUMP MY bag at the door, and I don't even bother turning on the lights as I put the dogs out and wait for them, shrugging off my jacket and beanie. The dogs come back to the door scratching, and I let them in and close up the house.

I undress, leaving my clothes in a puddle at the end of my bed, and I literally moan when I slip between the sheets and sink my head on the pillow. Looking over at the clock, I see it's almost four a.m.

For another night, I go to bed with Zara on my mind. I go to bed asking myself if she is going to come to casino night. I go to bed actually missing her. This week with me traveling and her working on the West Coast has been a mess trying to connect, and I was beyond frustrated. I set my alarm to wake me at ten to call her and see what she is doing! Tomorrow I'm going to get the courage and the balls to ask her if she is coming.

When her face fills the screen, it always takes my breath away. Always. When she told me her flight was soon, I finally asked her the question I've wanted to ask her all week, yet didn't because I didn't want her to think I was pressuring her. When she told me she was coming to Dallas and landing at four, I about lost my shit. I was so excited. I got out of bed right away and started making all the plans.

I went into the guest bedroom and made sure everything was okay for her. Even though I wasn't sure if she was staying here, I wanted it to be perfect. The last person to stay in this room was my mother two months ago. The big king-size bed sits in the middle of the room with a beige headboard. The white duvet fluffed up with six pillows all lined up in two rows. The beige throw blanket at the end of the bed half rests on bench in front of the bed.

The bed sits in front of the two windows that show the front of the lawn. I walk into the en suite bathroom and make sure there are clean towels. I'm so nervous.

"Lilo, Stitch." I call for them at three thirty when I'm just about to leave to go and get her. My heart hammers in my chest. "I'm going to pick up a friend," I tell them, and they both sit in front of me with their tails wagging. "Wish me luck," I tell them, grabbing the bouquet of roses I picked up earlier.

I get in the car and make it there in record time. As I walk into the baggage area, my palms are almost dripping with sweat from my anxiousness. My heart beats so irrationally and fast, I'm surprised I'm not having a heart attack. I walk to the screen and see that her plane has just landed. I didn't text her to tell her I was picking her up. I didn't text her anything. I look around the baggage claim area and see maybe seven people lingering.

Standing in front of the escalator, I wait anxiously for her. My leg starts to shake as I watch for any signs of her. My finger taps the stems of the roses I hold by my side. I spot her shoes before anything else, and slowly, like I'm unwrapping a beautiful gift wrapped present, she finally comes down. Her hair flows down loose, and I want nothing more than to bury my hands in it. I wonder if it feels as silky as it looks? I can't help the smile that forms on my face. I can't help the beating in my chest, and I can't help that my mouth is dry.

Our eyes lock, and no one else exists. The room could be on fire, and I would only have eyes for her. I walk slowly to the escalator, my eyes never leaving hers. When she finally walks off it and is in front of me, my heart that was pounding just a second ago is now beating perfectly. I hold out my hand with the long stem roses in them, and her eyes finally see them.

"Welcome, my sweet Zara." She smiles at me shyly and reaches for the roses, our fingers grazing each other, and it's another shock to my heart. She looks down at the flowers and then up at me, and I'm suddenly so close to her I can smell her soft citrus smell. I can hear her breathing. Her eyes come back up to mine, and I want nothing more in my life than to kiss her.

I get even closer to her, but I stop myself from kissing her. I stop myself because the only thing going through my mind is how I'd get lost in her kiss. So lost that I'd pick her up and leave without her luggage. Instead, I lean in, and I swear her breath hitches, and then I kiss her softly on the cheek.

"Beautiful, sweet Zara," I whisper to her, and I want to trail my nose along her cheek to her neck, but I stop myself. I look at her eyes again.

"I can't believe you're here," I say, and she just laughs. "Let's get your bag and get out of here," I tell her, and she nods. We walk over to the carousel, and her bag is already out.

"Is that yours?" I ask, pointing at the black Louis luggage with the bright orange priority sticker. She nods her head, and I walk up to it and roll it beside me.

"Ready?" I ask, and she nods.

We walk to the underground parking lot, and I lead her to my black BMW. I unlock the doors and load her luggage into the trunk. She stands next to me the whole time. I turn and look at her again, and I see her shiver. "Are you cold, sweet Zara?" I ask her, rubbing up and down her arms.

"No," she says softly, "not one bit."

I smile again. I seem to be always fucking smiling when it comes to her. I put my hand at the base of her back and hold out my hand for her to walk ahead of me. When we get to the passenger door, I open it and wait for her to get in before slamming it shut. When I get into the driver's side, she is reaching in the back to put the flowers on the back seat. Her white silk shirt pulls across her chest, giving me a glimpse of the white satin bra she is wearing under it. My cock suddenly starts to wake up, and I take a full ten seconds to count before turning back around, and when I do, luckily, she's sitting straight and putting on her seat belt.

"So where are you taking me?" she asks me as I pull out of the parking spot.

"I'd love to take you to my house and introduce you to Lilo and Stitch," I tell her. She's met them through FaceTime. "But if you aren't comfortable, I get it."

"It's fine," she says, and I nod and make my way to my house. "Have you lived there long?" she asks me, looking out of the window.

"It's been a year, but with my contract up for renewal, I don't know how long I'll actually be living here."

She turns to look at me, leaning her back against the door. "Do you not think they will renew?"

"Oh, they want me to sign the contract now," I tell her something no one really knows except my agent and me, "but I'm not ready yet."

"I think you should hold out," she says. "Wait and see how you finish the season." I laugh at her. "For the reporters, you are the leading scorer in the league. You have a great plus minus thingamajig, and you are also high on the charts for minutes played."

"Thingamajig?" I repeat, and she rolls her eyes.

"That is the best sports talk you will ever get," she says, and I nod and continue to look out the window. When we finally make it to my house, I shut off the car and see her hand reach for her handle.

"Don't you dare," I tell her and get out of the car, going to her side and opening her door. Then I open the back door so she can grab her purse and the flowers. I wait for her to finish and shut the door, then walk to the trunk and grab her bag. I wheel the bag beside me to the front door, and I already hear the barking. "They are just as excited as I am that you're here," I tell her, and she bumps her shoulder into me.

"That is very smooth, Mr. Richards." She laughs and holds her purse in one hand and the flowers in the other while I open the front door.

"Sit," I yell to the dogs, and they follow the command. Sitting side by side, they slap their tails against the floor when they see someone with me. I shield her in case they jump all over her, but they don't move. When the door is closed behind her, I leave her and go to the dogs, grabbing them by their collar. "This is Lilo," I say, rubbing her head, "and this is Stitch."

I'm expecting her to stand there and greet them; what I'm not expecting is for her to drop her purse and the flowers and then come over, bending down to rub their faces. "Aren't you two the cutest dogs in the world." And then all bets are off. Lilo looks up at her, licking the side of her face, while Stitch tries to get in there.

"Okay, enough," I say and walk into the house. "Out," I say, and they leave her and both charge outside.

"Sorry," I say, going to her. "Let me show you around." Taking her room by room, I show her everything and even take her upstairs to the other two guest bedrooms, the media room, and the game room.

"My nieces and nephews would go nuts in this room," she says, and I bring her downstairs and show her the guest room where I hope she will stay. She sees the big vase of white roses on the side table.

"This is where my mom stays when she comes down," I say. "I wasn't sure if you had a hotel reservation or not."

She walks into the room and smells the flowers on the table, and then goes to sit on the bed. "I actually did book a room," she tells me and kicks off her shoes and crosses her legs. Her toenails painted a bright pink. "I have it booked until Tuesday."

I lean against the doorjamb, my hands clasped behind me so I don't do anything stupid like grab her and push her down and get lost in her. "That's almost four days."

"Yeah," she says. Her stomach grumbles, and she laughs. "Guess I'm hungry."

"What do you feel like eating?" I ask her, and I'm so afraid to say or do something that will have her running. "I will order you anything you want, sweet Zara."

She gets up now, walking toward me, and stops in front of me. Her hands go to my chest as I suck my stomach in. "What is your favorite thing to eat?" she asks me, and now it's me who gives her a sly smile. "Food wise." She laughs, her hands not moving off me.

"Zara," I whisper and look at her hands on my chest. "I'm trying not to do anything that will make you run," I tell her. "I'm trying to get you to be so comfortable here that you don't want to go to your hotel. I'm fucking trying," I hiss when she steps a touch closer.

"Evan," she whispers my name, "I'm not going anywhere." My hands reach around and hold her hips.

"I can't kiss you right now," I tell her honestly, and she looks almost sad. "I can't kiss you right now because I won't stop." I touch her hair with my hands, wrapping it around my finger and thinking to myself it's softer than silk. "I need to get you fed." I look into the depths of her green eyes and see she's watching my every move. "I need to let the dogs in, and then," I whisper, "then I'm going to kiss you, sweet Zara." Her eyes cloud over when I say the last part. "Then the house could fall down around us, the dogs could eat the couch, and the world could come to an end, but the only thing I'll be doing is kissing you."

"I'm not that hungry," she says, and I laugh. "I can eat later."

"Will you stay with me?" I ask her, and then the dogs bark. "In my house."

"You promise me that you are going to kiss me?" she asks, tapping her index finger on my chest.

"Yes," I say softly.

"Then yes," she says, "I'll stay with you." She whispers the last part. "Now feed me so we can get this kissing on the road." And just like that, I throw my head back and laugh.

FIFTEEN

ZARA

I'VE NEVER WANTED anything more in my life than to be kissed by Evan. I love that he doesn't want to rush me, and I love that he almost walks on eggshells around me. But I'm here. I'm here for him and only him.

"Let's get you fed," he says, dropping the hair he's twirling in his fingers. He grabs my hand and pulls me to the kitchen. I walk through his house and can honestly say it's a total bachelor's pad. He walks to the living room, going to a hallway and closing the gate that is there. "That's my bedroom," he says, and I smile.

"You didn't show it to me," I tease, and he walks to the back door where the dogs are barking up a storm.

"That is part two of the tours." He laughs and walks around the counter into his kitchen. The only touch that shows he lives here is another bouquet that is pink. I mean, don't get me wrong, everything he needs is here, but it's not a home. There are no soft touches of things on the fridge; there is no mail tucked away on the counter. No flower on the windowsill over the sink. He walks to the side of the fridge to open a drawer and grabs a bunch of menus to bring to the counter.

"What do you feel like?" I look at him, and I take the biggest step I've ever taken in my whole life. I've never run after the boy. I've never wanted to kiss a man this much before. I used to make fun of my parents for always kissing, but I get it now. The need to touch that person, the desire to have that person touch you.

I walk around the counter and go to his side, my fingers grazing his as I play with the menus. Menus I'm not even looking at. If you ask me what kind of menus they were, the only thing I could say is food. In general.

"I don't know." I pretend to look through them, my pinky wrapping around his when our hands are side to side. The movement slowing down once we touch. My stomach flipping every single time he touches me. He looks down at our hands as I move mine again, reaching out to grab another one. I place my hand down next to his, and now he reaches for my hand. His pinky rubs my hand, and I don't even see the words on the menu.

I drop the menu on the counter and turn to him. He looks at me and turns with his back to the counter, and I finally step in front of him, his eyes looking into mine. "This past week, the only thing that kept me going was knowing I was coming to see you," I tell him softly. "Our crazy time difference, the travel schedule." I put one of my hands on his chest, my palm opening flat, the beating of his heart thumping against it.

"I knew that come Friday I would be with you." I take a deep breath, and I really wish I had a couple of shots of tequila before doing this. "I didn't care where I was going to stay, and I didn't care what I was going to wear. The only thing I cared about was seeing you." I say the next part almost in a whisper.

"The only thing I cared about is kissing you. Having you kiss me." My hand moves up now from his chest, and I slowly touch his face. I lean in just a touch, and he bends his head now, his eyes turning almost black. My fingertips in his scruff ignore the pinch. He leans in, and our noses touch from the side as he leans his forehead against mine.

"Sweet Zara," he says, and I can feel his hot breath on me. His one hand goes to my hip, pulling me closer, while the other one goes to my neck. The heat from his hand makes me shiver, knowing he's going to kiss me. I wait for it as he moves my face up to his, and then the moment I've been waiting my whole life for. His lips touch mine softly, his bottom lip touching my top lip as he tries not to rush the kiss. I bring my other hand up and wrap it around his shoulders and get on my tippy toes in front of him and finally his mouth touches mine. I think I sigh as my eyes close, and his tongue slowly moves into my mouth. His hands don't move from my hip or my neck as he groans into the kiss. His tongue slowly rolls over mine, the kiss so slow that I savor it.

I'll remember this kiss forever. It's a kiss I've dreamed about; it's the kiss that my sisters would tell me about that I never had, a kiss that every single little girl dreams about having. It's a kiss that even if I wanted to tell them about it,

I couldn't do it justice. I softly move my head from one side to the other, hoping to deepen the kiss and get more of him. He lets go of my lips when we are both so breathless we can't breathe. Both of our chests are heaving. He finally lets go of my hip but only to move the hair from my face.

He cups my face in his hand. "Ruined," he says softly, leaning in and kissing me again softly. His kisses are soft. "If I don't get away from you, no one is going to be eating."

My fingers play with his hair at the nape of his neck. "I'm totally okay with this plan." I kiss him again, and now his hand moves to my back, rubbing it up and getting lost in my hair. My stomach, however, has other plans and takes this moment to gurgle.

"I'm going to honestly kill my stomach," I say between pecks. My eyes remain closed.

"My sweet Zara." He chuckles, and now I open my eyes to see him. The softness of his face makes me lean in and kiss his chin now. "Why don't you take the dogs outside, and I'll order some food for us?"

"Even If I say no, my stomach is going to say yes." I reluctantly release him and turn to see the two dogs sitting by his feet. "Do you guys want to go out with me?" I tell them, and Stitch gets up first, going around in a circle while wagging his tail. "Let's go," I say and turn to walk to the door. Opening it, I let them walk out ahead of me. I look over my shoulder, and Evan is there just staring at me.

"Order food so we can do that kissing thing again." He shakes his head with a smile. "Chop-chop." I clap my hands and walk out onto his concrete patio. His yard is huge, and the dogs run in the distance. I walk to the hammock hanging right at the edge of the covered patio and sit in it softly, my feet never leaving the ground. I lean back in the hammock, watching the dogs run back and forth after each other. My hand touches my lips as his kiss lingers.

"Food should be here in twenty minutes," he says from behind me. The dogs now run full force toward him. He grabs their silver bowls and fills them up with water. "There you guys go," he says and looks up at me. "Hope you like Mexican."

"I do." Turning in the hammock, I look at him.

"Good because it was the one that took the least amount of time," he says. Coming over, he bends over and softly kisses my lips. Not with tongue, just a kiss, and just because. He stands by the hammock, and the dogs finish drinking and come around us. I stand only so I can hold his hand. Once my hand is in his, he brings it to his lips. We say nothing to each other, and when his phone rings in his pocket, he tells me the food is here.

I walk into the house and wash my hands and make my way around the kitchen looking for plates. I finally find them walking to the table with them the same time he comes in with the huge bags. "How much food did you order?"

"I didn't know what you ate, so I told him to bring a little bit of everything," he says and unloads the food while I go in search of utensils. I also get a couple of water bottles from his fridge.

"It smells so good," I tell him, sitting down and seeing all the containers he has opened.

"This is chicken tacos." He points at one. "Fish tacos." I listen to him tell me all the different things he ordered while

I grab a chip and dip it in the queso.

"I'm not listening to anything you say," I tell him, and he laughs. He sits down in front of me. "This is the first meal we've had together alone," I tell him, grabbing one of the shrimp tacos.

"It is," he says, grabbing a taco and then loading it with some guacamole.

"So what are we going to tell everyone tomorrow?" I ask him, and he looks at me with his eyebrows pulled together.

"What do you mean?" he asks.

"I mean, people are going to ask if we are together," I tell him. "I mean, the whole world knows. And now we got through the first awkward kiss part."

"There was nothing awkward about our first kiss," he snaps. "If you want, I can show you what I mean right now."

I laugh out loud. "Relax there, cowboy. I'm not saying that it wasn't a good kiss," I joke with him, and he glares at me. "It was better than good. What I'm saying is that people are going to be there, probably members of the press, so what do you think we should tell them?"

"I don't give a shit what we tell them or if we tell them anything at all," he says between bites. "I'm good with what-ever you want to tell them."

"We could play it off as I'm visiting a friend." He raises one eyebrow. "Jesus, relax there," I tell him. "You need to calm the male hormones please and listen to me."

"Not sure I want to hear what you have to say."

"I'm saying that we don't have to go in there and play tonsil hockey and have people taking a picture of us. We can go in there and be like I'm visiting and I decided to swing by," I say, and he laughs.

"Tonsil hockey," he says between laughter, and I shake my head. "Sweet, sweet Zara."

"Oh, good God," I say annoyed. "Can we just keep this on the down low until I tell my family?" I ask him. "I mean, we've spent two days together at the most."

"It's been two weeks," he counters.

"I said we've spent two days *together*. Not that we have known each other," I tell him.

"I'm not going to hide that you're mine," he says, looking straight at me.

"First thing, I'm my own person," I tell him. "Second, we aren't hiding anything. We are being private." I grab another chip and dip it, waiting for him.

"You kissed me," he states. "You kissed me. You made yourself mine when you did it."

"Oh, for the love of everything," I say out loud, looking up at the ceiling. "What is it with hockey men?" I hear his chair scrape back and watch him come to my chair and push my chair back.

"You done eating?" he asks me, his eyes staring straight into mine.

"What?" I whisper.

"Are you done eating?" he asks me, and I nod. He bends down and literally picks me up and tosses me over his shoulder.

"What the hell?" I shriek, and the dogs go crazy, thinking it's a game.

"I'm showing you my bedroom, and then I'm going to show you how you're mine," he says and then he opens the gate and closes it behind him. "Go lie down," he tells the dogs, and then I look up at them and see them sitting there watching.

"Can you put me down?" I ask him, and he slowly puts me on my feet. "Have you lost your mind?" I huff.

"When it comes to you, sweet Zara, my mind is a mess," he tells me softly, pushing my hair back from my face. "The only thing that I think about is how long I can keep you to myself."

My hands now run through his hair. "You have me until Tuesday."

"Well, then it's enough time to show you that you're mine," he says and bends his head at the same time as I tilt my head up. When our lips smash together, this kiss is different than the last one. This one is all hands—my hand in his hair, his hands buried in mine as he moves my head side to side to deepen the kiss. He lets go of my lips, and I swear I forget everything when he touches me.

"I didn't bring you in here for anything more than a kiss."

"Just kissing," I tell him. "Just a kiss." I kiss his lips, and one of the dogs barks. "Are they going to be okay?" He turns and walks to the door, and then I finally get to look at his room.

His king-size bed is very, very masculine. The covers make it feel homey, but you know this room belongs to a bachelor. I turn to look out the window and see the dogs running in the backyard and then hear him coming back. I turn to look at him. "Do you want to go outside with them?"

"We don't have to," he says, coming into the room. "Do you want to change?"

"I actually would love to take a shower," I tell him, looking down to see that it's almost nine already.

"Okay, let me take you to your room," he says, holding out my hand. He brings me to the room, grabbing my bag on the way. "There are fresh towels," he says and then grabs one side of my face to kiss me again.

"Text me when you get out." He turns to walk away. "Or you can come find me on the couch." He closes the door behind him, and I have to sit down to allow my heart to settle before I get up and take a shower.

Sixteen

Evan

I CLOSE THE door softly behind me and walk to my room and sit on my bed. My hands still smell of her. I've kissed girls before, but nothing that rocked my world the way it did when I finally kissed Zara. It was an out of this world, kick you in your balls, holy shit hat trick moment.

My heart speeds up when I think of her in the shower. I get up and unbutton my pants before my cock gets strangled. Turning on my own shower, I think of her in hers, and I have no choice but to fist my cock and take care of myself. I get out, and I swear my cock doesn't go down. I take my time putting my boxers on and also my gym shorts, hoping she won't see my half-mast boner. Running my hands through my hair, I walk into the living room, and I stop mid step. She's sitting on the couch in a gray top and pants, her hair piled on top of her head, but that isn't what stops me. It's the fact that she has Lilo on one side and Stitch on the other with her feet tucked under her.

"What do you guys want to watch?" she asks them. Lilo places her head on her legs, and she holds the remote with one hand while she pets her with the other. She must sense me because she looks up, and the dogs don't even move. "Hey." She smiles. "Are they allowed on the couch?"

"Yeah," I say, walking to the couch and sitting down on the other side of the dog. Much farther from her than I want to be.

"I don't know any of the channels," she says, handing me the remote, but I pull her to me at the same time. Picking her up over the dog, I have her sit on my lap. Might not have been my smoothest move, and I swear it was not with her almost falling off the couch. The dogs think it was a game and rush over to us, causing her ass to fall off my lap and onto the couch. The dogs now are all over her, but she doesn't do what I'm expecting her to do like shriek and yell. Instead, she full-on belly laughs while the dogs lick her face.

"Down," I command them, and they jump off the couch and sit right next to her. She turns on her side, and this time, her feet are in my lap.

"I'm only supposed to kiss your master," she whispers to them. "I'm his." She looks over at me, and it takes me only a second to cover her with myself. What I'm not expecting is for her to open her legs for me and wrap them around my waist with her hands up by her head. My hands slip into hers, and I lower my mouth to hers. I tasted her not long ago, but the taste of her again makes me groan. I hold my weight up, and she arches her back up to me. I let her go now, kneeling on the couch between her legs. Her shirt rose up, so you see her smooth stomach, and I look down mesmerized with it. My thumb slowly rubs it. Her skin is silky and smooth and hot, and I'm in a trance at this point.

I want to raise her shirt a bit more just to rub her skin. "That tickles," she finally says breathlessly.

"I think we should go to bed," I say, getting off the couch. She props herself up on her elbows, looking at me, her cheeks flushed and her lips swollen from my kisses.

"Are we going to bed together?" she asks me, and it takes everything in me to answer her.

"No." I shake my head. "I said I wanted you here, but I'm not going to push you to sleep with me."

"You can't force me to do anything," she says, getting off the couch. "But if you don't want to sleep with me, it's all good." She smirks at me.

"I'm going to let that slide," I tell her, "because I don't think you're ready for me to tell you how much I want you." Her eyes cloud over. "I don't think you're ready for me to take you to my bed because when I finally get you in that bed …" I walk to her, tilting her head up by her chin. "We'll be in there for a while."

"A while, huh?" She smiles, and I peck her softly on the lips. "Fine, I'll go to my room." She turns around, and I watch her swing her hips. "If you change your mind, you'll know where to find me." She looks over her shoulder. "I also should warn you I sleep naked," she says. I squeeze my hands into fists, and she just laughs.

"Good night, Zara," I say through clenched teeth and watch her walk to the bedroom wiggling her hand in the air. I look up again and turn to go to my room. "This is going to be fun," I say sarcastically to myself. I throw the covers off the bed and slide in, grabbing my phone.

I text her.

Me: Is everything okay?

She answers right away.

Zara: This bed is so comfy.

Me: I'm here if you need anything.

I send her the message, and I hope to fuck she doesn't push me.

Zara: I do need someone to tuck me in. ;)

Me: I take back that you're sweet.

I reply, smiling. She is better than fucking sweet.

Zara: HA HA HA

I turn on my television, flipping through the channels, and I don't even know what the fuck is on television at this time. I stop at *SportsCenter* and watch the highlights of the games from tonight. I see the highlights of the game from New York.

I don't care what anyone says; Max and Matthew have the best chemistry on ice, and just watching them play, you wonder why they are going to retire, but hey, they both have more than one Stanley cup ring, so why not. Go out on a high note is what I always said. I watch *SportsCenter* for thirty more minutes and then realize that the dogs aren't in my bed. I get out of bed and look on the couch and still don't see them.

The back door is not open, so I walk to the front door, and I see her door open. But most importantly, I see her sitting up in the bed watching television with both dogs on the bed. "What is going on in here?" I say, standing in the doorway.

"I was sitting in bed, and I heard sniffing at the door. When I went to open it, she was lying down." She pets Lilo's head. "Then I came back to bed, and she followed and so did he." She points at Stitch who is lying down, but his eyes are on mine, expecting me to tell them to get down. "Would you like to join us and watch this movie?" she asks me, and I look at the television. "It's *The Proposal* with Ryan Reynolds and Sandra Bullock."

I shake my head. "Why, why are you testing my limits, woman?" I tell her and walk into the room. The dogs still don't leave her as she lies in the middle of the bed.

"Don't be like that. I'm sure you can be the perfect gentleman." She leans over and folds over the cover and scoots over, making the dogs groan and move over. "Don't worry, I'm fully dressed," she says, and I swear this woman is going to be the death of me.

I get under the covers next to her, and Lilo lies between us almost like she is guarding her. "You are supposed to love me," I tell her, and she just lays her head down. Zara puts her hand on Lilo's back.

"Don't talk to my girl like that," she says, smiling. I grab her hand in mine, and just like that, we watch a movie together in bed. Like it's been done for years except I haven't even known her for a month. She moves her legs and that makes Lilo also move, but she gets up and goes to the other side of Zara and lies down on top of her, and Zara has to move closer to me. She does all this while laughing. I open my arms and reach around, pulling her close to me. She looks up at me, the little freckles on her nose that you don't really see except if you are really close.

"Hey," she whispers.

"Hey," I say and lean down to take her mouth again. Her tongue slides into my mouth and then we both moan. We scoot down and make out while the remote falls on the floor. The dogs get off the bed, and then it's just the two of us. My mouth never leaves hers. I'm lost in her, lost in the kiss, so lost that the television turns off from inactivity. Her leg hitches up over my hips, my cock against her core, and our clothes the only barrier stopping me from sliding into her. My hands roam from her ass to her back to her hair. I manage to get the elastics out and then bury my hands in it. I don't know how long we kiss for, and if you ask me, it's not long enough. She lays her head on my shoulder and just pulls me closer to her. Our chests are flush together, and with our feet intertwined and her in my arms, I fall asleep.

The next morning when my eyes flutter open, I have to take a second to get my bearings. I look beside me and see the bed empty, but the sheets still feel warm. I toss the blankets over me and get out of bed in search of my woman. I don't have to go far before I hear her talking to the dogs.

"Now where does he keep your food?" she asks them, and I hear the cupboards open and close. "You guys must be hungry, right?" I stand by the counter and watch her as she gets to know my kitchen with both of my dogs watching her. Both their tails wagging. "Oh, I found the treats," she says and hands them both a treat. "Don't tell on me."

"Too late," I say, and she jumps back.

"Shit, you scared me," she says, holding her hand to her

chest. "I can't find their food, and they are starving," she tells me.

I walk into the kitchen and take her in my arms. "You left me," I say. I bury my face into her neck, and she moves her head to the side, giving me access.

"They had to pee, and so did I," she says. "Go feed them, and I will make us coffee." I nod my head and turn to the dogs.

"Let's go, you two," I tell them, and they follow me to the garage where I scoop out their food. I open the door for them and then walk back into the house.

She is making her coffee, and I walk behind her and wrap my arms around her waist, kissing her neck because her hair is tied up again. "You know what you are missing?" she tells me, and I just grumble. "A nice couch outside."

"So let's go buy one," I tell her, grabbing my own coffee. Taking her hand, I lead her outside, and we watch the dogs run around. I sit in one of the rocking chairs and then look at her. "Yeah, we need a couch out here," I tell her, and she sits in the rocking chair next to me, tucking her feet under her.

"What time is the event tonight?" she asks, taking a sip of her coffee and watching the dogs run.

"I have to be there at six thirty," I tell her. "There is a red carpet." She turns her head to look at me. "You don't have to walk with me," I tell her, "but you can if you want to."

"Um," she says. "I'm good with watching from the side-lines."

"I thought you would be," I tell her, "but make no mistake about it, everyone is going to know you're there with me." She rolls her eyes at me. We spend the day lounging on the couch while I buy a round couch for outside. We also have a heavy-duty make-out session that leaves me rock hard and has her running to take a shower.

I slip on my suit jacket when I see it's almost six. It's the suit she sold me, and I smile when I look into the mirror. I grab my Rolex and slip it on and then go in search of her.

Her bedroom door is closed, and I find Lilo lying in front of it. "Did she kick you out?" I ask her and then knock softly on the door.

"Come in," she shouts, and I'm not ready for the sight that greets me. Sitting at the end of the bed on one of the white benches, she is leaning over and tying the strap to her gold heels. But all I see are her legs—her long, lean, and soft fucking legs. Her head turns toward the door, and I see that she has makeup on. Not a lot but the perfect amount to make her green eyes pop even more. She's left her strawberry blond hair loose with soft curls. "I'm almost ready," she says, and all I can do is stare when she gets up, and I finally see her full outfit. It's a pink gold colored outfit in all sequins. The sleeves are long and tied tight at her wrists, making the sleeves baggy. It's a V-neck in the front, and the waist looks like it's crossed over. The kicker is it reaches her mid thigh, so her legs are all out. I have no idea what the fuck she is wearing, but I do know she isn't going out like this. "I have to just get my purse," she says, walking to her purse, and I see the skirt slink around her legs.

"You can't go out like that," I finally tell her, putting my hands in my pocket. "What else do you have?"

"What is wrong with this outfit?" she says, looking down. There is nothing wrong with it, and now that she's facing me, I see it's a wrap dress.

"Well, for one, it's not long enough," I tell her, and she just laughs, making me glare at her. "For two, it's not long enough," I repeat because besides the length, she looks amazing. "Three, it's not fucking long enough, Zara," I say, now running my hands through my hair.

"Oh, you are wearing the suit you got," she says, walking over, and all I see are her legs and the fucking dress that just brushes against her. Then to top it all off, she's wearing fucking gold stilettos. A single gold strap over her toes and then another around her fucking ankle. "You look amazing," she says, smoothing the jacket. "We should get going. You are going to be late."

"Zara," I say through clenched teeth.

"Actually"—she turns and looks at me—"can we get a picture so I can send it to Zoe?" she asks and walks ahead of me toward the long mirror hanging in the entrance. She stands there and holds the phone up to snap a picture of me looking at her. "You have to smile and not glare." She laughs and then I just shake my head.

"Can you please, please go change?" I ask her. I'm not opposed to begging.

"Don't be silly," she says. "Besides, the slip under is shorts so you can't see anything." She turns to look at me and then tilts her head back. "I really want to kiss you right now, but I'm wearing lip gloss." My hands grab her face, and I kiss her, smudging her lip gloss. My hand in her hair now making it more wild than before. I see little soft red dots where my scruff pricked her.

"Is there any chance you will go change?" I ask her softly.

"Not a chance," she says, wiping off her lip gloss from her lips. "But there is a good chance I can show you what I'm wearing under it when we get home."

"This is not helping right now," I say and grab her hand, almost pulling her out of the house. I walk to the side passenger door and open it for her. She stops beside me and kisses my cheek.

"Well, you look handsome," she says, and then steps into the car and sits, making her skirt go higher.

"This is going to be the longest night of my life," I say, closing the door and walking to my side of the car.

Seventeen

Zara

I TRY TO hide my laughter while he gets into the car, and all he does is grump and pout. The outfit is short, but it's so slinky and sexy and sassy I had to wear it. Plus, after seeing his face when he saw me, I had no choice.

"Is there going to be food there?" I ask him. "I'm getting a bit hungry."

"There should be," he says, looking over, and now it's my turn to look at him. The black suit did not do him justice when he tried it on in the showroom. Having it on him tailored and perfect with his white shirt under it and the gold cufflinks, he was so hot as fuck. I look down, sending the picture of him scowling to Zoe.

Zoe: I think I saw that same look on Matthew and Max.

"My sister says you look nice." I laugh at the comment. He pulls up to the arena and heads to the underground parking. He scans his badge that is in his middle console, and the black doors open. He makes his way down to where the players park, and I see that it's almost full. He puts the car in park in his reserved parking spot, his name on the concrete wall in front of us. I grab the lip gloss from my little purse to reapply it. I put it back in the purse, and he opens the door, coming to me and kissing me. "I just put my lip gloss on," I tell him, grabbing a tissue and wiping it off his mouth.

"I know," he says and then comes back in for a little peck. He then holds out his hand, and I grab it to help me down. He presses a button on the keys, making the car beep. We walk to a black side door with my hand in his the whole time. He opens the door with his free hand and holds it open for me to walk in before him, my hand slipping out of his.

"Oh shit," someone says, and I look up at a guy who looks the same age as Justin. "Goddamn."

Evan stand beside me and looks at him. "What's up, Patterson?" he says, doing the chin up.

"Hey, Richards," Patterson says, and that is all he says. He's too busy staring at me.

"Hi," I say, and I'm about to put my hand out when I'm yanked away and just look at Evan. We walk down the carpeted hallway, and he says hello to a couple of people and then finally we get to the locker room where the guys are all waiting.

"Hey," he says, sticking his head in, and I hear a guy laughing.

"Oh, New York is going to be so much fun," he says, slapping the bench next to him. "Dude, you are going to die." I shake my head and hold the purse up to my mouth to hide my laughter.

I lean in, and whisper, "I'll protect you."

"Okay folks, we are about to do the introductions, and then there is the red carpet." A man who I think is the PR guy comes in and then looks over at us. "Everyone in place please." He claps his hands. "By number please except captain and assistant," he says and walks over to us.

"Can you take her out there?" Evan says to him. "Zara, this is Tristan." He motions to the man wearing a Gucci suede suit that was on the runway last season.

"We've met." I look at Evan. "He came to collect me in Jersey."

He smiles and then nods his head when he sees that the reporters are watching. "I have to go."

"See you out there," I tell him and then wait for Tristan to lead the way. We walk down the hallway, passing the reporters, and I keep my head down as well as my eyes. This is his night, and I don't want to overshadow it by being here. He walks me out to the ice that has been transformed into a casino. A black carpeted floor covers the ice with different tables set upon one side of the ice. He walks me to where a crowd is forming.

"These are all the season ticket holders," he tells me. "There are also some contest winners and of course the Dallas oil billionaires." I smile at him when I see someone I recognize.

"Excuse me," I tell him and walk up to the woman who is staring at her date's face. "Well, well, well, Cori," I say, trying to hide my smile. "If it isn't the woman who had to rush off." I joke with her when she turns and see me. Cori started out as Kellie's assistant, and when her manager got fired, she took his place.

"Oh, fuck," she says. "I had no idea you would be here." She looks at her date. "Harry, this is Zara." The man who is wearing this year's Armani suit holds out his hand. He has his black hair pulled back, and I swear he could be a model, but I know who this is.

"You must be Brian's brother," I say, and he just smirks. "I see the resemblance."

"Well, there goes that secret love," he says to her and brings her close to him. I see her outfit now. It's a champagne color that goes low in the front and has an accordion skirt. A black satin belt makes the whole outfit.

"What are you doing here?" she says, bringing her glass of champagne to her mouth. "Doesn't your family play for New York?" I smile and look down but grab a champagne glass from the passing waiter.

"Testing one, two." I hear from the speaker and look toward the spotlight that is on a man standing on the stage. "Oh, that's bright," he says, laughing. "I want to take a second and thank you all for coming out for our annual casino night." I look around while the man speaks, and I spot the wives right away. All well dressed and stuck together away from anyone who isn't them. I've seen it time and time again; Karrie has to deal with the cattiness all the time, but with Allison and Vivienne in her corner, no one fucks with her, and we all socialize. "It's my honor to introduce you to the dealers tonight." The man starts introducing the players, and when he introduces Evan, I have to smile as I silently clap my hands. He walks up the step to the stage and looks out, waving as he walks over to the other guys and stands with them. The last one out is the captain of the team. "Okay, it's time to raise some money," he says. "The players will be around all night, and some might even be your dealer."

Everyone claps, and the guys come to mingle with the crowd. I watch him make his way around, shaking hands with certain people. I see him passing the "wives crew." He stops to say hello to who I am pegging as the captain's wife. It's almost like watching the movie *The Godfather*. I see her throw her head back and laugh at something he says and then see her husband come over, and she is, in fact, the captain's wife. He grabs his wife around the waist and tells him something. The wife calls over a woman who is tall, totally bleach blond, a touch of Botox, a touch of lip fillers, and a lot of tits. She plays shy, and I am so ready to roll my eyes, especially when she tosses her hair.

"This is going to be good," Cori says next to me. "And to think you wanted to stay in." She looks at Harry.

"You were the one who didn't want to come to this," he says, laughing and then leans in to whisper. "You made me sign a certain contract," he says, and she turns and puts her hand over his mouth.

"Shut up," she hisses, and I laugh now. I don't know how I know Evan's close, but I do, especially when I feel his hand on my back. "Oh, hello there," Cori says. "Harry, I would like to spend some of your money, and then I want you to take me for a burger."

"Excuse us," he says, looking over at us. "It was a pleasure meeting you, Zara, and it is always nice to see you," he says to Evan who shakes his hand.

"Thank you for coming," Evan says to him and then grabs

a water bottle from a waiter passing by. "I was looking for you."

"Well, you found me," I say, and I'm trying not to let the blonde get to me, but it's me, so she does. "This looks nice," I say, looking around, and a reporter comes up to us.

"Hey Evan, how are you?" he asks, and I stand there holding my drink in my hand.

"I'm good. Thanks for asking." And he walks away. "Did you get anything to eat?"

No, I got out here and saw Cori," I tell him, and he comes closer to me, "and I came over."

"Well then, let's go find something to eat," he says, "and I want to introduce you to a couple of people." I follow him to the wives' circle, and I swear I'm ready for it, but one look from the leader and I know this will not end well. "Hey guys," Evan says, and the woman just looks up, doing a very obvious up and down.

"Oh, look, y'all," she says with her Southern accent.

"Corey," Evan says to the guy. "Paige, this is Zara."

I hold out my hand to Paige first who takes it with a smile on her face. "Nice to meet you." And then I do the same to Corey.

"We've met a time or two before," Corey says and then looks at his wife. "Honey, do you remember Max Horton and his wife, Allison?"

"From New York, right?" she asks him, and he nods.

"This is Allison's sister," he says, and I can see the look of shock come over her. "Karrie is your sister-in-law as well?" she asks, and I smile

"Yes, she's married to my brother Matthew," I say.

"I met Karrie and Allison last year when all the wives joined forces for a calendar," she says. "Wait a second, are you the one Zara's Closet?" She now has her mouth hanging. "You were the one who got us all that designer stuff?"

"Yes," I say, "that would be me."

"I had no idea," she says, and I'm almost tempted to mumble under my breath, *I bet you didn't*. But I don't for Evan and also for Karrie and Allison's sake. "So what are you doing in Dallas?" she asks me, and now her blond friend comes back.

"Oh, there you are." She smiles at Evan. "We meet again."

I try to hide my eye roll and can hear my mother's voice in the back of my head. *"Be nice, Zara."*

"Taylor." Paige turns to her friend. "This is Zara Stone from Zara's Closet." Her friend opens her mouth in shock. "We were just looking at your stuff the other day," Paige says.

"I love the look you put together for Jessica Beckett for the Oscars this year," Taylor says. "And your dress is fabulous."

"Thank you," I say and then look over at Evan, who is glaring at the woman now.

"So what are you doing in town?" Taylor asks the same question Paige asked but I didn't answer.

"I came in to visit this guy," I say, pointing at Evan with my hand holding the champagne glass while he slips his pinky into mine with our free hands. From the look of shock on both their faces, it takes everything in me not to do a mic drop and then a boom.

"I have to go and do the blackjack table," Corey says. "Come with me."

"It was great meeting you, Zara," Paige says, and Taylor just smiles and nods and walks away with them.

"Well, there goes her hopes and dreams of going home with you tonight," I say under my breath, and he just laughs while he leans in and kisses my lips. I look around after to see if anyone saw us. "Down low," I hiss at him as he walks away, and he looks over at me.

"Don't care," he says, whispering. "Let's eat something. I have to do the roulette table in fifteen minutes." He leads me to the food, and we grab a couple of things, then go and sit at an empty table, but it isn't empty for long as some of his teammates join us. "Okay, we have to be at the roulette table."

"Who is we?" I look up at him, and he just smiles.

"Want me to show you again?" He looks around. "I think I see a couple of people."

"Bully," I say to him, getting up, and he just laughs. "Let's go win some money."

"I get to go home with you tonight," he says, smiling as we walk side by side through the crowd of people. "I've already won," he says, and he winks at me. It's at this moment I realize I'm in way over my head. This crazy thing is starting to snowball, and I'm afraid I won't survive the end of it.

EIGHTEEN

Evan

"OKAY, PLACE YOUR bets." I look at the twenty-five people standing around the roulette table. I look up at Zara who has been the center of attention to everyone who came to the table.

"I'm going to try my luck with number four," she says, putting two red chips on it. Before we came to the table, she walked to the donation table and dropped five thousand dollars and got the chips for it. No one actually wins any money tonight; whatever chips you cash in at the end of the night will be matched by the owner of the team.

She started with five thousand, and she's way over seven thousand right now. "Well, if you say four, I have no choice," says Trevor, the fifty-year-old man who has been itching to touch her, always leaning in to whisper to her. The only thing I can see in my head is me throat punching him.

"All bets are closed," I say right as he puts his chips on

the table and take the white little ball and spin it. I don't even watch the ball spin, the only thing I'm watching is Zara standing next to him with her hand holding her purse.

"I'm here for my shift," Peter, my other teammate, says from behind me, and I look over at him.

The ball finally falls and jumps from one number to the other landing on 00. "The winner is 00," I announce and see everyone lose their bets. "Thank you, guys, so much for playing. I'm going to be handing it off to my boy Peter," I say with a smile and walk around the table to see Zara collecting her chips.

"Don't tell me you're leaving already," Trevor says, and she just smiles.

"Hey, babe," I say using the nickname I've never used in my life because my father always calls my mother that. She turns to me, and I see a sparkle in her eyes. Fuck, maybe I need to call her babe more often.

"Hey," I say to Trevor, then turn to Zara, kissing her cheek. "You did good." She puts the chips in her hand purse, and now it's bursting.

"Yeah." She smiles. "We should try blackjack." I nod at her and grab her hand in mine. "Trevor, it was a pleasure meeting you." She smiles at him, and I just turn and pull her away.

"I swear if he touched you one more time, I was going to throat punch him," I tell her, and she just laughs.

"Please, you had that bleach blonde all over you laughing up a storm." She stops walking. "Tell me, what did she say that was so funny?"

I look at her, and she folds her hands over her chest, which is the wrong move 'cause it pushes up her perfect tits. "Which blonde?" I ask, knowing she is talking about Taylor.

"Playing stupid is not a good look on you, Evan," she says, her eyes squinting as she glares at me.

"I have no idea what you're talking about," I tell her, and she now comes closer to me.

"I'm not the jealous type," she says. "Not in the least. Never was, never am going to be." She looks right and left and then comes back to me. "But if we are seeing each other, and I find out that you are also seeing other people, it won't bode well for you." Fuck, her words get my cock stirring.

"One, I'm not a cheater. Never have been, never going to be," I tell her, picking up a strand of her hair and twirling it with my fingers. "Two, there is nothing that she could have said to get to me because the only thing I was interested in was finding you," I tell her, getting really, really close to her, so close our chests touch, and she leans down. "Three, I was going to make damn sure everyone here knew you were with me." I look down at her now, my fingers trailing across her face. "Now, do you really want to play blackjack, or would you like to cash out and head home?"

"That depends," she says. "Are you going to feed me?" she asks me, and I tilt my head to the side and smirk at her. "I mean food."

"I can feed you that also," I reply to her, and she leans up and kisses my chin.

"Then let's blow this popsicle stand," she says. "I should say bye to Cori and Harry." She looks around the room and doesn't spot them. "They must have left already."

We walk to the cashier table, and she hands them her

chips with her name. She made twenty-two hundred dollars in thirty minutes. I grab her hand and start walking out, saying good bye to the people we pass. A couple of the fans stop me and ask to take a picture. She is happy to take it for them, and they all thank her. We finally walk into the back and head toward the garage. The sound in the garage is eerily quiet with just her heels clicking on the concrete. I see that almost all the cars are still there. Walking to her side of the car I click the button to unlock the door, but I don't open it for her. Instead, I turn her around and push her back against the car. My hands go on either side of her head, my palms flat against the car instead of buried in her hair.

"You still have lip gloss on," I tell her and then see her eyes change from a light green to a dark gray right before my eyes. "It's shiny," I tell her, leaning in and nipping her bottom lip and then trailing my tongue along it. The tip of her tongue comes out just a touch to touch mine.

"It drives me crazy." I kiss the side of her lip, and the tip of my tongue comes out again and now so does hers, trying to catch my tongue. "All I want to do is kiss it off," I say, going to the other side of her lips and kissing her there, but her tongue is already coming out to get mine. "All night it drove me crazy," I whisper to her. "All night," I say and finally tilt my head to the side and attack her lips, her hands holding the lapels of my jacket while our mouths attack each other. My tongue fights hers, the need greater than it's ever been. My hands now coming off the car to hold her face in them. I turn the kiss to the other side, somehow hoping to get it deeper.

Our tongues go around in circles. I don't want to stop

kissing her, but if I don't, I'm going to take her in the back seat, and we are never going to leave this garage. When I finally pull my head back, her chest heaves and her hands still hold on as she tries to pull me again for a kiss.

"Sweetheart," I say. She opens her eyes, and they are blue green now.

"I think I still have some lip gloss on," she says softly, trying to get my lips back on hers, and I laugh.

"I think I got it all. Now let's get you in the car and get home." Her eyes blink a couple of times, and she comes out of her daze.

"You are a total buzzkill, Richards," she says, using my last name, and I step back and open the door for her.

"Total buzzkill. I'm telling my sister." I watch her get in the car.

"Maybe even Karrie and Allison." She mentions them, buckling her seat belt.

"Even my mom." And once she says her mom, I tilt my head back and belly laugh while she glares at me.

"You are not helping your case right now, Evan," she huffs out, and I close the door and walk to my side of the car. I get in, then lean over and kiss her neck.

"Nope, you get no access to any of me until you feed me." She turns with her back to the door. "I want a nice big greasy cheeseburger."

"Are you okay with diners?" I ask her, backing up and pulling out. I make my way over to the little hidden treasure that everyone knows about and is always open.

"We may be a touch overdressed," I tell her, and she just shrugs. "But they have the best root beer floats." I watch as her eyes get wide like saucers.

When I pull up to the parking lot of the little diner, I see about ten cars there. "If we come during the day, they have people bring it to your car." I park my car under the awning and turn off the car. Getting out, I make my way to her door, and I get there while she's getting out.

"What did I say about waiting for me?" I scowl at her.

"Evan, I think I can get out of a car without you helping me." She puts her hand on my cheek. "Besides, I'm so hungry I'm dying." She is the best at turning the story around so you forget what you were talking about in the first place. She reaches her hand out for me, and I grab it, loosening the tie around my neck and unbuttoning the first button.

"Take off your tie." She stops walking and waits for me to do it and then holds out her hand.

"I'll put it in my purse." I hand it to her, and she folds it, placing it in her bag. I walk to the small brown brick building with a lot of windows showing you inside. With a brown door on each end, I grab the brass handle of the closest door and pull it open. The bell over the door rings, and once the door closes, the open sign hanging in the window shakes.

"Two guests," someone yells, and I look over at the woman. "Take a seat wherever you like, and I'll be right there," she says, and I look at Zara. "Do you want a booth, or do you want to sit at the counter?" I point at the counter with ten stools, and only three are occupied. Looking around the rest of the restaurant, I see that one booth is open.

"The counter is good," she says. Walking to the end, she slides on the moving stool and places her purse on the counter, and I sit next to her. She reaches for a menu tucked between the ketchup bottle and the salt and pepper shakers.

"What are you getting?" she asks me when the lady comes to us.

"Welcome, what can I get you?" she asks us, grabbing her pad from her white apron.

"I'm going to have a double cheese with bacon, basket of onion rings, fries, and a root beer float," I tell her and look over at Zara.

"I'll have a cheeseburger with bacon," she says, then looks at me. "Will you eat all your fries?" I shake my head. "I'll also have a water please." She smiles at the woman who just turns and walks away.

"I'm sharing your root beer float." She turns her stool to face me and leans in. I turn my own stool and open my legs, keeping her legs between mine to block anyone from ogling her legs.

The lady comes back and places the frosted glass in front of us, the root beer bubbling with a scoop of ice cream in the middle slowly melting and two red straws sticking out. She grabs her phone and snaps a picture, then leans in and takes a sip.

"I might have to get my own," she says, taking another sip. I grab my straw and take a sip, and she snaps a picture.

"Zoe always says if there isn't no photographic proof, then it didn't happen." I shake my head and lean in to kiss her lips.

The food comes in no time, and between the two of us, nothing is left. She has about fifteen napkins all balled up from the grease that she cleaned off her.

"That was so good," she says, getting up once I pay the bill and thank the woman.

"You lovebirds come back again," the waitress says with a huge smile on her face.

We walk out hand in hand, and I open the door for her. "Thank you," she says, getting in the car. When I slip into the car, she is leaning over, and I see her untying her shoes.

"Okay, it's time to take them off," she says. "It's been six hours." I look over at the clock on the console and see it's almost midnight. I make my way home and look over at her when she reaches for the door handle. She sees me and takes a deep breath.

"Oh God, hurry up then." She snickers, and I get out of the car and already hear the dogs barking. I open her door, and she gets out, holding her purse in one hand with her shoes hanging by the straps.

She walks with her hand in mine, and I swear it feels like it's always been like this. I open the door and wait for her to walk in. She greets the dogs with hugs, and they get all excited. "Let's get you guys outside," she says, dumping her stuff at the front door and walking into the house, leaving me to lock the door and follow her. They didn't even come and see me.

She unlocks the door, still talking to them while I walk to the fridge and grab two water bottles. The light from over the stove on giving some light to the room. "How long do they stay out there?" she asks, coming over to me, and I hand her a water bottle. I lean back on my counter, watching her drink her water bottle.

"You're beautiful," I tell her, and she looks at me, walking over to me. I lean in and kiss her neck right where I can feel her heart beat. When I feel its fast beat, I'm happy I'm not the only one feeling like this. "Hands down the most beautiful woman I've ever met in my life."

Her hand roams up my chest to the top of my shirt where it's unbuttoned, her fingers going inside the top as her fingers rub my collarbone. "I believe I told you that I would show you what I was wearing under my dress," she says.

Her hand leaves my chest and goes to the side where she unsnaps the little button on the side, and I see a little bit of her pink bra strap. My whole body is on alert. My heart picks up speed, and my cock strains to come out. I watch her delicate hands reach the other side and unsnap another button, and then it just hangs open. She takes both sides in her hand and slips it off her shoulder, and I am holding my breath. *If I died at this moment, my life would be complete* is the only thing I can think. She is so much more than exquisite, and I can't come up with the words. No words can do her justice.

She is standing there in a pink see-through bra with gold stitching all over the cup, but you see her light pink nipple puckered and pebbled. My hand reaches up, and my thumb rubs the swell of her breast, going from one to the other. "I have no words," I tell her softly. "I keep trying to come up with words to describe your perfection," I say to her, my thumb now slowly going down to her left nipple and running over her nipple. Her head falls back, and she softly moans. I grab her, picking her up, and her legs wrap around my waist. Her arms going around my neck, and she attacks my mouth. My hand goes straight to her ass as I make my way to my room.

NINETEEN

ZARA

I CAN'T GET enough of his kisses. I swear his kisses are everything. He walks through the house, and I hear barking. "The dogs," I say, almost panting.

"They have the doggy door in the garage," he says, burying his face in my neck. "They can get in the house," he says, walking to his room and closing the gate behind him. His scruff against my neck makes me shiver.

"Evan." I moan his name. He loses his grip on me, and I slide down him. My hands go to his jacket, slipping it off him, and it falls to the floor at his feet. My hands shake when I reach out for his buttons. I really wish the lights were brighter in his room. The only light on is the bedside table, and it's on dim.

"The first time I saw you without your shirt on." I talk my way through the nerves, one button at a time. "I had to turn around and then go sit down." I look at him and see his eyes on my fingers watching my every move. I pull the shirt out of his pants and finish unbuttoning it. Touching his chest, I lean in and kiss it softly at the same time I shrug his shirt off.

"Fuck," he hisses when my hands go to his belt. His hands grasp my hair, pulling it back so he can kiss me, his tongue slipping into my mouth. My hands work frantically to unbuckle the belt and then get his button open. Our panting and our moans drown out the sound of his zipper. One hand leaves my hair and trails down to my breast. My nipples ache when he rubs them through the net material.

"Evan." I whisper his name, and he bends his head, taking a nipple into his mouth through the bra. I have to close my eyes to focus on just this new sensation. My stomach is so tight, my hands shaking, my toes tingly. "Evan," I say again when he switches sides, and I take a deep breath. My hand slips into his pants, and I have to stop because I don't think I've ever felt something so hard before. My hands work the waistband of his boxers, and when I slip my fingers in, he groans when my fingers graze the head of his cock. A cock that is hard, a cock that is soft, and a cock I really hope he lets me suck. "Evan," I say his name, and he looks up at me. "We never really discussed foreplay."

He smiles at me. "I didn't think we need to discuss it." He comes in. "Besides, it's much more fun doing it." He kisses my neck and then nips it and sucks in. "Much more fun," he says, backing me up and the back of my knees hit the bed. "Don't you think?"

"Yes," I say excited. "Much more fun doing it," I say and then get on my knees, but he stops me and pulls me up. "Evan, you said we can do it." I swear I sound like a kid who just got told there was no snacks after school.

"You will get your chance to do it"—he laughs—"but I get first dibs." He pushes me back, and I fall on the bed sitting up.

"Oh, this is good also," I say, looking right in front of me at his cock. "Me first," I say and grab his hips.

"Woman, don't you dare," he says, shoving my hands away. "You first." He gets down on his knees, and my legs open for him. "You always first." He takes his right hand and traces my pussy from the outside.

"Lie back," he instructs me, and I lean back on the bed but hold myself up on my elbows. I watch his eyes as he takes in the matching panties with a clear pink net and gold embroiders, the landing patch very visible. He picks up one leg and puts it over his shoulder and then the other, and then ever so fucking slowly, his mouth covers me. The heat and the wetness of the tongue on the mesh makes my head fall back.

"How bad do you love these panties?" I look at him, confused. "Can I rip them off you, or do I have to move them to the side?" The question shocks me because I've never been with someone who wants me so badly that he needs to rip off my panties. "Okay, I'll push them aside, but from now on, no panties in bed ever," he says.

I can hear the words, and I can understand the words, but nothing is clicking into place. The only thing I can focus on are his fingers moving the panties aside and then his groan right before his tongue licks all the way up my slit. "Fuck," he says.

I slowly open my eyes, watching him as he eats my

pussy like a hungry man. Not only does he eat my pussy, but he loves it. He bites my clit and then sucks it into his mouth, making my thighs squeeze his head.

"Sweetest pussy in the world," he says, and then I feel him insert his finger into me. Slowly, so fucking slowly I can feel anything, and now it's my turn to hiss out.

"Fuck," I say and then he pulls it out and puts another one in. He finger fucks me the same time as his tongue twirls around my clit. My hand comes out and goes into his hair, and my hips rise on their own.

"I want you to come on my tongue, sweet Zara." He says the word, and his fingers start going faster and faster, and I become wetter and wetter. I feel it happening, the tightness in my stomach as my pussy starts to give out, and then just like he wanted, I come on his tongue

"I'm …" I moan, not even finishing the sentence, and I just ride the wave. His fingers go faster and faster while I slowly start to come down. His face doesn't leave my pussy until my legs finally go limp on his shoulders. He places my feet down and gets up. I watch him as he takes off his pants one leg at a time, and then he stands there in front of me, wearing only his black Hugo boss boxers.

The tip of his cock peeks out while I sit up and bring him closer to me. I peel his boxers over his hips, and his cock springs free. I look at it, and I suddenly wonder if cocks can be beautiful, because his is beautiful. I fist him in my hand, and my fingers don't touch. I lean down and lick the tip of his cock and look up at him while he moans. I put the tip in my mouth and roll my mouth around it. I take him deeper into my throat, my hand working what my mouth can't reach. He puts his hands into my hair and slowly starts to fuck my mouth, and I fucking love it. The power to make him lose his mind. I'm making him do this. I take him to the back of my throat and then let him slip out of my mouth and then lick down his shaft. My hand never stopping up and down. "You have a beautiful cock," I finally tell him, taking the tip into my mouth. "Long."

"I'm not sure I'm okay with you calling my cock beautiful," he jokes while I try to take it all the way down but fail miserably. "Maybe sexy or manly." He stops talking when I roll the tip of his cock with my tongue.

"Thick." I swallow him again, and I take my time doing it. This is getting me hot again, and I'm ready to come again. I want to close my legs and add some friction. I look up at him and see his eyes closed, so I take my free hand and move it down, slipping it into my panties. The minute I touch my clit, I groan, and he opens his eyes.

"My sweet Zara," he says when he sees that I'm playing with myself. "What's the matter?" he asks and now his hands come out of my hair and move to my breast. He pushes the cups down, pushing my tits higher in the air, and he tweaks my nipple. I have to stop moving for just one minute before I continue.

"Is it possible you're the perfect woman?" he asks as he rolls my nipples with his thumbs and forefinger. "Perfect face, perfect mouth, perfect fucking tits, perfect pussy." My hand moves faster and faster on his cock and in my panties as his cock gets bigger in my mouth.

"I'm going to come," he says and tries to take his cock out of my mouth, but I squeeze his cock harder so he doesn't.

"I'm there," he says. He comes in my mouth, and I swallow every single fucking drop. He pulls out of my mouth, leaving me shocked, but what he does next shocks me more. He goes back down to my pussy.

"I'm so sorry about this," he says and rips my panties off me, and his mouth takes my pussy again until I come on his tongue for the second time in one night. He comes over me, his mouth covering mine, then he falls next to me on the bed, and I lie there like a limp noodle.

"I struck the mother lode," I say to the ceiling while he lies there looking at the ceiling with his hand on his chest.

"No," he says. "I struck the mother lode." I turn to look at him. "I also owe you a pair of panties."

"Are you crazy?" I tell him, getting up and picking up the shredded pink panties. "I'm having these framed." He gets on his elbow, his cock at half-mast and his abs on point and perfect. I walk to the bed and put my knee on the mattress, and his cock suddenly goes from half-mast to full-on raging. "Are you ready to go again?"

He looks down at his cock. "I think that would be a yes." He gets up. "But this time, let's do it in the shower." It's something he doesn't have to ask me twice.

By the time we finish in the shower, my fingers are wrinkled, and I'm almost an icicle. I wrapped myself in his huge terry cloth robe, and I'm heading out of the room when I hear him behind me. "Where the fuck are you going?" I turn to see him as he glares at me, a white towel wrapped around his hips, the outline of his cock that I just sucked. AGAIN. My eyes fixate on the sight again, and I'm eager to try different things. "Zara?"

"Yeah?" I say, blinking my eyes.

"I said where do you think your going?" he asks me again. This time, he's right in front of me.

"I was going to get my pjs," I tell him, my fingers coming up to trail up his abs. It's the same trail I did with my tongue not too long ago.

"No," he says, untying the sash of the robe. "You sleep naked."

I laugh. "But what if there is a fire?' I ask him as he peels the robe from shoulders.

"We will leave the robe by the bed." He takes the robe and tosses it to the end of the bed. Moving back up to the bed, he lifts the cover and then kisses my neck. "Get in, beautiful."

I slip into his bed, and it's like sinking into a cloud. I watch him walk around the bed, slip off his towel, and get into bed with me. He scoots to the middle of the bed and pulls me to him. "Good night, sweet Zara," he says, and I settle in his arms and fall fast asleep.

TWENTY

EVAN

I HOLD HER hand on my lap, her fingers entwined in mine. Picking it up, I bring it to my mouth and kiss it, looking over at her and seeing her smile at me. I'm driving her to the airport, and I fucking hate it. I wanted her to stay longer, but she couldn't. The past four days have been the happiest I think I've ever had. We woke up Sunday reaching for each other. Fuck, I want her all the time, and we haven't even had sex yet. I don't want her to think I asked her here for that.

We got up, fed the dogs, and I took her out to buy a couch for the backyard. She was in heaven when they delivered it that afternoon. A round couch that you could lie on, and it comes with a half sun umbrella. I found her sitting on it with the dogs right next to her on Monday when I came home from the rink.

We made dinner side by side, watched television together, fell asleep together, and now it's all coming to an end. "What time do you land?"

"At three thirty. Zoe is coming to get me," she says, and I swear I want to turn the car around. "What time do you have to be at the rink?"

"As soon as I drop you off," I tell her and take the exit to the airport. "Our game is tonight, and thank fuck we are home the whole week."

"I have a crazy week." I look over at her and take another mental picture of her. I've taken a million mental pictures of her. She is wearing regular light blue torn jeans with a white shirt that I know is going to be covered with her black leather jacket. Her feet in her Converse making her sporty and classy. "I have to make portfolios for five clients."

"Are you working from home, or do you need to go into work?" I ask her.

"No, I'm working from home the whole week," she says. "I do have to go in on Saturday to fit the girls for their gowns for the retirement gala that they are throwing." I turn into the parking garage, and she huffs next to me. "You don't have to walk me in."

I pull into a parking space and then unclip my seat belt and lean over and kiss her. "I listen to half of what you tell me to do." Then I go to her ear. "Unless it's the words make me come again."

She pushes me away, and I see that her cheeks are now flushed. "Shut up. You said the same thing to me right before we left." I laugh now, thinking about how she took my cock into her mouth right before we left the house. "*One for the road*," she said with a glitter in her eye. I get out of the car and walk to her side to open the door. When she gets out,

I hug her, and her arms go around my waist. "I don't want you to go."

"Me either," she says into my neck. We stand there like that for as long as we can until her phone beeps with a notification. She grabs it from her pocket. "My flight is on time."

I nod at her and walk to the back of the car to grab her bag while she gets her purse and jacket out of the back seat. We walk into the airport holding hands, our fingertips loosely holding each other. I wait for her to check in her bag, and I walk with her until I can't go anymore. She turns to look at me, and I tuck her long, wavy hair behind her ears.

"My sweet, beautiful Zara." She holds on to my wrist as I cup her face in my hand and bring her close to kiss her. Softly, gently on her lips, but not the way I want to. "Call me when you pass security," I tell her, and she just smiles.

"I have flown before, you know," she jokes. "I will call you once I get to the gate."

"Fine," I huff and kiss her neck. "Be good, sweet Zara," I tell her, and she turns to walk away from me. Going into the TSA pre-check line, she walks right up to the agent who takes her ticket and her ID from her. He scans it, and just like that, she is gone away from me. I walk back out with my head down, my lips still tingling from her kiss, and my hand still warm from her fingers.

When I get back home, the dogs are barking and jump up on me, and I see Lilo look behind me for her new favorite friends. "She's gone, girl," I tell her, and I swear she pouts. She puts her head down and then walks away to the kitchen. She calls me when she is boarding the flight and tells me she'll call me later.

I force myself to nap before the game, and when I get up at three, I see that she texted me twenty minutes ago that she landed. I get up and get my suit on and make my way to the rink. I walk in the room, and I see Denis is already there and so is Corey. "Hey," I say, tossing my keys on my shelf with my phone and my wallet.

"You're here earlier than normal," Corey says, drinking a protein shake in his workout clothes.

"Yeah, I figured I'd eat here," I tell them, and then a couple of the rookies come in.

"Did you take your girl to the airport?" Corey asks, and I just nod my head.

"Is that really Matthew Grant's sister?" Thomas, one of the rookies, asks and sits down at his place. Corey tries to hide his smile.

"Yeah," I say, shrugging off my jacket.

"Dude, no offense, but fuck is she hot." He goes on, and I glare at him. "Her legs? Fuck, they go on forever."

"Hey, Thomas," I say, and he looks at me while he takes off his tie. "How many teeth are your own in your mouth?"

"What?" he asks confused. "They are all mine."

"Then unless you want me to knock them all the fuck out, I suggest you change the topic," I tell him. Corey falls over with laughter while Denis just sits there laughing silently.

"I didn't mean anything by it." He holds up his hands. "I was just saying."

"I get what you were saying, and now you get what I'm saying." I glare at him, and he just nods and then walks out of the room.

"Jesus, I thought he was going to piss himself," Corey says. "You need to go easy on him. He didn't mean anything."

"I don't give a fuck what he meant," I say, changing into my workout clothes and making my way to the kitchen. My phone rings the second I sit down. I look and see it's Zara

"Hey," I say, the smile on my face huge.

"Hey," she says breathlessly. "I just got home. Traffic was horrible."

"I'm at the rink," I tell her. "Lilo is pouting and misses you."

"Aww, my girl," she says, and I can see her smiling in my head. "Is Lilo the only one that misses me?"

"I slept on your pillow when I took a nap," I say, looking around to make sure I'm by myself.

"I took your T-shirt home," she says quietly. "The one you wore yesterday." I laugh now. "What time is the game tonight?"

"You don't have to watch the game, Zara," I tell her, knowing she hates hockey. I put on the game yesterday that New York was playing, and she fell asleep in thirty seconds flat.

"I know I don't have to, but I'll tune in," she says, and then I hear Zoe in the background screaming her name. "Okay, go and get into the zone. Call me after the game."

"Will do," I say, and she hangs up. Putting my phone down, I eat my food when my phone beeps, and I look at it. She sent me a text.

Zara: For every goal you get, you will be rewarded with my mouth.

Zara: On your cock.

I groan inwardly because my cock thinks it's now and

starts waking up. And I text her back.

Me: I'm going to have to take care of myself before the game just thinking about it.

She answers me right away.

Zara: Well, then our chat after the game is going to be very interesting. I miss you.

I don't answer her because my phone rings, and I see it's Candace. "Hello," I say to her. "Are you alive?"

"Ha, ha, ha," she says sarcastically. "Trust me, if I wasn't, Mom would be on your ass to come and find me."

"This is very true," I tell her, knowing that my mom would be on my ass to go get her.

"Did you just get back?" I ask her, finishing my food.

"Yeah," she says. "I was going to come to the game tonight and bring a friend."

"Okay," I tell her. "I'll catch you after the game," I tell her and put my phone down.

I warm up a bit before I have to get into my gear and take the ice. When I skate on the ice, I see a couple of the fans waiting by the glass and toss a couple of pucks to them. I look down the ice at the number one team.

"This is going to be a rough night," Corey says. "They are going on a six-game winning streak."

"Well, it ends tonight," I say, taking a puck and moving it back and forth with my stick.

The warm-up finishes, and we skate back into the dressing room. The coach comes in, and he has shots of some plays that he wants us to work on. I sit on bench with my pregame drink in my hand, my fingers strumming the bottle. "Let's break out of the streak, boys," he says, clapping his hands, and we get up and get into the line to skate out. We wait in the hallway as Corey gives his speech every game. I bounce on my skates and then tie my helmet and wait for my turn.

I get on the ice and take my place on the blue line, taking off my helmet and waiting for the anthem to be sung. Once it's done, I skate to the middle of the ice as the fans on their feet start stomping. I skate in a circle with my stick in both hands and get into the zone. I block everything out, and when the referee comes over with the puck, I get into position and wait for him to drop the puck. I win the face-off, passing the puck back to Denis who slowly brings it up to the three of us skating toward their goal. He passes the puck to Jari as I try to skate around the defense to the right. I make it just a touch past their defense and toward the left side when I look at him to pass me the puck. As soon as the puck hits the blade of my stick, I just shoot it on the goalie, not expecting anything but to give everyone a chance of a rebound play. Except it goes in off the goalie's shoulder, and just like that, seven seconds into the game, it's one to nothing for us. I skate to the back of the net, and my teammates come out to me. Corey is the first one to me. "Guess someone is fired up," he jokes with me, and then we skate to the bench. We high-five everyone and then do a shift change.

For the rest of the period, we hang on to the one goal lead, but when we start the second period, either they are out for blood, or we are just dragging our asses because in the matter of twenty-seven seconds, they are up two to one. We get caught up in our zone more times than we want to, and clearing the puck is like pulling fucking teeth. We finally do it, but it's not enough to score that tying goal.

When we go back to the dressing room at the end of the second period, the shots on net are twenty-one for them and six for us. "We need to get more shots on net," the coach says. "You guys need to stop getting caught up in our zone."

The guys around me just look over at him, and when we get on the ice for the third period, the game shifts. We end up in our zone as usual, but this time, we intercept the puck and we haul ass toward the goal. Corey enters the zone with a two on one, and I make my move and shoot up past the second defense man. He makes a shot on goal, and it bounces off the goalie, but I'm right there on the right for the rebound, and I slip it into the empty side of the net.

"One more," I say to them, and we skate to the bench again doing the line change. "We need to get one more." I grab the Gatorade water bottle and squirt some into my mouth, and in the blink of an eye, the other line ends up scoring, making us go up by one goal. We finished the game ending their winning streak. I end up being the first star and going out and doing a lap around the arena, throwing the pucks to the crowd.

When I skate off, I get into the room as soon as the journalists make their way in. A couple of reporters ask me questions, but then I rush into the shower. I look at the clock and see it's almost ten my time, so it's eleven her time. I wonder if she's in bed. I grab my phone and text her.

Me: Are you still up?

I put my phone down and get dressed when she answers me right away.

Zara: Barely.

Grabbing the phone, I walk into a quiet room and then call her. She picks up right away, her voice sleepy, and I'm suddenly sad she isn't going to be home when I get here. "Hey, superstar."

"Hey, beautiful," I say softly, and I can see her smile in my mind.

"Are you in bed?" I ask her and think of her in my bed, and the times I woke up with her and took her in my arms.

"I am," she says, and I hear the sheets ruffled in the background. "I set an alarm just in case I feel asleep."

"I miss you," I tell her. "I wish I was going home to you tonight," I tell her the truth.

She laughs now. "That is only because you are owed two blow jobs." She laughs, and it settles me.

"Oh, don't you worry, sweetheart, I'm keeping track for next time," I tell her, and I hear her yawn. "Why don't you go to sleep, and I'll call you tomorrow when I get up?"

"Okay, Evan," she says softly. "I'll speak with you tomorrow."

"Night, beautiful," I say to her and disconnect. I walk back out into the dressing room and see it's almost empty.

"Your sister was looking for you," Corey says as he shrugs on his jacket, and I nod at him. I put the phone in my pocket and put on my own jacket.

"There he is," my sister says from behind me. "The number star of the game." I turn around smiling, and then my smile goes away when I see who her friend is.

"Hey," I say to her and then look over at Sophia, my

ex-girlfriend. I knew they were friends, but I didn't know how close.

"Hi," Sophia says, and I just nod at her.

"You did good," my sister says, and I just look at her, hoping she sees the disdain on my face.

"Thanks," I say and then grab my keys. "Where are you two off to?" I ask her, and she looks at me and then Sophia.

"We were hoping that you would take us out," Candace says, and I smile at her.

"Sorry," I tell her. "I'm beat and on my way home."

I turn and walk out of the room, and my sister and Sophia follow me. "Oh, come on," Candace says, and I turn around and see the two of them.

"Cand, I have no idea what you're trying to pull, but it's not going to happen," I tell her. Not only am I pissed that she brought Sophia into this, but now I'm also pissed she is putting me in an awkward situation. "Sophia, it was nice seeing you. Cand"—I turn and look at her—"you can call me tomorrow." Without bothering to wait for her to answer, I just walk away and head home.

Twenty-One

ZARA

"I WILL GET right on that, Mrs. Kitch, and then I'll send you all my ideas by next week," I say into the phone while I write down the details in my book.

"Thank you so much, dear. Kellie can't say enough about you," she tells me, and I smile. If you would have asked me last year if I ever thought that my client list would be more than ten, I would have laughed at you.

Today, I walked into Nordstrom and handed them my resignation letter. I was taking the huge leap and betting on myself. It was with a heavy heart, but I couldn't keep up any-more. My client list that started with four, which was just my family, was now at seventy. Between the Hollywood stars, to the hockey wives, to the oil tycoon billionaires, to every-one who read my name in the papers—everyone wanted to get in and have something from Zara's Closet.

"I'll be able to see you in Dallas some time next week," I

tell her, checking my schedule.

"Perfect. I look forward to seeing you," she says, and I disconnect the call.

It's been two weeks since I've been in Dallas, and I'm actually anxious to get back there. I miss my man something fierce, and even though we talk four to five times a day, there is nothing like having him close by.

Yesterday, I couldn't smell him anymore on his shirt, so I called him and was a bit frantic about it. Well, what did he do? He sent me another T-shirt that he wore by FedEx so I can smell him. I mean, he has not been happy in all this, and it's the only thing we argue about. Me not being there; him not being able to come here. Long-distance romance sucks balls.

But I mean, there is FaceTime, so we have dinner together whenever we can, and even Lilo and Stitch join us. I miss his touch, and I miss his kiss, but this weekend, his team is coming in for the big game, and I can't freaking wait. He has been on the road most of the week, and they are ending their road trip in New York. Only he doesn't know that I'm going back with him.

I'm writing in my agenda when the doorbell rings, and I go downstairs and see it's the FedEx guy. I smile at him and sign my name, carrying the huge brown box inside. *What did he send me?* I think, walking upstairs to my bedroom and putting it on my bed. I run up to my office, grab the scissors, and then run back downstairs. I run my hands over where he wrote my name.

Slicing open the tape on the top of the box, I place the scissors beside me and open the box. I grab the first thing wrapped in tissue paper, and as I unwrap it, I see it's a frame of Lilo and Stitch with notes hanging from their necks. Lili has "I miss you," while Stitch has "please come back." I laugh and bring it to my chest, blinking away the little stinging behind my eyes. I put it on my bedside table and then take out the next thing wrapped again in tissue. This time, it's a frame of the both of us. It was taken on his new outdoor couch. He is sitting up, and I am lying on his chest, my hand on his chest over his heart. A little card tucked into the frame.

I have this beside my bed and thought you might want a copy.

I miss you.

E.

I'm tempted to kiss him in the picture; that is how much I miss him. Instead, I rub the glass with my finger, then place the frame next to the other and take out the next one. It's wrapped in tissue with a pink ribbon. I untie the ribbon and see it's another jersey.

I was hoping you would do me the honor of wearing this on Saturday. It smells like me!

I can't wait to kiss you.

E.

I hug it to my chest and laugh. I know I'm going to get heat about it, but nothing is going to stop me from wearing this. The next thing that comes out is heavy, and when I open it, I laugh. It's a round crystal bowl with a cover, and it is filled with Hersey's kisses. The little paper on the front of it.

Some kisses for when I'm not around.

I laugh and put it right next to the frame and then finally

take out what I've been waiting for—his T-shirt. He sent two, and I bring one up to my nose and smell him. My stomach flips, and I smile as my heartbeat speeds up. I take off the shirt I'm wearing and put on his. I bring it back to my nose and smell him. I grab my phone and take a picture of me lying on my bed with his shirt on with the frame in the background, and I send it to him.

Me: How many more days until I'm back in your arms?

I don't know where he is, or what he's doing. I know today was a travel day, but that's all I know. He doesn't answer; instead, I see the FaceTime ring. I pick it up right away and wait for us to connect.

"Hey," I say when I see his face fills the screen. "I got your box."

"Did you?" He smiles, and I see that he is walking somewhere.

"I did," I tell him, turning to my stomach and looking at him. "Where are you?"

"On my way to the plane," he says and turns the camera around for me to see the jet waiting. "First stop Philly," he tells me, "then Buffalo and then New York."

"When do you arrive in New York?" I ask him, counting down the hours at this point.

"Saturday morning," he says, and I'm bummed. "We get in at ten, and then we have skate right away, and then I have to be back at the rink at five." I'm about to ask him when I'm going to finally see him when he looks at me. "Beautiful, I have to call you back."

"Okay," I say to him. "Fly safe." He smiles and winks at me and then disconnects.

I'm about to go back to work when I hear the front door open and close. "I'm here." I hear Zoe from the front door. "I come with gifts," she says, and I get up and walk down the stairs. "What are you wearing?" she asks me, and I look down at the Adidas shirt that is obviously too big for me.

"It's Evan's," I say, and she shakes her head. "What? I miss him."

"So I see," she says and then she holds up the brown paper bag. "I brought you bagels."

"Oh, good," I say, grabbing the bag and feeling the warmth coming from the bag. "Fresh too."

"Straight out of the oven," she says as she follows me into the kitchen. "I want mine toasted," she says, grabbing one and then putting it in the toaster while I do the same to mine. I walk to the fridge and grab some cream cheese.

"How was today?" she asks. She stands in front of me wearing perfectly pressed black pants with a white silk shirt tied at the neck. Her black sandals complete her classy and professional outfit.

"Bittersweet," I tell her. "But it was time that I let go of one."

"It was way past time," she tells me. "You need to take the leap, and now is the perfect time."

"Everything happens when it's supposed to happen," I tell her, and she just nods. "When are you going back to Dallas?" she asks me.

"Sunday," I answer her. "I booked a flight in the afternoon."

"Does that mean you're bringing Evan to the after-game party?" she asks with a twinkle in her eye, and I can just imagine what she's thinking.

"I haven't asked him, but if he wants to, I'll bring him. If not, I'll skip it," I tell her, grabbing the bagels that have popped up.

"You never miss the after-game party," she says. "This is a big deal, isn't it?"

I shrug my shoulders. "I like him," I tell her. "Like really, really like him."

She doesn't ask me anything else, nor does she push me. She eats her bagel and then goes to raid my closet again, leaving with another outfit. I lock up after she leaves and go to take a bath, and when Evan FaceTimes me, I'm just slipping into bed.

"Hey," I say once his face comes on the screen, and I see he looks tired.

"Hey, beautiful." He greets me the same way each time.

"Did you just get in?" I ask him, getting comfy, and he nods. "So," I say and try to come up with the words and then see him looking at me. "My family is having an after-game party get-together on Saturday."

"Okay," he says, and I see him shrug off his jacket. He is in his hotel room, and he gets on the bed.

"I was wondering if you would like to come with me?" I watch his face for any hesitation.

"It's up to you, beautiful," he says softly. "I'll go and do whatever you want."

"Well," I tell him, "I want you to meet my mom and dad."

"Then we'll go." His smile fills the screen. "Are you in bed?"

"I am." I turn the phone for him to see me lying in bed.

"Are you wearing my shirt?' he asks, propping up the pillows

"I am, and it smells just like you," I tell him, smiling. "Four days, right?"

"Four days," he repeats.

I try to cram as much work as I can in the days to make it go faster, but it doesn't. Every day is worse than the next, and I swear I don't even sleep on Friday night. I toss and turn, and when I finally fall asleep, I wake up forty minutes later only to see that it's not even five a.m. At seven a.m., I give up on sleeping and go downstairs. I'm about to start my coffee when I hear a soft knock on the front door. I look down and see I'm just in Evan's shirt, so I grab a towel from the laundry basket and wrap it around my top half as I make my way to the door. The knock coming again, this time a bit louder.

"I'm coming," I say and unlock the door and swing it open, not expecting to see him.

"Morning, beautiful," he says, holding a bouquet of roses in his hands, but I don't even care as I just fall into his arms. He barely has time to drop the roses before I launch myself. I wrap my legs around his waist and bury my face in his neck. I am pretty sure I'm choking him, but I don't care. He's here in front of me, and he is holding me in his arms, so nothing, and I mean nothing, is going to get me out of them. He walks into the house and closes the door behind him.

"Sweetheart," he says softly. "I'm going to need your lips." I lean back in his arms with my legs locked at the ankles. He has one hand under my ass and the other wrapped around my waist holding the flowers. "There she is," he says to me, his smile so big his eyes are crinkling on the side. "I missed you so much," he says, and I can't talk because I have a huge lump in my throat, and I know if I say anything, I'll probably sob 'cause I'm so happy. I put my forehead on his and my hands on his cheeks, his scruff longer than the last time. I lean in slowly and kiss his lips softly, so soft it's almost like it wasn't there. He turns to put the roses on the front end table. "Where do you want to do this?" he asks me.

"In my bed," I tell him. "Up the stairs." He walks up the stairs, and I finally get off him but not before my hands are going nuts at his shirt, ripping it over his head.

"When did you get here?" I ask him, and he doesn't answer. The only thing he does is take my face in his hand and kiss me. He kisses the shit out of me. The past three weeks catch up to me, and I don't stop kissing him until I can't breathe anymore. I don't stop until I am panting, and I'm in heaven.

"I only have a couple of hours before I have to be at the rink," he says to me between kissing my lips and then my neck and then his hand goes under his shirt to cup my tits that have been achy ever since I launched myself at him.

"I missed you so much," he says, taking a nipple in his mouth, and I swear I almost come. I'm that much on edge. My hand flies to the belt on his jeans, and before we even know what's going on, I'm on my knees, and I have his cock deep in my throat. Both of us groaning, I don't stop, I can't stop, and he comes down my throat with a roar.

Twenty-Two

Evan

NOTHING WAS GOING to keep me from her. I arrived last night at one a.m., but I didn't want her waiting up for me. The night just didn't go by fast enough, and finally, at six a.m., I got out of bed and headed to her house. I have to be at the rink at ten, so I technically only have two hours with her, but it's better than nothing. When she opened the door and saw it was me, she threw herself at me, wrapping her legs around my waist and making my cock go hard right away.

I watch her on her knees in front of me, my eyes finally focusing after coming in her mouth. I pick her up and literally throw her on the bed. I don't even wait for her to land before my mouth is on her pussy. Ripping her panties off, I add another set to my owe pile. Her sweetness hits me right away, but then her legs wrap around my head, and her hand flies to my head. My girl wants it so badly, she lifts her hips and rides my face, coming in record time, but I'm not ready to stop yet, so I tongue fuck her again. I add another finger, and I know it's only a matter of time until she comes again. I finger her so hard I'm afraid to bruise her, but she meets my thrusts. I go to her clit and bite down on it, then suck it back into my mouth, and she comes again.

"I can't," she whispers. Her clit is sensitive to my touch, so I climb over her, and I kiss her, and she takes it. She doesn't give a shit that she just came in my mouth and my tongue tastes like her; she just kisses me. My cock is so close to slipping in her, I have to take a step back, and I fall to the side of her.

"Well, that was a great way to greet me," I tell her, and she turns to look at me. "You are so beautiful."

"Why didn't you come here last night?" she says, coming close to me and putting her head on my chest. "I slept like shit."

"Yeah, I didn't think it would be a good idea to keep you waiting all night, so I slept at the hotel." I kiss her forehead. "A lot of good that did me. I swear I slept two hours."

"I slept twenty minutes," she says, yawning. "How about next time, you just come over and save us all the hassle?"

"Deal," I tell her, rubbing cheek with my thumb. "I am free as of noon."

"You are coming back here, right?" she says, getting up on her elbow. "You better say you're coming back here." She attempts to get up, but I bring her back to me laughing.

"It's not funny," she says. "It's been three weeks."

"Trust me, beautiful, I know exactly how long it's been." I had a countdown on my phone. I had the minutes on there, and it was freaking hell. I won't do that again, not for that long. But I'll discuss it with her tomorrow after I beg and plead with her to come back home with me. "Now can we just lie together before I have to get back up and head out?"

"Fine." She huffs. "But if you don't come back here on your break, I'm seriously going to be pissed." She starts to get back up again, and I grab her. "No Evan, I'm not kidding."

"Okay, beautiful," I tell her. "Can we just rest for the next hour before I have to go?" I ask her, getting comfortable. "I should set my alarm," I tell her, grabbing my phone from my pants.

"Now get back into my arms," I tell her, and she crawls next to me, and I feel everything from the past three weeks—the tension, the need, the want—leave me. Everything is okay 'cause she's in my arms. I rest my eyes for the hour that I have and hold her close with her head on my chest and her hand draped around my waist. When the alarm rings, and I have to go, I swear I can see her pouting. She walks me to the door.

"I'll call you when I'm on my way over," I tell her, and she just nods but looks down. "Sweet Zara, I need your lips one more time, and then you can go back to bed." She gets on her tippy toes, and I kiss her lips.

"Now go and hurry back," she says, and I walk down the steps and into the waiting Uber. I get to the rink the same time the bus gets there. I swear there is a spring in my step, and I can't wait to hit the ice and get it over with. Going into the visitor's locker room, I suit up for ice. The practice is light and lasts about an hour and a half with an option time on the ice if we want it. I'm the first one off the ice with Corey beside me, and I unclip my helmet.

"Heads-up," Corey whispers from beside me, and I look up. There they are, the two guys I was waiting to see, Matthew Grant and Max Horton. In other words, Zara's brother and brother-in-law.

"Hey, Richards," Matthew says first. He is dressed in his workout stuff, wearing his baseball cap backward, and has his arms folded over his chest.

"It's M&M," I say smiling, and they just look at me. "What can I do for you guys?"

"We just thought we would come down ..." Max starts, and I hold up a hand.

"You thought you would come down here and scare me away from Zara?" Taking off my helmet, I slide off my gloves. "Sorry, boys, but you can do whatever it is you want to me. I'm not leaving her alone."

"Is that right?" Matthew says.

"That is right," I tell them and then feel Corey stand at my back followed by half of my team mates. "I like her, and she likes me. Let's leave it at that."

Max looks like he is going to smirk at me, but Matthew walks forward and leans in. "If you so much as hurt one hair on her head ..."

"Yeah, I got it," I tell him. "You said this before. So let me say it again. I like her, she likes me, and I'm not backing down." He looks at me, not sure if he should push it or not. "Now if you will excuse me, my girl is waiting for me."

"She is far from your girl," he says, and I just shake my head.

"That's where we differ because the only thing she is, is mine." I smile at both of them. "See you later, M&M." I walk away from them, and I swear I breathe a sigh of relief. Nothing good would come of it if we got into a brawl before the game. My ass would be on that bench the whole night, and my skates would stay dry.

"I think you handled that right," Corey says from behind me, "but I think you just upped the stakes there."

"Yeah, I have no doubt about it," I tell him and then sit and undress. I take a quick shower and then take off to the hotel room, grabbing my stuff and leaving. By the time I get back to Zara's, it's almost two. She is there waiting for me wearing jeans and a sweater.

"I made you something to eat," she says once I let go of her lips. "Then you can go nap."

"Are you going to come with me?" I ask her, following her into the kitchen. "Eat," she says as she serves me eggs, bacon, and toast. When I'm finally finished, I push the plate away from me, walk over to her, and carry her to bed. I want to undress her and do all kinds of naughty things, but I need to honestly save my energy for the game tonight. I don't bother telling her about her brother and Max. Instead, I fall asleep with a smile on my face and her in my arms.

"What time are we leaving?" she asks me from her bathroom. "I need five more minutes."

I got up and showered with her, which took twenty minutes longer than I thought since there were hands and fingers and lots of tongue. She rushes out of the bathroom, and I just stare at her. Her hair that was wet twenty minutes ago is now dried all wavy and sexy. She is wearing a white little thong that I'm going to be adding to the destroyed pile and her lace half bra. She goes into the closet and then comes back out wearing blue jeans that are so tight she can't bend over and a white tank top. The lace bra can be seen through the tank top. "That isn't going to happen," I tell her, shrugging on my jacket. "Go change that top."

"What do you mean?" she says, looking down at her top.

"I mean you aren't walking out of this house wearing that top so"—I go to her and kiss her nose—"change it."

She stands there with her arms crossed over her chest. "Or else?" She asks me the question I'm only to happy to answer.

"Or else it gets put in the destroyed pile." I smile at her. "The car is going to be here in five minutes."

"You can't honestly think you can tell me that, and I'm going to listen." She glares at me, and I go to her, smiling the whole time.

"It would give me great joy to rip the shit out of the top." She huffs and turns around, going back in her closet.

"FYI," she says, "I was going to wear your jersey over that." She comes out now with a white button-up shirt with no sleeves and tight at the waist but then kicking out. "It's only 'cause I don't want you to be late that I'm changing. Otherwise, no ..." she says, huffing and grabbing her pink jacket and then the jersey I can't wait for her to wear. Seeing my name on her, God, it does crazy things to me.

"Sweet Zara," I say softly, and her eyes go soft.

"No, Evan Richards, you do not tell me to change and then be sweet with me," she tells me. "Now let's go or else you are going to be late, and I'm not going to have it blamed on me." She turns to walk out of the room, but I grab her hand and pull her back.

"Lips," I tell, and she rolls her eyes at me but not before giving me her lips. We walk out of the house, and she puts on her jacket, and we hold hands on the way to the game.

Once we arrive at the underground parking garage, I get out of the car and hold out my hand for hers. "How do you want to do this?" I ask her, not sure how to proceed and not wanting to make her do something she doesn't want.

She holds out her hand to me, and I take it. "I want to walk in there with you," she says, smiling. "Even though you are the most annoying man in the world, I'm here with you."

I grab her hand and slip my fingers with hers, bringing them to my lips. We walk into the building, and I'm shocked to see Matthew and Max walking in at the same time. The minute he spots us, he stops walking.

"Hello boys," Zara says when we are close enough. "Are we late?"

"Oh for fuck sakes," Matthew says, putting his hand to his mouth. "I don't want to know why you're late."

"It's not what you think, pervert," Zara says, and then Max tries to hide his smile. "Mister here made me change my top before we got here."

"What?" Matthew and Max both whisper.

"Whatever," Zara says, and then she lets go of my hand. "You," she goes to Matthew, and, "you," she points at Max, "no funny shit on the ice. Got it?"

I shake my head and bring her back to me. "Zara," I hiss, "I got it." She gets on her tippy toes and pecks me on the lips. "Good luck out there."

She turns back around. "Don't make me put shit in your shampoo." She glares at them and walks away.

"You made her change?" Matthew asks confused, and then Max asks, "Like her clothes?"

"Yeah," I tell them. "She was wearing this white shirt you could see her bra," I tell them and then turn to walk away. I go into our locker room and get ready, going through the same routine I always go through with my workout drills and then I suit up for the pre-game skate. I go on the ice and skate around, and then I see her. She is holding a kid in her hand that has to be Max's. Seeing my girl holding a girl, I swear my heart squeezes in my chest. I almost stop skating in the middle of the ice when it hits me. I love her. I've fallen in love with her. She is wearing my jersey, but the little girl is wearing the New York jersey, and I skate to the side where she is at. She whispers in the girl's ear, and the girl waves at me. I bring my glove up and bend my fingers to say hello. When I get the puck, I throw it over, and she picks it up for her, and the girl smiles from ear to ear.

Corey pushes me to move and do the play, and practice is over before I know it. I skate to the back and go over the drills in my head. The coach comes in and goes over a couple of plays. "It's our last game before going home," he says. "Let's win at least this one." We've had three loses in a row on the road. No one wants to make it four. When we take the ice, I'm ready. I skate onto the ice with the boos sounding in my ears.

We start at the center ice, and it's me against Matthew, Corey against Max, and I look over and see them talking. "I promise not to hurt you tonight," Matthew says, and I throw my head back and laugh. "I promised."

I shake my head. "Bring it," I tell him. "Do your worst."

Now he laughs, and we stop talking when the referee comes over. "Let's start the game, boys," he says, and I lean down, my eyes on his hand, and the second that he drops the puck, I move on Matthew. We both miss the puck, but I kick it behind me with my skate and push past him. He doesn't hit me, though he anticipates every move I make, so when I push, he just pushes harder. It goes on like that for two periods, and I'm so fucking tired, but I'm not giving up.

I look up at the jumbotron and see that two minutes remain in the third period. "I'd really like to win in regular time," I tell Corey, who just nods his head, and then it's our line's turn, so I jump over the board right when they are making a play in the neutral zone, and Corey intercepts it. Turning to go back into their zone, I'm there with him, and because we messed up their line change, we are with the fourth line instead of playing against Matthew and Max. Their defense man backs up while we are three on two. Corey passes it to me, and I see him speed up, so I pass it right back to him as he skates on the side and I rush the goal. He passes me the puck, and I shoot, hitting the side of the post. When the puck lands on my stick again, I flip it up and send it over the goal line. The red light behind the goal goes on, and I lift my hand and point at Corey. "All you."

We go to the bench and high-five everyone and then skate back to the center ice and now Matthew and Max come back on. "Got a lucky one there," he says, and I just shrug.

"Either way, I'll take it," I say, and for the next two minutes, it's head to head. They pull the goalie and one of the rookies slides it in to clench the win two to nothing. We skate off the ice, and I'm named first star, but I don't do the round like I do in Dallas. Instead, I rush to the room and change. The rest of the team are heading back tonight, but I'm staying back, and I booked a private plane tomorrow afternoon. I hurry up and shower, then grab my stuff, throwing it into my bag that is going back to Dallas. "Safe flight, boys," I tell them. I told the coach this morning that I would be going back home the next day because I had a personal appointment. He knew full well what my personal problem was, and as long as my ass was on the ice on Monday, he didn't care. So I walk out of the locker room in search of my girl.

I find her standing there with who has to be her mother and next to her none other than her father, Cooper Stone. She spots me first, and her eyes go soft. I walk to them, and the woman stands there with a smile on her face with Cooper holding her by his side. "Hey." She kisses my lips. "There he is, the first star of the game." I shake my head, and she brings me to her parents. "Mom, Dad," she says, "this is Evan." Her smile so bright. "Evan, this is my mom, Parker, and my dad, Cooper."

I put out my hand first for her mother and then for her father. "Mr. and Mrs. Stone, it's a pleasure to meet you."

"It's great to finally meet you," Parker says. "Zara has told me wonderful things about you."

"That was a good game out there," Cooper says to me. "We should get going, or they will close the kitchen."

"We are going to walk to the bar. It's right around the corner," Zara says, and we follow her parents all the way there. Cooper holds open the door Parker and then for Zara.

I hold out my hand to hold the door for him, and he nods at me and walks in after the girls.

The place is jam-packed, and I see Zara walking toward the back. Making my way through the noisy crowd, I walk by the bar and finally get to the back of the room where I see six tables with a reserved sign on them. People are filling the tables, and I spot a couple of the players who all see me and give a chin up. One of the tables is full, and I spot Zoe, who gets up and comes to greet us. Zara moves to the side so her parents can go find a seat.

"Are you okay?" Zara asks me, and I just nod at her. She grabs my hand and then pulls me to the table.

"Everyone," she says, "this is Evan." I smile at everyone and wave while Zara names everyone to me.

"Hey mister two in a row," someone says, and Zara just shakes her head.

"That is Vivienne." She laughs. "You have to ignore every-thing she says."

"Do you want to go to the bar and get something to drink?" she asks me, and Zoe finally gets to us.

"Hey there," she says to me and comes in for a hug. "Great seeing you again."

"Nice seeing you too. We are going to get something to drink; does anyone need anything?" Zara asks, and Park-er orders a glass of white wine while Cooper just asks for water. They are sitting side by side, but his hand is on her neck. I've noticed that every single time I look, he's holding or touching her.

We walk to the bar, and I get the bartender's attention and order a water for myself and a couple of glasses of wine. "You look beautiful," I tell her, and she looks up at me and smiles, and then she looks to the side and her whole face changes.

"Oh my gosh, Zara," a man's voice from beside me says. "Jesus." Then he looks at me, and his mouth hangs open. "Oh my, you're Evan Richards." He holds his hand out to me. "I'm a huge fan."

I look at Zara, waiting for her to say something, but she just looks at him. "Zara," I say to her, and she looks at me and then looks back at the man.

"Ed," she says, then laughs. "This is my ex, Ed." She points at the guy, and I now look at the man who broke her heart so badly she tweeted me. I want to reach out and shake his hand and thank him.

"Baby," a female's voice says, and I look over at the woman he must have left Zara for. She is smaller than Zara with brown hair and brown eyes. It is like night and day compared to her.

"Holy shit," someone says behind me, and I see Zoe coming toward us. She looks at the bartender. "Lou, give me five shots of tequila."

"Hey, pencil dick," Zoe says to him, then looks over at the girl. "My condolences to you."

He just looks at Zoe with his mouth pinched together. "Why is it no surprise you would be five steps behind?"

She shrugs. "Why am I not surprised that you would show up here knowing we are always here?" She leans on the bar and grabs the shot that the bartender puts in front of her. She hands one to Zara. "To the past," she says, and Zara quickly swallows the shot and then grabs another one.

I watch her, and she winces when she takes the second shot but then quickly takes the third one.

"Well, it was nice seeing you," he says and then ducks his head and walks out with the girl beside him.

"Oh, my God," Zara says, but Zoe just hands her another shot.

"I don't think that's a good idea," I tell her, and she just shakes her head.

"You have no idea what just happened," she tells me, "and I'm guessing she didn't either." She motions with her head to Zara who just finished her fifth shot and then looks at me, her eyes starting to glaze over.

I look at Zoe and then Zara, and I look to the side where I see Matthew and Cooper now standing next to us. "That's enough shots," Matthew says. "I hate when you girls drink, and I have to be on guard all night." I ignore him and his ire, and Cooper just slaps him on the shoulder and then looks at me.

"I think Evan has this handled." He smirks at me. "Let's get the M back to the other M." Matthew glares at him and then turns to walk away. "You got her, right?"

I nod at him and then look back at Zara. "Are you okay?" I ask her, and she shakes her head.

"I think I want to go," she says, and I just nod my head.

"I'll tell everyone you headed out," Zoe says, and I grab Zara's hand and walk outside. I hail a cab, and I look over at her and see that she is swaying to the side. The door behind her opens.

"She forgot her jacket," Zoe says, and then Zara just giggles.

"How much did she drink tonight?" I ask her, and she shrugs.

"Isn't he hot?" she says to Zoe. "Hooottttt," she hisses and then reaches out to touch me, but her hand falls, and Zoe holds her straight. She whispers in her ear, and Zara just nods her head. A car stops, and I grab Zara, and we walk to the cab. I get in after her, giving the guy the address.

"Are you okay?" I ask her as she looks out of the window.

"Yup," she says. "Peachy." I nod my head and look out my own window.

"I can't believe he showed up there," she says, her words about slurring. "Like he didn't know I was going to be there." She doesn't wait for me to say anything. "It's so shady."

For the whole ride, she goes on and on about her ex, and by the time I get out of the cab, my stomach burns and my anger is to the level where I just want this fucking day to be over. I grab the key out of her hand when she misses the key hole for the fifth time.

"I got it," I tell her, grabbing the keys from her. I unlock the door, and I wait for her to walk into the house. I close the door, and I don't have time to even turn on the light before she throws herself into my arms. I catch her before she falls, and she gives me a sloppy kiss.

"We need to have sex," she tells me, and I make a decision at this moment that is going to fucking suck. Her hands go to the top of my shirt as she tries to unbutton it, and I stop her, but she is so far-gone she doesn't even realize that the mood has changed. She tries to unbutton my pants, and I walk away to the stairs, holding her hand so she doesn't fall. "Yes, let's go to the bedroom," she says. "We need the bed to have sex in."

"Yeah, that's why we are going upstairs," I tell her, and as soon as I get into the room, she rips her shirt open and stands there in the same bra she was wearing before.

"Let's get naked," she says, throwing up her hands and then swaying. I look at her, and in the dimly lit room, I know she will always have a piece of me.

"Why don't you lie on the bed? I'll be right back," I tell her, and she smiles and goes over to the bed while I go into the bathroom and wait until I hear her soft snores fill the room.

I walk back into the room and see her lying in the middle of the bed with her pants on only one leg and her hand over her stomach. I pull the pants off her leg and then slowly tuck her in before I lie on top of the covers beside her. She's facing me, and I take a mental picture of her.

TWENTY-THREE

THE SUN IS hitting my face, and I can feel it. I try to swallow, and I literally can't. The pounding in my head comes full fucking force, and I groan. How much did I drink last night? I slowly peel only one eye open and look at the room. I groan and close my eye. "Here is water and ibuprofen," Evan says, and then my head turns to look at the side of the bed. He is sitting on the edge of the bed. I open one eye again, and this time, I zero in on him. He sits there in his jeans, his hands on his knees, and his shoulders slumped down. I close my eye again, trying to piece together what the fuck happened last night.

"You'll feel better once you take the pills." He reaches over and gets the water and the pills. I get up and have to fall back down on the bed 'cause my head spins. I wait a couple of seconds and then get back up. He hands me the water bottle and the pills. I sit up and swallow down the pills.

I keep drinking the rest of the bottle. My tongue feeling like shit. "Thank you." I smile at him. "I need to brush my teeth." I slowly roll out of bed and walk to the bathroom. I wash my face and brush my teeth. I feel slightly human, and I look down to see that I'm wearing nothing but my bra and panties. I walk back out and see him standing up and looking out the little window I have in my room. "I swear I still taste tequila." I walk into the closet to get my robe and then come out and see he is still looking out the window. "Evan?" I say his name, and he turns around, and I finally see his face. "What's wrong?" I say to him my hangover now not even bothering me while my heart starts speeding up.

"I can't do this," he tells me, and I have this sudden pain in my chest. I suddenly don't think I can breathe.

"What?" I say, and my hand goes to my chest.

"I can't be in a relationship with you when you are still pining for your ex." He says the words, and I just try to make them register while he continues. "It started as a joke, and I get it." He shakes his head, and I take him in. He's dressed in black jeans and a plain black T-shirt. He is wearing his boots, and I shake my head. He was waiting for me to wake up before he left. "But it's not a game to me anymore."

I hold up my hand now to stop him from talking. "Just a second." I swallow down. "What do you mean pining for my ex?"

"I saw you," he says. "The way you reacted."

"The way I reacted?" I'm repeating everything he's saying, trying to make sense of it.

"You haven't once led on that you wanted to have sex

with me until you were drunk," he says, and I hear the hurt in his voice.

"You think I got drunk because of my ex?" I ask him the question, and he just looks at me. "You think I only want to sleep with you because of Ed?"

"Well, look at it this way. You are totally fine, and then the minute you see him, you get shitfaced." His voice tight.

"Do you know why I took those shots?" I ask him, and I don't wait for him to answer me. "I took those shots because I finally realized that I'm in love with you." I'm angry now, and I don't wait for him to say anything. I just continue.

"I kind of thought I liked you," I tell him, "but then yesterday, it hit me. Like a cement truck." I lay it all out for him. "I was standing there with my niece, and I saw you, and my heart, I don't know, it got full," I tell him. "Then I went back into the lodge, and I saw my mother look at my father, and then it just was there. I was holding my breath the whole game while drinking wine, I might add." I throw my hands up. "I was getting the courage to tell you how I was feeling."

"Beautiful," he says to me, and I shake my head while a tear falls out, and I wipe it away so fast you would get whiplash.

"I watched the hockey game last night," I tell him, walking now back and forth in front of him in the middle of the room, "The whole game. I was actually cheering for hockey," I tell him. "I don't like hockey, Evan." I shout the last part. "But I did it because I love you."

"You love me?" he whispers.

"I do," I finally tell him. "I thought I loved Ed, I really did, but it's nothing." I shake my head. "It's nothing like what I feel when I'm with you." His eyes don't move from mine. "I won't get over this," I tell him softly. "I know what everyone was saying now." I throw my hands up. "I get it, that feeling like you can't breathe when you're not together. Or the missing them so much your heart aches. The whole my stomach is sick from not touching you. It all makes sense."

"You love me?" he whispers again, and I just shake my head.

"Yeah, jackass, I love you." I'm still aggravated. "That is why I got drunk."

"So it wasn't because you were doubting us?" he asks me, and I swear men are dumb sometimes. Most times, generally all the time.

"The only doubt I had in my head was if you felt the same way about me," I tell him. "There was no doubt about Ed. He wasn't even on the same wavelength as you."

"I'm coming to you," he tells me, and I just nod. He rushes to me, his hands going into my hair, his mouth crashing on mine, and my arms wrapping around his neck while our tongues fight a battle. His hands leave my hair and wrap around me, and I jump into his arms as he picks me up.

"I love you," he whispers to me when he finally lets go of my lips. "Loved you the first moment you walked into my house and sweet talked my dogs." His forehead rests on mine as I hold his cheeks in my hands.

"I didn't sleep a wink last night," he whispers. "I spent the night watching you." I laugh now, my heart a little less heavy than five seconds ago. "In a non-stalker way."

"Evan," I say his name. "I am so sorry you doubted me or us." I kiss his lips.

"Will you come home with me?" he asks me in a whisper.

"I already bought a ticket," I tell him, and he smiles.

"Good. Get ready," he says. "I rented a plane, and it leaves in an hour."

I look at him shocked. "What?"

"The team headed back last night, but I rented a plane for today so I could spend the night with you, but I have to be on the ice tomorrow morning," he tells me. "I was going to woo you, hoping you would come home with me."

"My bag is already packed," I tell him. "Any chance we can leave earlier?"

"Let me call the company," he says, letting me go. "Go get dressed just in case," he tells me, and I run into the closet and pull on a pair of yoga pants and a sweatshirt, his sweatshirt, and when I finish, he is hanging up the phone. "We are good to go in forty-five minutes," he says. "I have a car coming to get us, and it should be here in ten minutes." He looks up from his phone and sees me wearing his hoodie. "Beautiful."

I walk to him and wrap my hands around his waist. "Let's go home to my puppies," I tell him.

He kisses my lips and holds my hand while carrying my bag in the other. I had everything packed yesterday afternoon so my carry-on is already waiting at the door. "I'm going to text Zoe that I'm leaving," I tell him, grabbing my phone and seeing a couple of missed calls from her.

I dial her right away, and she answers on the first ring. "Thank fuck," she hisses. "Where the hell were you?"

"I was sleeping, and I just got up," I tell her and see that Evan has opened the door and is now carrying my bag out.

"Now I'm leaving."

"Where are you going?" she asks me, and I hear a guy in the background.

"Who is that?" I ask her.

"The contractor," she says. "I came home to a flooded apartment. The moron cat upstairs touched something, and the sink locked, and well, there is now a swimming pool in my living room." She then whispers, "He's so lucky that it wasn't my clothes." She takes a deep breath. "Anyway, I was wondering if I could come stay at your house while you're away."

"You don't even have to ask. You should have come over last night," I tell her, locking the door and then walking to the car where Evan is waiting.

"I thought you wouldn't want to be disturbed," she says, giggling. "I want all the details, but it is going to have to wait. I have to go and see how long this mess will take."

"Whatever. I'll call you tomorrow," I tell her and stop by the car to give him a kiss just because I can.

"All good?" he asks me, and I nod my head and get in the car. He gets in after me, and the man takes off.

"Yeah, all good." I smile up at him. "Zoe's place got flood-ed, so she's going to stay at my house."

He leans down and softly kisses my lips. "If she wants, she can come stay at my house in Dallas. How long can you stay this time?"

"Um." I smile. "I quit my job last week."

"What?" he asks shocked. "Why didn't you tell me?"

"Well," I start, "I officially decided to work with Zara's Closet full time, and I was going to surprise you by staying for a couple of weeks," I say, leaning in to him. "I mean, if you don't mind."

"Fuck." He grabs me to sit on his lap. "Don't leave." He buries his face in my neck, kissing it.

He kisses me the whole flight home, and when we finally touch down in Dallas, I'm starving.

"Do you want to grab something on the way, or do you want to stop?" he asks me, getting into the Yukon truck that is waiting for us.

"I just want to get home to my babies." I wink at him, and he just shakes his head. I look out the window while he goes nuts on his phone, and when we pull up to the house, I don't wait for him to open the door for me. I take charge and almost run to the door. "You really need to get the automatic door opener," I yell at him as he walks to me scowling.

"You always wait for me to open your door," he says, rolling my luggage and carrying my purse.

"Just open the door," I tell him, jumping. "Lilo." I say her name and hear her crying and barking.

"Calm down," he says, sticking the key and opening the door.

"Hey, my baby girl," I say, squatting down, and she comes to me and licks my face. She's so excited, she goes in circles and then comes back. "Oh come on, my boy," I say, and they both come to me, knocking me off my feet, and I fall on my bum.

"Enough," Evan yells, and then I see someone coming with two boxes of pizza. "Food is here." He picks me up from the floor and then grabs the pizza. I grab the suitcase, and we walk inside the house, the dogs following me the whole way. "Put your bag in my room this time."

"Really?" I look over my shoulder. "You were going to break up with me less than twelve hours ago."

"Yeah." He smiles. "But you love me so …" He kisses my neck, and Lilo barks at him. "I will share her, but she's mine."

I shake my head and walk to his room, dumping my bag in there and going to find my man.

TWENTY-FOUR

EVAN

I WAS GOING to walk away from her. I was going to cut my losses and move on. It was going to be hard, but I wouldn't be second prize. But when she stood there and gave me everything, my heart that was breaking filled so hard and so fast, I thought it was going to explode in my chest. I love her with everything I have. I love her like I have loved no other.

That moment you see the person who owns your heart, who can destroy you. Knowing that without her, you are going to be half the man you should be. Knowing that only with her, your heart beats normal; knowing that only with her, everything is going to be okay.

Seeing her standing in my kitchen, grabbing a water bottle while eating a slice of pizza with Lilo following her everywhere, I know that this is it. She's the one I've been waiting for. "What are you thinking about?" she asks me, sitting down in front of me. "What's going on?

"I'm thinking about you," I tell her honestly. "Thinking that you here in my kitchen with me." I take a sip of her water. "I got really lucky."

She tilts her head to the side. "You did get lucky." She smiles, grabbing another bite of her pizza. "But you are about to get a whole lot luckier."

"Really?" I ask, trying not to smirk. "How lucky are we talking about here?" Right here is another reason I love her. She can be serious and then just turn it around and make it funny.

"I'm talking about even better than a hat trick," she tells me, and I laugh because I know she has no idea what she is talking about when it comes to hockey.

"I mean, a hat trick is pretty incredible," I tell her. "I've had the privilege to have four in my career, and it's pretty hard to beat that."

"Really?" she says, chewing. "What about me spread eagle on your bed?" My throat starts to close up, thinking of her.

"Naked obviously." I don't take another bite. I just watch her as she bites another piece of pizza and licks the sauce off the side of her mouth.

"With one hand playing with myself." My cock hardens with this picture in my mind.

"Getting myself primed and ready for you." She even squirms in her chair.

"Do you think that could be better than a hat trick?"

"I mean, I would have to experience it to fully render my decision," I tell her, and she just smiles. "I don't think it's fair to make a half-ass choice."

She pushes away from the table. "Give me twenty and then come in the room."

"Twenty?" I ask her. "Minutes or seconds?"

She throws her head back and laughs. "Minutes. I want to take a quick shower, and then I should be good to go." She turns and walks out of the room with Lilo at her side.

"Lilo, let's go eat." I call her, and she stops following Zara and looks at me, then at Zara, making her own decision on what to do. She goes with food and comes back to me. I clean up the kitchen, go into the garage to feed the dogs, then go into the guest room to take my own shower. I make sure everything is locked and the dogs are taken care of when I walk back into my room with just a white towel around my waist.

I don't know what is going to greet me, but when I finally walk into my room, I have to stop and actually catch my breath. There in the middle of the bed is Zara. Not just Zara but a naked Zara, her long legs stretched to the side, her tits peaked and ready for me to bite down on them. But my eyes go straight to between her legs. Her one hand circles her clit while the one has two fingers buried deep inside her. I slip the towel from around my waist and fist my cock in my hand. She must sense me watching her because she tilts her head to the side and opens her eyes.

"Evan," she whispers my name, and I walk to her, her hands moving faster and faster. I get on the bed, kneeling beside her. My hand goes back to my cock, fisting it up and down while my other hand goes to her nipple where I roll it between my fingers. I lean down and take it into my mouth, and then I suddenly feel hot wet on my cock and look down to see she moved to get my cock into her mouth. I thrust my hips as I fuck her mouth, my mouth pulling her nipple into my mouth again, and she arches her back when I bite down. Her mouth takes me deeper, and I look down and see her hands going faster and faster. Moving down, I take my cock out of her mouth, and she groans. "No, you aren't having all the fun," she says sitting up now, her fingers now out of her pussy. I pick them up and bring them to my lips, licking them clean.

"I want you to sit on my face," I tell her, leaning down and sucking her tongue into my mouth. "Then you can suck my cock."

Her eyes hood over in lust. "Okay." I get on my back, and she throws her leg over. My patience has run out, so I grab her hips the same time I lift my mouth and suck her pussy into my mouth. She moans while I groan, and she falls forward and takes my cock in her hand and then down her throat. Our bodies take over as the both of us are full of need. My hips thrust up into her mouth, and her hips start grinding on my face.

"Oh my God," she says when she lets go of my cock, but her hand still works it. "I'm so close," she whispers right before she swallows me again. I lick up and down her slit, flicking her clit with my tongue. She moves her mouth faster and faster, and I slip two fingers into her. The slickness of her pussy makes them easy to move in and out, but two thrust in it gets tighter and hotter as her hips move against my mouth. Her mouth leaves my cock again to groan, and I know that she comes because my fingers get tighter and wetter in her. "Evan," she says, her hips moving to meet my fingers. I wait for her to ride it out and then slowly roll her to the side. She lies there, trying to catch her breath. Turning her head, she watches me lean over and grab a condom from the side table. I tear the corner off and slide the condom out and place it on my cock.

She opens her legs for me, her eyes still hooded over as she recovers from the orgasm I just gave her with my mouth. When I grab my cock at the base and slide it over her slit, her back automatically arches up at my touch. Her hand pushes mine away as she guides it straight to her opening. I don't even try to stop it, and I just sink all the way balls deep into her in one thrust. Her head goes back, and her eyes close. Her hand rests on the base of my stomach, and I don't move until she is ready. She is snug, tight, and perfect.

"It feels so good," she hisses, opening her hips wider, and then wraps her legs around my hips. My body lowers on her as I take her mouth, my tongue sliding into her mouth, the same time I pull out and then slowly start moving in and out of her. I don't move fast at first; I take my time, feeling all of her. Her arms wrap around my neck, and her legs squeeze my hips.

I slip one hand under her and slide down to kiss her neck, her fingers running through my hair as she pants. I try to keep the same pace, but when her pussy starts to squeeze me harder and harder, I can't stop my thrusting. Raising her hips, she tilts them back so I get even deeper. She slides one hand between us, and I look between our bodies, seeing her play with her clit.

"That's it, beautiful," I tell her, and she just moans. "Play with that pink clit." Her head moves side to side. "Flick it," I tell her, and she does. "Now do little circles." Her hand obeys everything I say, her pussy getting tighter and tighter, her hips squeezing me more and more. "Pinch it," I tell her. "Tight and don't let go till I tell you." She does, and I thrust hard one, then twice. "Let it go and rub it side to side now." She does it, and she takes off, coming on my cock so hard I can't move in her. I have to stay planted balls deep.

Her eyes open to look at me. "Are you going to come with me?" she asks me in a sultry voice. "Make me come again and then come with me." My body so ready to fucking release but not until she does it again.

"Come deep inside me." Her hips now moving faster than they did before, her middle finger moving as fast as her hips. "I need you." She looks at me, and I will give her whatever she needs.

"I need you to come with me." She moves her hand wrapping it around my neck as she meets me thrust for thrust. I pull out all the way to the tip and then pound it down, harder than I want, but she takes it. She takes each fucking thrust. "I need you deeper," she says between her pants. She tilts her hips and holds her legs back, and I sink so fucking deep it's all I can take. When she comes on my cock after the fourth thrust, I let her ride it out, and when she is almost done, I let myself loose. I plant myself balls fucking deep, and I come with her name on my lips.

Collapsing down beside her on the bed, I think I see stars, but I'm not sure. When I blink my eyes, I see black spots. She kisses my shoulder softly, and my cock twitches. "I just need a couple of minutes." I try catching my breath, and she licks her way to my ear.

"I want to ride you," she tells me, and my eyes open, looking down at her. "I want to ride you, and I want you to let me do what I want to do."

"Yeah," I tell her.

"I want to come again." She moves her hips, and I have to hold her in place. "I want to come while sitting on your cock."

"I need to change the condom," I tell her, and she looks down as my semi erect cock slips out of her.

"Then I want you take me in the shower, and I want to suck your cock again." She smiles at me, and I roll off the bed.

"I am going to need to hydrate." I look over my shoulder at her and see her hand slip down between her legs. My cock not getting any memo except to get back into her.

"Don't you make yourself come without me," I tell her, and she looks up at me. "You come with me, or you don't come at all."

"That's not fair." She almost pouts. "What if you can't ...?"

"Then you come on my fingers," I tell her. She closes her knees, and I know she is so fucking far-gone. I ignore the condom and walk back to the bed, standing on the side of bed.

I move her hand away from her clit, and I lick my thumb to wet it and then rub her clit. "My sweet Zara," I tell her and lean over as she spreads her legs, and I take her clit into my mouth, sucking it deep. Her hands gripping the sheets beside her.

"Always sweet," I tell her as I nip her clit, and she arches her back.

"Beautiful." I watch her eyes when I slip two fingers in her.

"Always fucking beautiful." Her hand reaches out to fist my cock, but I move away, and her hand falls on the bed as she groans in frustration.

"Let me have your cock. Please."

"After you come on my fingers," I tell her, fucking her with them and watching her look down at my fingers. It's the most exotic sight I've ever seen, her eyes following my fingers as they disappear in her. I bend my head down again and suck in her clit harder this time, and she pants out my name. I slip my tongue in with my finger, and she's two seconds away from coming. "You come on my fingers, and then you can sit on my cock all night long."

"Promise?" she hisses, then looks down, and she comes on my hand. "Fuck."

She rides my fingers, and then I pull them out of her and lick them clean. I'm expecting her to take time to recover, maybe get up and go get water, but what I'm not expecting is for her to roll to the side of the bed and grab another condom out of the drawer. "Come on, cowboy, it's time for me to take that ride." She winks at me, and my cock is suddenly rock hard solid.

TWENTY-FIVE

ZARA

I NEVER KNEW sex could be this much fun or that the need and urges would totally take over my body. I never ever in a million years thought I would be the one begging for it. For his touch, for his mouth, for his fingers, and more importantly, for his cock.

I woke up with my body sore in places I didn't know were possible, but then I think back to the night we had, and the amount of times I begged for it. After he let me ride him, and ride him I did, he bent me over in the shower with his hands fisting my hair, and I came so hard I thought my legs were going to give out. The night was filled with hands and mouths. I woke once to him sliding into me, and he woke once with his cock in my mouth. Looking over at the clock, I see it's almost seven and know he has to be up at eight.

He faces me with his eyes closed, and his hand rests on his chest as it rises and falls. I slowly reach into the side table and grab another condom. I tear open the condom and grab his cock in my hand. I hear him groan, but his cock is already up and ready for me. I roll the condom down his length, and he groans again. I don't wait for him to open his eyes before I throw my leg over his hip and slowly slide down him until he's all the way in me. My hands cup my tits and tweak my nipples. There are little hickeys over them from the last time I was in this position. His eyes open, and he looks down to see me squat up and then down again, his hands going to my hips.

"Beautiful," he mumbles, his eyes closing again, but this time, one of his thumbs finds my clit. "So wet already," he says, and his fucking dirty talk will get me off faster. He knows it, and I know it.

"You want to ride my cock?" he says and now my hands fall to his stomach as I grind my hips and rotate them. "Fuck," he says when I clench my pussy on his cock. "Wanted to wake you with my face in your pussy," he says, and I'm so fucking close I can almost touch it. My stomach gets tight, my toes curling.

"Look at us," he says, looking at my pussy. "Look at how your pussy takes my cock." My eyes watch how I ride him. His cock disappears, and I hurry up to see it again.

"Take my cock, beautiful." My legs burn as I squat on top of him, one of my hands going to meet his thumb as we both play with my clit. He lifts his other hand and squeezes my tit. Moving my hand away from my clit, he causes me to moan out in frustration 'cause I'm so close to coming. He squeezes and twists my nipple at the exact time as he squeezes my clit, lifting his hips. He twists my nipple again, but this time, he lets go of it and also lets go of my clit. I'm a rag doll at this point, and he grabs me around my waist and flips me on my back and fucks me so hard. It takes four thrusts, and I lean up and bite his pec right before he plants himself in me, and we come together.

"Jesus fucking," he hisses, and I laugh. "That was so fucking hot." He leans down taking a nipple in his mouth, sucking it in and then leaving a little bite mark next to it.

"Stop with the marks." I push him off me.

"Never," he says. "Those just show you're mine." I look over at him as he rolls off me and walks to the toilet. I look over and see it's almost seven thirty, so I roll out of bed, and my legs literally feel like I spent four hours in the gym.

I walk to my luggage and throw it down. "What are you doing?" I look over, and he is standing there naked, his cock at half-mast.

"I'm getting clothes," I tell him, and he just shakes his head. He walks back into his walk-in closet and comes back with one of his shirts.

"Here." He hands me the gray shirt with the team logo on the front and his name on the back. "How would you feel about having my name tattooed on you?" he asks me, and I shake my head.

"How would you feel about going hunting with my family dressed as a duck?" I grab the shirt and slip it over my head. "I still need panties," I tell him, and he shakes his head. "Evan, the dogs are going to be all over me, and I don't want their snouts in my vagina."

"Fine," he says, putting on a pair of gym shorts. "But make sure they can be easily ripped off."

"We just had sex five times in six hours," I tell him, laughing and slipping on a pair of pink lace boy shorts.

"I lost track," he says. "Before I leave, we need to do it twice more."

"You need to save your energy for the ice," I tell him, getting up and walking out of the room. The dogs jump off the couch and come over to me.

"Hello, my loves," I tell them. "Are you ready to go out?" Stitch is going in circles while Lilo is up and licking my face. "Okay," I say and walk over the door and open it so they can run outside.

"Leave the door open so they can come back in," Evan says as he walks to the garage probably to fill their bowls and start the coffee.

"Do you eat here or at the rink?" I shout and then jump when I see he is back already. "Jesus."

"I can eat here," he says, coming to me and wrapping his arms around me. "Good morning, beautiful." He kisses my neck.

"Good morning," I whisper to him, and he kisses my lips. I need to call someone and ask them if the need to climb him like a fucking tree is a normal thing because, let me tell you, I would climb him for hours. I watch him walk to the fridge and pull some things out, and just like that, we make breakfast side by side. I mean, there are times when I accidentally have to lean over, just like there were times he needs to slip his hands into my panties and slip a finger in. "Behave," I tell him while I scramble some eggs. "No sex till after you come home."

"That's in about six hours," he huffs, and I plate us both

some eggs, his serving bigger than mine. I cut some fresh avocado and make his two slices of toast.

"What is the plan for the day?" I ask him, putting the plate down on the table and feeling him behind me.

"I have practice from ten to noon, and then I usually go to the gym until one thirty, so I'll be home at two," he tells me, sitting down next to me.

"Okay, perfect." I look at the clock and see it's a bit past nine. "I'll have my work done before you get home."

"Do you want to go out and eat dinner tonight?" he asks me, and I just shake my head.

"No," I tell him. "I want to lie with you outside on my couch." He nods his head, smirking. "Then I want to come in and take a bath."

"Sounds like a plan," he says, picking up his plate and bringing it to the sink and then putting it in the dishwasher.

"Leave it. I'll clean up. You go get ready," I tell him, and he comes over and leans in front of me. I kiss his lips, and he turns to go get ready, running out of the house ten minutes later. Leaving me almost panting.

"Don't touch yourself while I'm gone," he says, winking at me and walking out.

"Asshole," I say to the closed door, and I clean up the kitchen and go grab my phone. I open my FaceTime and decide this has to be a group chat. So I open my app and start adding people. The first one to pick up is Zoe.

"Hey," I tell her. "I'm adding a couple of people since I don't want to repeat this story seven times." She nods her head, and I see her reading the computer screen in front of her.

Karrie is the next one to pick up. "Well, well, well," she says with a smile.

"She's adding people, so say the you're a ho chant when everyone picks up," Zoe says, smirking and grabbing her coffee.

"Vivienne and Allison are both here," Karrie says, but they answer on their own devices. "Why are you answering?"

"Because I want to see how good she got it," Vivienne says, her face filling the screen. "She did good. Look at those cheeks." I raise my hands to my cheeks. "Her eyes are still floating on orgasms."

"Damn," Allison says, "she's not lying."

"Okay," Zoe snaps. "Let her talk." And everyone just looks at me.

"I think I'm a nymphomaniac." I come out and tell them. Zoe's eyes open big, Karrie's mouth drops, Allison rolls her lips, and Vivienne just throws her head back and laughs.

"She got it so fucking good," Vivienne says, slapping her hand on the table.

"I swear we had sex five times, and I must have had ten orgasms," I tell them. "And as soon as we finished, I craved it again."

"Snap," Zoe says, "does he have a brother?"

"I swear, this morning, I woke up, and the first thing I did was pounce on him." I shake my head. "He was sleeping, and I put a condom on him and rode him."

"Jesus," Zoe says. "I don't think I've ever wanted it that bad."

"Then you aren't getting it right." Allison shocks us all. "Max is always up for it." And I now cringe when Zoe yells,

"Ewww."

"What? She's allowed to talk about Evan and her pound town, but I can't?"

"Yes, because she isn't married to him," Zoe says. "I don't have to sit at the table next to him wondering if you banged him before we have Sunday dinner."

"The answer is yes." Allison sticks out her tongue. "If he is home, we have had sex at least once a day."

"Same," Karrie says, and now I hold up my hand.

"You are not allowed to tell us that because he is our brother. And isn't he getting close to the age where he can have a heart attack from going at it that much?"

Karrie rolls her eyes. "I fucking wish." Zoe, Allison, and I just cringe while Vivienne smiles. "I came home from the gym the other day. I was sweaty and I stank, and he looked at me and said 'You in the mood?'"

"There has to be a cutoff age," I tell them.

"Not here," Allison says. "Not even close."

"Anyway, can we focus on me for once?" I ask them. "What do I do?"

"You fuck," Vivienne says, laughing. "You bang and bang and bang again and again and again and again." Then she looks at us. "I haven't had sex in five months." Now it's our turn to look at her shocked. "I've been busy."

"Liar," Karrie says, and now Vivienne glares at her. "But it's not about her."

"Why don't you just enjoy the moment?" Allison says.

"He says I'm not allowed to touch myself if he isn't here, and he left so many marks on me I am going to have to wear turtlenecks for the next week," I tell them, and they all laugh.

"I remember once I left a hickey next to Max's dick, and Matthew saw it." Allison laughs out loud. "He didn't know I was the one, and when he found out, he threw up."

"Matthew is only allowed to leave them in places the kids can't see," Karrie says. "So basically I can't go topless."

"Why is it these men are all about branding their women?" Zoe asks. "It's a bit too much."

The rest of the chat goes smoothly, and I tell them about how I love him, and Zoe is the only one not surprised by this. When we finally hang up, it's almost noon. I go back into his room and unpack my stuff, hanging what needs to be hung but leaving the folded clothes in the luggage by the wall. I grab a pair of yoga pants and a top and go to shower. Then I take my laptop and a notebook and make the kitchen table my office space.

I'm so into booking my schedule and returning a bunch of emails I don't even notice the front door open and then slam shut. I look at the clock and see that it's only one thirty. I get up and walk around the counter and stop when I come face to face with a blonde. My heart speeds up.

"What the fuck are you doing here?" she asks me, and I look to the side and see Lilo sitting beside me. "I can't believe he would bring you here."

"I'm sorry." I finally find my words. "Who are you?"

"Me, sweetheart?" she says sarcastically. "I'm the one who is supposed to be here and not you."

So this is what it feels like to be mature. This is what it feels like not to fly off the handle and to take a second. "That doesn't answer my question." I fold my hands over my chest. "Who are you?"

"I'm Candace, Evan's sister." She rolls her eyes, and I just look at her. "I swear he thinks with his dick all the time." The words coming out of her mouth sting. I'm not going to lie, they also fucking hurt.

"Now that you've answered the who you are question, perhaps you would like to answer why you are even here," I ask her, looking around. "This isn't your house." Her eyes just glare at me. "I mean, unless you were here to pick something up."

"It's our weekly meeting," she hisses. "Jesus, aren't you a sharp one."

Now, I've about had it, and my back goes straight and the little bit of maturity I have is about to go out the window. "I guess your weekly meetings just aren't as important as you think they are since he didn't even mention you coming over."

She laughs now. "You don't really believe that he likes you, right?" she asks me and doesn't wait for me to answer. "I mean, it's all about publicity. He is banking on the biggest contract, and well, you just make it that much sweeter." I was wrong before. Those other words were nothing because these words gut me. I don't have a chance to say anything because the door opens and closes, and Evan looks at the sight before him. The smile leaves his face when he sees that I'm not smiling. I'm about to throw something across the room.

"What the fuck is going on?" he asks, his eyes never leaving mine.

"I was just telling her—" Candace starts, but I'm done

with this bullshit right now, so I cut her off.

"Yes, she was informing me that I'm not the smartest, that you always think with your dick, and let's see, that this thing between us"—I point at him and then at myself—"is a publicity stunt." I look at him and then look at Candace who just swallows now. "Am I missing anything?"

"Candace," he hisses, and I shake my head.

"I'm going to just step outside," I tell them, and she just rolls her eyes. I grab my phone and open the door and the dogs follow me outside. I walk to the couch in the middle of the yard, and I sit down, the lone tear rolling down my cheek. Lilo gets on the couch with me, putting her face on my legs, and Stitch sits in front of the couch looking at the door.

"Well, that was fun," I say to myself because the dogs don't understand anything. "You see, the old Zara would have told her to fuck off and kicked her out of the house." She looks up at me. "But the mature one who loves him and doesn't want his family to hate me just got kicked in the vagina." She tilts her head to the side. "Yeah, I liked the old Zara also." I smile at her and rub her head. "She'd have a plan B just in case," I tell them, opening up my American Airlines app.

Twenty-Six

Evan

I SLAM THE door behind me with a smile on my face, knowing in five seconds my lips will be on hers, and then I see the scene before me. She tells me what was being discussed and then turns on her heels. I watch her walk out of the house with the dogs behind her, and I count to ten before I turn on my sister. What started out as an amazing day is quickly going to shit. I turn to my sister, taking off the baseball hat I was wearing and throwing it on my couch.

"Candace," I say her name between clenched teeth. "I really fucking hope that what she said isn't true."

"Oh, please," Candace says. "You can't tell me that this actually means something."

"I'm going to forget you just said that," I tell her and then finally turn my head away from the window and turn to stare at my sister. "You came into *my* house." My voice starts going a touch louder as my patience snaps. "And you said the most vile things to a woman you don't even fucking know."

"Oh, I know her kind," she says, and she must see my face because she stops talking.

"Her kind?" I repeat her words. "You mean a smart, independent woman?"

"I mean a puck bunny. God knows how many hockey guys she's—"

I put my hand up. "I'm going to stop you there before I do something that will be very bad for both of us," I yell at her. "If you ever disrespect her again …"

"Disrespect her," she huffs.

"Don't make me choose between you and her," I tell her, shaking my head. "I called Mom today. Told her that she needs to come down this weekend to meet her." She doesn't say anything; she just lets her mouth hang open. "I love her, Can." I tell her what I just told my mother. "It started out as a fluke, but fuck, I fell in love with her."

"You can't be serious," she finally says.

"If it wasn't crazy, I would ask her to marry me today," I tell her. "If it wasn't crazy, I would beg her to spend the rest of her life with me." I finally take a deep breath. "I'm that serious, Candace." I don't know what I was expecting, but it was definitely not her turning and walking out the door, slamming my front door. I take my phone out and call my mother who answers on the first ring.

"Twice in one day," she says to me, laughing.

"I'm giving you a heads-up." My voice comes out harsher than I want, and my mother's laughter stops. "I just walked in to a showdown between Candace and Zara."

"Oh my," my mother says.

"Mom, if I have to choose, I'm going to pick Zara," I tell her. "Candace came into our house and said things I'm not even going to repeat."

"I'll call her," she tells me. "You know she is only looking out for you."

"I know that," I tell her, walking to the door that leads outside, "but I'm only looking out for Zara."

"Go and make sure she is okay and then call me back so I can meet her," she tells me. "Let me talk to Candace."

I put my phone down on the table next to Zara's stuff, and I have to smile, seeing her stuff mixed with mine. I open the door and walk outside toward her couch. She is on her phone, and when I get closer, Stitch sits up and looks at me, and I swear I can hear Lilo growl at me.

"Hey there," I say. Walking to her, I lean down and kiss her lips. She kisses me back, which is almost a win. "Whatcha doing there?" I say, sitting next to her. Throwing my arm around her, I bring her close to me. I look at her phone and see the American Airlines app. "What is that?"

"I was just looking at flights," she says with a softness I've never heard from her.

I turn in the couch now, and she still doesn't look up. Reaching out, I lift her face to look in her eyes, and I see she is crying. "What is going on?" I bring her to me, hugging her. "Talk to me." I move back so I can see her eyes, but she still won't look up.

"It's stupid," she says softly and uses her sweater to wipe her nose.

"Nothing is stupid, sweet Zara." I move her chin up again. "Please tell me why you're crying."

"The things she said, Evan," she says, and she blinks wiping away a tear. "They were harsh, and I just stood there." She shrugs her shoulders. "The old Zara would have throat punched her, grabbed her bag, and took off. After she smashed her car by backing into it five times."

"Candace was out of line," I tell her. "One hundred percent out of line and I told her it was unacceptable."

"I don't even know her," she says. "I've never met her in my life. She said I was a publicity stunt."

"I left practice thirty minutes early, and the first thing I did was call my mother," I tell her, and she opens her eyes bigger. "They are flying in on Friday night for the game."

"I'll go stay at a hotel," she says, sitting up

"Over my dead body. You sleep where I am," I tell her. "I called her because I want her to meet you." I grab her face in my hands. "I want her to see how amazing you are and how we are together. I just …" I try to find the words. "I want her to meet you 'cause I'm head over heels in love with you, and I want everyone to know it."

"But …" she says.

"There is no but," I tell her. "Do you love me?" I ask her, and she nods. "What would you do if that happened to me?"

"What do you mean?" she asks me, tilting her head.

"If you walked into the room and saw Matthew there, and he said stupid, he doesn't know what he's talking about stuff."

"I would put Nair in his shampoo bottle, and then put itching powder in his skates," she answers without hesitation.

"Jesus," I say, laughing but knowing she probably would.

"Three years ago, he pissed me off for, I can't even re-member, but we put gorilla glue on his hockey stick." I can't stop laughing now. "We still have the stick with the gloves stuck to it."

"I'm so sorry she hurt you," I tell her, and she just shrugs. "I don't ever want to be the source of your tears. I want to be the one who wipes them away."

She smiles at me. "Oh, you're good." I lean down, kiss-ing her cheeks where the tears streamed down. "I'm sorry I doubted you," she whispers, looking up at me. "I'm sorry that I doubted us."

"I'd really like to make it up to you?" I get off the couch and reach down for her, picking her up and tossing her over my shoulder. Her laughter fills the yard, making the dogs excited.

"This is not the way to start foreplay." She laughs, and I swat her on the ass. "Okay, that's a start," she says. I walk into the house, and the dogs follow me. I close the gate leading to the bedroom, and Lilo gives a little whine. I walk into the bedroom and see her suitcase opened by the wall.

I drop her to her feet, and she moves the hair away from her face. "Why haven't you unpacked?" I ask her, walking to the suitcase.

"I did," she tells me. "I hung up what needed to be hung."

"But what about this stuff?" I point at the luggage, and she shrugs.

"I was going to put it in the guest room, but I didn't know if I had to clear out drawers." She sits on the bed.

"Guest room?" I ask confused. "What?"

"I can just leave them in there." She points at the luggage, and I hate it. I walk over to my dresser and open a drawer, grabbing everything out.

"There is a drawer," I say, carrying all my clothes with me into my walk-in closet and dumping them on the floor. I walk back out and do the same thing with three other drawers. "Is that enough space?"

"Are you crazy?" she shrieks. "Now I have to fold all your clothes. You could have just asked me to share it with you."

"Put your clothes in the drawers," I tell her. I'm almost tempted to just grab everything from her luggage and shove it in there.

She gets off the bed now, coming to me. "I thought you were going to make it up to me?" Pulling her shirt over her head, she's standing there in just a bra. "I believe you said—"

"I know what I said." My hand reaches out and pulls her to me, my tongue slipping in with hers. My body releases the tension I felt when I saw her crying, when I saw her trying to leave.

"I missed you," I tell her, kissing her neck and then trailing kisses all the way down to the swell of her breast. Seeing my little red mark peeking out of the white bra, I touch it with my finger. "I don't know what it is," I tell her. "Seeing my mark on you."

"We have to talk about that," she says, and I look up at her. "You can't just leave them everywhere you please." My eyebrow shoots up looking at her. "I work in fashion, so it's going to be hard not wearing an outfit because I'm branded."

"What kind of fucking outfit are you wearing that they see my marks on you?" I ask her. "Who cares?"

"I care," she tells me. "How about a compromise?"

I lean down and suck in another part of her flesh, leaving it red. "I'm listening," I tell her, going to the other breast and leaving the same mark.

"One a week," she says, her voice going low when I move the cup of her bra off and her nipple pops out and into my mouth. "One a week." She trails off, and then I feel her hands in my pants cupping my cock. There is no talking after that, but when I finally finish with her, she has more red marks, and I'm not even sorry about it.

We finally pull ourselves out of bed when it's dark out, but only because the dogs have to eat. I watch her put her stuff away while I order food for us on my iPad. "I'm going to go feed the dogs," I tell her, walking to my closet and grabbing a pair of shorts. When I come out of the closet, she is bent over, grabbing her stuff. "Now that is a sight," I tell her, and she looks over at me, her hair failing down. I see the glitter in her eye as she opens her legs a tad more. "I need to eat, then I'm taking you just like that."

"Promises, promises." She laughs when I walk out the door but not before biting her ass cheek.

"Let's get you some food," I tell the dogs that are lying on the couch. I pick up my phone and see that I've missed a couple of texts from my mother.

Mom: Spoke with your sister.

Mom: I hope she listens.

Then there is one from my sister.

Candace: We have to discuss the rest of the season. I'm not going to do it at your house if she's there.

I shake my head and answer back.

Me: So does this mean you quit?

I am not going to let her act like a spoiled brat.

She doesn't take long to answer.

Candace: I guess you are the one who has to decide that.

Me: Candace, tomorrow at my house at eleven. If you aren't here, that means you aren't interested in working.

I turn off the phone and make my way to the garage. The lights are on in the living room now, and she has turned on the television. "We need to go over a couple of things," she says, coming into the living room from the kitchen. I see her wearing shorts and one of my shirts.

"What's that, beautiful?" I ask her, turning the channel and stopping on the New York game.

"We need to go over our schedules," she says. "I am going to be here until Monday, I think, or Tuesday, but then I have to fly back to Chicago."

"But then after Chicago, you are coming back here, right?" I ask her, and she just shrugs her shoulders.

"I don't think it makes sense to be here if you aren't here," she says, sitting on the couch, and Lilo running back to lay with her. "Hi, pretty girl." She pets her head. "We need to get you a collar with some bling on it." Lilo's tail hits the couch as she wags it.

"So what are you going to do?" I ask, sitting next to her.

"Well, we can go over our calendar and see." She looks at me. "I mean, I think the season is almost done, right?"

"Another couple of weeks," I tell her, "then it's play-off time."

"I have Max and Matthew's retirement gala the second of

July." Her face fills with a smile. "Wanna be my date?" I nod, afraid to say anything that would scare her away. "My parents are throwing them a surprise getaway at their house in Mexico."

"Tell me where, and I'll book us a house." I watch the screen.

"That makes no sense. We have the house."

"Beautiful," I tell her, "we aren't staying in the same house as your parents."

"And why not?" she asks angrily.

"Because we have sex, lots of it," I point out, "all the time. I don't see that changing." She glares at me. "If normal sex with you is sky rocketing, can you imagine vacation sex?" I put my head back and close my eyes, my cock finally moving in on the action. I feel a pillow hit my face.

"Who says we are still going to be having sex by then?" She turns to look at the television.

"I say we will be having even more than we are now." She looks like she is going to argue with me, and the doorbell rings. "Oh, food is here."

"Your father thinks he's a slick one," she tells the dogs. "No blow job for him." I put my head back and laugh, knowing full well she enjoys it as much as I do.

TWENTY-SEVEN

ZARA

"I'M BACK," HE says from the front door, and I walk out. He left this morning to go to the rink and said he had run an errand afterward. Tomorrow, his parents get here, and I'm not going to lie, I'm an emotion mess. His sister came over the day after our face-off, and I left before she got here. I made up a phony excuse about meeting with a client. I got in the car and went to the Starbucks and worked from there.

"I hope you brought me food," I tell him and stop when I see who is behind him. "Zoe," I yell excitedly and run to her. "You're here."

"Well," she says when she steps out of our hug. "I couldn't let you get thrown to the wolves without me." Then she turns to Evan. "Not that your family is a pack of wolves."

I shake my head. Evan comes to my side and kisses me. "You did good," I whisper in his ear when he hugs me, and I smell him. Yeah, I smell him because it's my thing. He's my man, so I can do what I want.

"So this is where you hang your hat," Zoe says, looking around, and the dogs rush in full force to her, and then Lilo steps back, wondering what is going on. She finally comes to my side.

"This is my girl, Lilo." I bend down and kiss her, and she licks my face. "And this is Stitch." He's still debating which one of us to go to.

"I'm going to take your stuff into the guest room," Evan tells Zoe. "I'll put you upstairs so you have your privacy."

Zoe just nods her head, and she waits for him to go upstairs with her luggage. "You landed a good one," she says, and I go and hug her. I've missed her so much, but I didn't want to say anything to either of them. Even though we don't live together, we would not go more than two days without seeing each other unless I was traveling.

"I still can't believe you're here," I tell her. "Let's go sit outside." I turn and lead her outside. She is wearing jeans and a sweater with a light jacket. "Are those my clothes?"

"Um, yeah," she answers like duh. "I live in your house. Surely, you didn't expect me not to go through your closet?"

I shake my head and walk to the couch that I made him buy. "Look at all this land," Zoe says, and I'm sure she's evaluating his property and how much it would go for in her head. "This is at least a good three million, maybe even four point five if we can make an outdoor oasis."

"How did you get here?" I ask her. I sit down, curling my feet under me, and she does the same next to me, turning to face me. Some say we are identical if they don't know us, but Zoe's eyes are greener than mine. She also has a dimple right where she has a freckle.

"Well after you called me from Starbucks, I was thinking of just coming down, but then Evan called me and asked if I wanted to come down." Zoe starts talking, and now Lilo jumps on the couch and sits next to me, putting her head on my lap. "It was a no-brainer."

"I'm so nervous about meeting his parents," I tell her, and she smiles.

"Mom and Dad are coming too," Zoe says, and my eyes widen.

"What?" The question comes out in a whisper.

"Well, Mom was worried about you," Zoe starts, "and well, you know how Dad is when it comes to Mom." I nod my head. There is no doubt in the world that my father loves my mother. That he cherishes her right down to his soul. If she is sad, he makes her happy; if she is worried, he moves heaven and earth to make sure she isn't. "So Dad is calming her down by bringing her here and letting her see for herself that you are okay."

"I have to tell Evan." I am about to get up.

"Dad already called him and set things up," Zoe tells me, and I just look at her. "He just wanted to make sure that Evan wasn't blindsided with them coming. So Evan set up a lodge for them and also his parents so they could mingle and get to know each other."

"But I just started dating him," I tell her. "This is crazy. Is it really time for the parents to meet?"

"Oh, you silly, silly girl." Zoe laughs, shaking her head. "He's the one." I stare at her, not saying anything. "He is the one, and your heart knows it. Your head, not so much."

"It's too soon." I don't know if I'm telling her or myself. "I've only known him for a month."

"Who cares how long you've known him? When you know, you know," Zoe says. "There is no textbook or manual that says when you can and cannot fall in love."

"It just seems a bit rushed," I tell her, and she shrugs.

"When it happens, it happens. No one can control that." I know she's right. "You just have to embrace it and admit it."

I roll my eyes at her. "Don't be all wise and shit." She laughs, and then I see the back door open, and Evan comes out toward us.

"Is it okay that I'm here?" he asks. "Do you want sister time?"

"My parents are coming?" I look at him. I've looked at him a lot over the past couple of days. I've memorized how he looks when he smiles, when he smirks, when I make him come, and how his eyes now shine at my question. "Where are they going to stay?"

"I told them they could stay here," he says, sitting next to me and kissing my neck, "but your mom didn't want to burden me, so I rented them a house two blocks over."

"And we are having a family lunch on Sunday," I also remind him.

"It's the perfect time," he says, pulling me to him. "I was going to order the food, but my mother lost her shit."

"I can't cook," I say, my heart starting to beat faster, and I now get up. "Like I can cook, but I can't cook for your mother." I start shaking my hands.

"Oh, here we go," Zoe says, and Evan looks over at her with worry on his face. "This is her 'I'm freaking out' voice."

"Why?" he asks the question. Yes, a stupid question indeed.

"Why?" I shriek.

"You shouldn't have said anything," Zoe tells him.

"Why? Because the way to a man's heart is through his stomach."

"That is so not true." Zoe shakes her head. "It's usually through your vagina."

I put my hands on top of my head, then look over at Evan, who is about to start laughing but stops when he sees my face. "This is why we can't do the lunch."

"Beautiful," he says softly. "My mother doesn't care if you can cook for me."

"Lies." I raise my hands. "She'll want someone who can take care of you."

"I'm pretty sure he can take care of himself." Zoe puts in her two cents that I don't really want to hear right now.

"I have been taking care of myself." Evan looks at Zoe, who raises her hand like you see.

"I don't mean like that," I tell them, and now I start to pace. "I mean, I can take care of you if you're sick."

"Eww," Zoe says. "If he's sick, leave the house."

"Shut up, Zoe," I yell at her. "Every mother wants to know her son will be taken care of. She wants to know I can cook for you when you're sick."

"What is wrong with you?" Zoe says. "It's 2019. I'm sure he can order his own fucking soup."

I watch Evan as he gets up and comes to me, grabbing my hand in his. "Beautiful," he whispers, his voice calming me. "My mother couldn't care less if you can cook. She cares that you love me, she cares that you stand by my side, and she cares that I treat you the way you are supposed to be treated."

"I do love you," I tell him, and Zoe claps her hands.

"Ahhh, so sweet." I turn to glare at her.

"My sisters don't know how to cook," he tells me. "Besides, you won't be the one on the hot seat." I tilt my head sideways. "Your father will be sitting there making sure I treat you right. No father wants to sit at a table with a man who is sleeping with their daughter."

I laugh. "Max does it."

"I know, but he's Mad Max," he says, and now I step into his space. "I just want him to know you're okay here."

"I'm more than okay here," I tell him. "Besides I'll go back home sometimes."

"Wait a second," Zoe interrupts again, "are you moving here?"

"Not really," I tell her and see Evan's face. "If he's here, I'll be here, but when he travels, I'll go back home."

"What about the summers?" Zoe asks. "Your whole life is in New York."

I shake my head and think about what she said. When you love someone, you love someone, and there isn't a timeframe or a manual; there is nothing but what you feel. "Not my whole life."

"God, I wonder if I can move into your place." She looks up and taps her lips. "It would be so good to have no neighbors."

"You know if you move into my house, I move out my clothes," I inform her.

"Why would you do that?" she asks, and I shake my head. "That would be mean."

"Do you want to go eat?" Evan asks me, and I nod, then look at Zoe. "I want to have the greasiest burgers of life."

"Is there any other kind?" she asks as she gets up. We walk inside to lock up, and then I take her to visit my new hometown.

"What time are you parents getting here?" I ask Evan when he comes out of the bathroom. I'm sitting in the middle of the bed with my white cami and matching panties on. My hair hangs wet from the shower we just took together. The towel around his waist showing his semi erect cock that was just in my mouth.

"Why are you dressed?" he asks me confused.

"I'm not dressed. I'm in pjs." I look down.

"You know the rules," he tells me, getting in bed naked. "No clothes when we sleep."

"I'm not sleeping in the house naked with your parents here," I tell him. "Also, there will be no sex of any kind."

His eyebrows pull together. "Why?"

"Because they already think we are having sex," I tell him, getting under the covers.

His hands pull up my camisole. "I'm pretty sure they know we are having sex and not just thinking it," he says while he takes a nipple into his mouth, and my thoughts start to get hazy.

"That's the point. I don't want them to look at me and wonder if I just banged their son before I sat at the table."

"You do have a glow on your face after I bang you," he says, taking the other nipple in his mouth. "I can't go three days without having you."

"Yes, you can," I tell him, and he pushes me down, my legs opening for him. "I mean there is the nighttime."

"Yeah," he says with a smirk, moving down my body.

"I mean if we have sex before we go to bed, then no one is going to see my face." I think but not to hard 'cause his mouth lands on my pussy, his tongue moving my panties to the side so he can lick my clit. I moan silently. "We would have to be very, very quiet," I say in a whisper.

"Can you be quiet?" he asks me. I look down at him feasting on my pussy, seeing his tongue disappear inside me.

"We could try now and see." I open wider, my hand going to his head as I try to rub my pussy on his face. We have sex many times a day, and sometimes I'll wake with him sliding into me in the middle of the night. Or he wakes with either me blowing him or riding him. Either way, it's a win for everyone. We spend the rest of the night seeing exactly how quiet we can be.

TWENTY-EIGHT

Evan

"HOW DOES THIS look?" Zara asks me again, walking out of the walk-in closet. This time, she's wearing a pair of black jeans and a white shirt with a scarf the same color as my jersey.

"Much better," I tell her. The outfit she put on before was white pants and a black see-through shirt. There was no way in fuck she was wearing that out.

"I still like the other outfit more," she says, going back into the closet.

"You are not leaving the house in that outfit," I shout at her, and I hear Zoe's laughter from somewhere in the house. Having her here is an eye-opener, I knew they were close and that they shared a strong bond, but I had no idea how strong. They finish each other's sentences, and they know what the other person is thinking just by looking at each other.

"What was wrong with that outfit?" she asks, folding her arms over her chest. "It was nice."

"I saw your bra," I point out to her, grabbing my belt and putting it on.

"Oh, I think I have another outfit." She turns around and goes back in the closet. I know she is super nervous about meeting my parents, and I'm super nervous about meeting hers again. I'm also nervous about Candace. When she came over the next day, she smirked when she found out that Zara wasn't here. I don't know what she thought, but then she saw her jacket on the chair in the kitchen. My mother told me she will be at the Sunday lunch thing, and that she will behave. Normally, I don't care what she does, but if she fucks with Zara, there will be a showdown no one wants to see. "What about this?" I look up to see her in black jeans now and a peach and black top that is loose and criss-crosses.

"That is nice also," I tell her, and she just shakes her head and walks out of the room, yelling for her sister. I look at Lilo lying on the bed. "Who else is excited for Monday to be here?"

I grab the jacket to my suit and shrug it on. "Zoe said I look like a schoolteacher in this." I walk to her.

"Beautiful, relax. Everything is going to go okay." I try to calm her. "I have to get to the rink."

She nods her head. "What if they hate me?" she asks, her voice soft, and I know what she is going through. "I mean, your sister had never even met me and she hated me. What if she told your mother?"

"Beautiful," I say, tucking her hair behind her ear. "My

mother isn't going to hate you, and I can bet money that once Candace gets to know you, everything will be good."

"I just …" she starts saying, and her voice cracks. "I won't let you be in the middle."

"I'm not in the middle," I tell her, knowing that I couldn't care less if they like her. I would love nothing more than my mother to love her, but if push comes to shove, I can't let her go. "Now go put on whatever you want to wear." She smiles. "Except that first outfit and then we can go."

"I love you," she says, and I kiss her lips. "I have to change."

She spends the next five minutes changing her outfit, and when we leave, she is wearing blue jeans and a white shirt with a leather jacket. Her black high-heeled booties make her legs look even longer. "Okay, I'm ready," she says, wrapping a scarf around her neck, and we walk out to see Zoe sitting on the couch.

"Finally. I was beginning to sweat," she says, getting up, and I inwardly groan. She is wearing tight blue jeans, lighter than Zara's, but her shirt is white and falls off one shoulder.

"That's my shirt," Zara says.

"Not anymore," I say, walking to the front door.

"I'm going to have no more clothes left," Zara says, huffing.

"And I'm going to have a brand-new closet. I like him," Zoe says, and I walk to the truck and open Zara's door first and then Zoe's. "Does he do that all the time?"

"Yes," she huffs and kisses me right before she gets into the car.

"If you get tired of her," Zoe says, getting into the car, "we could always date." She winks at me, and I close the door.

These two together are crazy. I get in the car and hear them laughing. "I'm just going to date him," Zoe says to Zara who glares back at her. "I'm not going to sleep with him."

"Zoe," she hisses.

"What? Even though he can go five times a night, I won't cross that line," she says, and I look at Zara.

"You told her about that?" I ask shocked.

"Dude," Zoe says from the back, "I'd put your picture on a billboard in Times Square."

"She probably would," Zara says, and I don't say anything else as I make my way to the rink. Once we park, I get out and walk around. Zoe steps out, blocking me from going to Zara's door.

"You really are that chivalrous," Zoe says and moves out of the way when I glare at her. I open the door for Zara.

"Evan, I could have opened my own door," Zara huffs. I grab her hand and start to walk inside when my phone beeps. I look down at it and see it's from my mother.

Mom: *We are waiting for you inside.*

"My parents are here," I tell them, and Zara puts a hand to her stomach.

"I think I'm going to be sick," Zara says, and Zoe stands closer to her. I pull open the door that leads to the dressing rooms and walk down the red carpeted hallway.

"Holy shit, there are two of them." I hear someone say, and when I turn around, there is no one there. I walk out to the arena where I know my parents always wait for me, and I smile when I see my mother dressed in jeans and one of my jerseys.

"There he is," my father says, and my mother now looks

over at me smiling. Her eyes go wide when she sees Zara.

"Oh my," she whispers.

"Mom," I say, hugging her on the side, not letting go of Zara's hand. She is squeezing it so tight I think it's going to turn blue soon. My father stands beside my mother with his hand on her shoulder. "Dad," I say, and he just nods at me with a beaming smile on his face. "This is Zara." I pick up her hand in mine and kiss it. "And that is her twin sister, Zoe." I take a deep breath. "This is my mom, Jackie, and my father, Patrick."

"Mr. and Mrs. Richards," Zara says, reaching out her hand to shake my mother's. "It is so good to finally meet you." My mother reaches out and hugs her.

"She is so beautiful," my mother says, and I can see tears in her eyes, then she looks at Zara. "You are so beautiful."

"Jackie," my father says, "don't scare her away."

Zara laughs, and then Zoe talks. "She doesn't scare away that easily. I've been trying since we were in utero." I shake my head, and I'm about to say something to her when I hear talking coming from down the hall, and I look up, and all I hear is Zara.

"Oh, my God," she whispers when she finally looks down the hallway. There walking down the hall is Cooper, Parker, Matthew, Karrie, Max, and Allison. Zara turns to Zoe. "Did you know about this?" Zoe just shakes her head. They make their way to us, almost like a flying vee with Cooper and Parker in the front and Max and Matthew with their wives on each side.

"Well, well, well," Matthew says. Karrie nudges him, and he looks at her.

"Behave," Karrie says and smiles.

"Sweetheart," Cooper says, and he comes forward to hug his girls, my hand never leaving Zara's. She actually squeezes it tighter.

"What are you guys doing here?" Zara asks when her mother comes to hug her, and I look over at my father who is watching everything with his back straight.

"We had four days off, and I thought why not come to Dallas," Matthew says, and I watch him as he looks at my father and then my mother.

"Excuse us," Parker says, smiling and going to my mother. "You must be Evan's mom." I don't know what my mom is expecting, but I'm sure it's not the hug that Parker gives her. "You raised a true gentleman," she tells her, and my mother now beams with pride. "And I see he's just as handsome as his father."

"Excuse my wife," Cooper says, pulling her away from hugging my father, and I want to laugh. I think my father would do the same, and I sure as fuck know I would also. "Mr. Richards." He holds out his hand, and my father smirks and does the same. "I'm Zara's father."

"Mr. Stone," my father says, holding out his hand. "It's a pleasure to meet you." If you have been on the ice or have even watched hockey one time in your life or even if you haven't, you know who Cooper Stone is.

"I have to go get ready," I whisper to Zara who just nods her head. I lean in and kiss her lips not even caring that her family is there. She is mine now, so they better get used to it. Because I'm not going anywhere.

"Skate hard," she tells me, and the boys chuckle. "I heard

Dad tell you that all the time." She glares at them.

"Yeah, when I was ten," Matthew says, and I just shake my head.

"I'll see you when I get out." I look back at Matthew and Max. "M&M, want to tour a winning locker room?" I joke with them, and they just glare. "I didn't say it." I look at Cooper who just smiles. "The stats did."

"Can I tag along?" Cooper asks, and I nod.

"Well, in that case, I'm not staying with the women," my father says, and we both walk toward the dressing room.

My father and Cooper walk behind us, and Matthew and Max walk with me in the middle. "So you guys had nothing better to do than to come all the way to Dallas to watch a hockey game?" I ask them when we walk into the hallway and then turn on them. Looking over my shoulder, I see that Cooper is already being recognized and is shaking hands.

"What can I say?" Matthew starts. "I live for the game."

"I just came because it meant I got to spend the week-end alone with my wife," Max says, shrugging.

"That's gross. She's still my sister," Matthew hisses at him.

"Your other sister is living with him," Max says, pointing at me.

"Do you guys ever not fight?" I ask them.

Matthew and Max both answer at the same time. "No."

"So why the sudden need to come to Dallas?" I ask them again. "Cut the bullshit, will you."

"Zara called my mom, and she was almost in tears about meeting your mother with your sister there."

"She was in tears?" I whisper. "She never said anything."

"That is just the way those women handle things," Max

tells me. "You are always the last one to know."

"We came to show her that we have her back," Matthew says, and I glare at him.

"I have her back," I tell him, and he holds up his hands.

"Relax, there," he says. "I know that feeling when you want to kill everyone who thinks they know your woman better than you do."

"Oh, I remember that," Max says, leaning on the wall now. "My wedding day was one of those."

"You eloped with my sister," Matthew snaps at him. "Not cool."

"Never going to apologize for it," Max says, smiling. "Best day of my life."

"I love her," I tell them both, and they just look at me. "I told her I love her, but I haven't told her she's the one yet because I don't want to scare her off. But I'm not going any-where." I look around and then look back at them. "She's mine. There is no other way to put it."

"What are you going to do about your contract next year?" Matthew asks me, and I don't answer him. "You know that she comes from a close family. Her twin lives in New York, and those two cannot be separated for long."

"I'm not deciding anything without her," I tell them the truth. "I won't even sign a contract without her approving it." Matthew looks at Max, and they share a look.

"How serious is this thing with your sister?" Max asks me. "I'm not saying anything, but you push one of those girls against the wall, and it's almost like you are taking them all on."

"My sister is worried about me," I tell them. "Same as you

are with Zara." They nod. "I have to get ready." I turn and walk away.

"Skate hard," Matthew says, laughing, and I flip him the bird over my shoulder. When I finally get into the locker room, there is chatter everywhere.

"You going to be okay?" Corey asks me, and I just nod at him.

"Never better." I shrug off my jacket. "Never fucking better."

Twenty-Nine

Zara

IT FEELS JUST like it does when I'm home. Sitting in the box with my girls, my father standing there watching every single play, but this time with Matthew and Max. Patrick and Cooper stand side by side as they discuss whatever it is they are discussing, both of them with their hand in front of their mouth. Just in case the cameras spot him and try to read his lips. It's like he has all the secrets. They actually had him on the jumbotron when the game started, and everyone turned to clap and stand. He got recognized the minute we started walking to the lodge as did Matthew and Max. But nothing can compare to my dad.

"What do you think we should make tomorrow?" Jackie asks me, and I look over at her. I'm sitting in a chair with Jackie on one side and my mother on the other, nursing the same glass of wine since we got in. My nerves are on edge, and every time the door opens, I think it will be his sister.

Zoe is sitting behind me with Karrie and Allison laughing away.

I mean, I guess if I were kid free for the weekend, I probably would be living it up. Karrie told me that Doug has her kids while Denise, Max's sister, is babysitting their kids.

"I don't know how to cook," I say, my voice not coming out strong. Zoe senses it right away, and my mother reaches for my hand. "I don't know how to cook," I say again, looking at Jackie. "I tried to learn, I did, but …" I have to blink away tears. "And I know that I'm not the perfect person you would want for your son."

"Oh dear God, it's happening," Zoe says from behind me, and Allison and Karrie both lean in and squeeze my shoulder.

"I can learn." I look down at my hand, then back up at Jackie. "I'll learn for him, and I'll take care of him if he gets sick."

"It's almost like she has diarrhea of the mouth," Zoe says, and I turn to glare at her. She looks at me. "You need to stop, or you're going to make yourself sick."

"I love him." I look back at Jackie. "Like love, love him."

"Oh honey," my mother says, and she puts her arm around me, and I've never been more scared in my life than I am right now waiting for Jackie to say something.

"Will you be there to hold his hand if things get rough?" she asks me, and I nod my head. "Will you be willing to go wherever this takes him?"

"Without ever looking back," I tell her.

"Taking care of someone is more than just cooking for him." Jackie grabs my hand in hers. "I didn't really cook when we got married, and well, it was a learning curve. I remember once I thought it would be a good idea to make meatloaf, and I broiled it instead of baking it." She shakes her head, laughing. "Those were the days. It's about being there when things are on a high, and then they go so low it takes everything you have in you not to try to fix it yourself." She leans over. "'Cause men don't always get things."

"True story," Karrie says from behind me.

"Before I met him, I was dating someone," I start telling her, and I know I shouldn't, but she has to know. "I thought I loved him. I really did." I look at my mom, who smiles at me and nods her head. "But then he broke up with me, and I thought it was the end of the world. I thought there was no way I would be able to go on." I blink away the tears. "I know now that isn't the case." A tear escapes me, and Zoe passes me a tissue that my mother holds for me.

"The reason I know it now is because I went on. Sure, it stung, but I was able to breathe. I was able to go about my day." The crowd gasps, and I look up and see that someone is on the ice, and he's down. I don't know who it is, all I know is that he's wearing green. I jump out of my chair, and my father looks back at me.

"It's not him, honey." He smiles at me.

I sit back down, gather up all my nerve, and finish. "I know because every day without him there was a pres-sure on my chest. A heaviness that I couldn't understand, and then, I finally was in his arms and the heavy was gone. I could breathe again." I look at my mom. "I get it. I get what you and Dad would talk about. How Dad would pout when you would go away for the weekend with the girls to a spa."

"I don't think he would pout," my mother says.

"He would start a timer on his phone with the hours of when you would be coming back," Zoe says from behind me.

"Remember the time he did the hours chart on the fridge, and every hour, he would cross off a number?" Allison says, laughing.

"I'm here," a voice says behind me, and I look over to see Candace coming in followed by another girl. She spots us, and her mouth drops when she sees Zoe, Allison, and Karrie.

Matthew and Max turn around and then look at each other, then spot the girl behind Candace. "What in the hell?" I hear Patrick say, and then Jackie gets up.

"Candace," Jackie says between clenched teeth, "what in the world were you thinking?"

"I didn't think," she starts saying, and now I get up.

"You didn't think that I would have anyone at my back," I tell her, my voice soft. "You thought I would be a sitting duck." Jackie looks at me, then at Patrick. "Hi, it's nice to meet you. I'm Zara."

The blonde behind her sticks out her hand, and I look at her up and down. We are like night and day. "Sophia." She says her name, and my stomach hurts. She looks at Candace and then back at Jackie. "I think I'm going to go and ..."

"That would be a good idea," Jackie says and then looks at me. "I'm so sorry."

I shrug my shoulders. "Nothing to be sorry about. I get to go home with him tonight." I fold my arms over my chest, and I feel my family at my back. "If anything, I should have thanked her."

"Everyone, this is Candace." I look around. "This is my family." I smile, and she just nods at them.

"If you will excuse us," Jackie says, "I need a moment alone with my daughter." She turns and grabs her arm to walk out of the lodge. I'm about to say something to Patrick, but I don't because the arena goes crazy, and everyone jumps to their feet. I look on the ice and see that Evan is skating with his stick in the air.

"Woohoo," Patrick says, clapping his hands, and they look at the replay, and even Matthew and Max agree it was a good play.

"I need a drink," I tell the girls who are all around me.

"I think someone needs a kick in her vagina," Zoe says.

I shake my head. "It is what it is. Nothing is going to make that whole thing better," I tell them and walk to the bar and pour myself a shot of tequila.

I take the shot with shaky hands, then put the empty glass down on the counter. I close my eyes and let the liquid burn. "The things we do for love," Jackie says from beside me, and I look over at her. She is wiping away a tear. "I'm so sorry that she did that."

"It's not your fault," I tell her.

"She is really a nice living person," she tries to tell me, wringing her hands.

"I'm sure she is." I am not going to put her in the middle of this.

"He won't forgive her for this," Jackie says to me. "She was already walking a fine line."

"Then we won't tell him." I smile at her. "He doesn't have

to know this happened."

"You love him," Jackie says. "That right there. Taking your pain and hurt and putting it aside to not have him know." She comes to me and gives me a hug. "That makes you worth everything."

"I really hope so," I whisper to her, and then I turn to my mother who is watching me with my father behind her.

"What is Evan's favorite meal?" I ask his mother.

"I think it has to be beef stroganoff," she answers, and I look at my mom.

"Will you show me how to make it so I can make it for him?" I ask Jackie, and she smiles. "I mean, I won't cook it, but I will watch and take notes."

"Oh, thank God," Zoe says.

"Why don't we all meet at Evan's place at noon, and we can all help?" my mother suggests, and Jackie just nods her head.

"That sounds like a wonderful plan," Jackie says, and the rest of the game is uneventful. They end up winning four to one, and we all sit in the lodge chatting. Then the door opens, and I look over and see Evan walk in. He looks pissed, so pissed that no one says anything, and the talking stops. He looks around the room, and his eyes finally find mine.

"Are you okay?" he asks when he's stand in front of me. I'm still sitting on the stool.

"What?" I ask shocked. "Of course, I'm okay." I smile at him, but there is no smile on his face. "What's the matter?"

"Candace texted me," he says, turning to look at his parents now. "It was not okay." His teeth clench when he says this.

"Hey." I turn his face to mine. "It's not a big deal," I whisper and get up to stand in front of him. "Now, how about we take the goal scorer to get some food?"

"I'm dying to eat," Matthew says, then looks at Evan. "Good game out there."

"Thanks," he mumbles, and everyone gets their things together. "Go ahead. We will meet you there."

Everyone walks out, leaving us alone together. He cups my face and kisses me. "Are you okay?"

"Yes," I tell him, trying not to feel sorry for myself. So what if his sister hates me.

"She was going to blindside you," he says, and I look down, not sure of myself. I don't think I can mask that hurt. "She said she wasn't thinking."

"Please don't make it a big deal," I whisper.

"It's a big deal," he says, getting loud. "It's a huge fucking deal. You were nervous to meet my mother and father, and then she brings my ex-girlfriend." He looks down. "I dated her for a month."

I shake my head. "I honestly don't even care," I tell him. "Truthfully, I don't care." Then I look at him weirdly. "Wow, must be what it's like to be mature and shit." I laugh now. "I mean the old Zara would have been putting sugar in her gas tank." I hold my stomach. "But now I just don't want you to be bothered with it."

"I love you," he tells me.

"I know," I answer him. "Everyone is coming over tomorrow, and your mother is going to teach me how to make beef stroganoff." His smiles now, and I wrap my hands around his neck. "I'm going to try to learn."

His arms go around me, and he brings me in close, his forehead resting on mine. "I'm sorry that she did that."

"Do you love me?" I ask him.

"With everything," he answers.

"Then in the end, I win," I tell him, going to get my coat. "Now can we go eat please? I was so nervous I didn't eat anything, and I had a shot of tequila." He takes my hands in his, and we walk out of the lodge and toward our waiting family.

"Shh," he whispers when he slides into me from behind. His hands grip my hips, pulling them up. "It's almost seven," he says, and my eyes stay closed.

"One more time," he says, and I bury my face into the pillow while he fucks me. So fucking slow, I try to meet his thrusts, but he stops me. "Not yet, beautiful," he says to me, and I slip a hand under me. My chest still lying on the bed, the only thing up are my hips, my finger finds my clit that is already wet. I know he played with me before sliding in, I felt it softly. "Are you playing with your clit, beautiful?" he asks me, whispering still.

"Hmm," I mumble as my finger goes slowly in a circle. We've already done this three times since we got home. The both of us always needing the other one.

"Fuck," he hisses. "Get there, beautiful." I know that tone— he's waiting for me to go before he does—so I work myself faster.

"You're right there," he says. "I feel your pussy getting

tighter." He isn't wrong; I close my eyes, and I'm right there. I finally let go and so does he. He collapses beside me.

"I didn't want to wake you," he says, "but you did a sound."

I laugh, asking him, "What sound?"

"That little sigh," he tells me, and I watch him get up and walk to the bathroom.

"You mean breathing?" I say, laughing, and he comes back out. "You know I'm on the pill, right?" He grabs me, pulling me toward him. "We don't really have to use condoms."

"Beautiful," he says, and we hear the dogs bark and then the back door open.

"I guess my mother is up," he tells me. I think back to the dinner we had. No one touched the topic of Candace. But having a meal with everyone as we chatted and laughed, and Jackie told us that Evan actually had a trading card of my father was funny. He actually blushed.

I throw the covers off me and try to get up, but he pulls me back to him. "Where are you going?"

"Your mother is up," I hiss at him while he kisses my neck. "I'm going to get up and see if she needs anything."

"She doesn't need anything," he says into my neck. "I need something." He pushes his cock into my backside.

"You got what you needed, and now your mother is up, so the chances of you actually getting that thing in me are slim to none." I push him away and go into the closet to dress in yoga pants and a top. "Why don't you rest, and I'll come wake you in a bit?"

"I don't like sleeping without you," he huffs, but I bend and kiss his lips. "Don't be a child."

I walk out of the room, leaving him in the bed with his eyes shutting. "Good morning," I whisper, looking in the kitchen at Jackie who stands there basically wearing the same thing I am.

"Oh, I'm so sorry. Did I wake you?" she says, smiling at me, and I shake my head and go to the door, opening it for the dogs.

"Hello, my girl." I pet Lilo. "Did you eat?"

"I was just going to do that," Jackie says.

"I'll do it," I tell her. "Come on, you two, let's go get you something to eat." I walk to the garage and put some food in their bowls and then walk back into the kitchen.

"I don't know how you take your coffee," Jackie says, handing me a cup of black coffee.

"Thank you," I tell her and go to the fridge, grabbing the milk.

"Why are you up so early?" I ask her.

"I was going to run to the grocery store before everyone got up," she tells me. "Grab the stuff we need for today."

"I'll come with you," I tell her, and she smiles while we write a grocery list. We walk out of the house and make it back just as Zoe is coming down the stairs.

"How are you up already?" she says, rubbing her eyes. "It's just after ten."

"We went to grab the food for lunch," I tell her, and she just shrugs. "There are sill some bags in the car." I hand her the bags in my hand and go back out for another trip.

"Evan is going to be pissed you lifted a bag all by yourself," Zoe says when I put the last bag on the counter in the middle of the island. "Speak of the devil," she says, looking over at Evan who is walking into the kitchen rubbing his eyes. "Evan, your woman lifted her own bags."

"Why didn't you wake me?" He hugs me from behind, burying his face in my neck. "I would have gotten the things from the car."

"Because you were sleeping," I tell him. "Do you want coffee?"

"Yeah," he whispers to me, and I get him coffee. I get him coffee, and his father comes into the kitchen just as we are preparing the ingredients. I sit at the stool, making a list of what she's preparing. I'm so into it I don't even notice that the front door opens and closes, and I look over to see Candace coming in the house.

"Hey," she says to everyone. "Mom told me that we were cooking at noon." She looks around, and I can tell she is uncomfortable. "I hope it's okay that I came."

Zoe pffts out behind her coffee cup, and I look at her, but Candace doesn't stop speaking. "Can I speak with you?"

I look at Evan who is glaring at her. "Sure," I tell her. "Why don't we go outside?" I get off my stool, and Zoe gets up also. "I've got this," I tell her, and she just sits back down.

I walk outside, and Candace follows me, and I look behind her to see Evan coming out. "You don't need to come."

"No way in fuck you are going to be outside by yourself," he hisses, and the dogs follow him.

"So what's the story, Cand?" Evan asks her.

"I wanted to apologize for yesterday," she says softly, wringing her hands. "I was out of line, and I never should have brought her with me."

"Damn fucking straight," Evan says, and I shake my head

at him.

"Evan," I tell him, and he just looks at me. "Would you please just give her a chance to speak?"

"Give her a chance?" he huffs out. "Twice she did that to you. There is not going to be a third time."

"He's right," Candace says. "There won't be a third time." She looks at her brother and then at me. "I don't know what came over me."

"I do," I tell her. "You were the only woman in his life, and you thought I would come in and shake shit up." I take a deep breath. "Head bitch in charge." She laughs now. "I don't want to take your place or step on toes."

"Trust me, I know," she finally says. "I got read the riot act yesterday from everyone. Even Chloe and she is the silent one."

"I know I was a total bitch," she says, "but I swear …"

"You were a bitch," I tell her, "and what you did was hurtful." I swallow. "And I won't take it anymore. If you can't be in the same room as me without containing yourself, then …"

"I can contain myself," she tells me then looks at Evan. "I swear one more time."

"You aren't getting another after this," I tell her, "and if you pull shit today with my family here, I won't be held accountable for what happens."

"Deal," she says. "One more chance."

"We should go in. Your mother is a nervous wreck. She's been to the door seven times," I tell them. "Did you have coffee?" I ask her.

"Not yet. I came right over after I got up," she tells me.

"Let's get you some coffee," I tell her, and we walk back

in the house. I was not wrong about Jackie being a nervous wreck. She is sitting at the island now with Patrick behind her. "Let's get Candace some coffee."

THIRTY

EVAN

"**T**HE CAR IS going to be here in ten minutes," I shout at the bathroom while I shrug on my tux jacket. We've been back in New York for the past three weeks. The season ended when we went head to head against Washington and lost five games in.

"I'm almost done," she shouts from the bathroom. When she comes out, I stop and look at her. Her hair is tied to one side, and she's wearing her makeup heavier than usual. "I just have to get into the dress, and I'm ready." She rushes to her walk-in closet and comes back out, and I look at the dress. "Can you zip me?" She smiles at me. I walk to her and zip her dress up in the back, kissing her neck.

She turns and smooths down the dress. "How does it look?" she asks me, and I look at her as she stands in front of me in a rose gold gown to the floor. The mesh around the legs gives you a look at her legs. A peekaboo effect.

"You look stunning," I tell her, "as usual."

"Are you packed?" she asks me, and I nod my head. We are on our way to Matthew and Max's retirement party. Lunch at my house went off with so many hitches. The onions got burnt to a crisp because Mom was talking and Zara was taking notes, and by the time they noticed, it was too late. So they started again, and this time, it went smoothly until they added the cream, and by mistake, the heat was turned up, and it boiled over onto the stove. Then talking and talking, they forgot the pasta on the stove, or actually one thought the other was taking care of it, and it turned out no one was, and the water had boiled out. I'm surprised the fire department wasn't called. But in the end, we sat at the dining room table eating pizza, and I took a look around and knew that this was my future. I just had to ask her the burning question. My parents are also coming tonight, along with Candace who has done a three sixty, and the two of them are thick as thieves when she's in Dallas.

"I'm packed," I tell her, my bag to Mexico at the door. "My parents said they would come and meet us."

"Oh really, that will be so nice," she says. "Will they stay with us?"

"Fuck no," I tell her. "I don't like fucking you when you're quiet."

She glares at me. "You better watch yourself," she says, and I know she's lying. Our sex life didn't slow down. In fact, it is more active than ever. "How are Lilo and Stitch?" she asks me.

"They were fine when I dropped them off, and we can always log in and see how they are doing." Another thing,

Lilo and Stitch came with us when we came to New York.

"Lilo is not going to be happy when she comes back," Zara says, putting on one shoe and then the other. "Last time, she ate my pink Louboutin." I laugh and get a notification that the car is here.

We walk out of the house, and I open the car door for her, and we make our way to the gala. "How big is this thing going to be?" I ask her.

"Knowing Karrie and Allison"—she looks over—"massive." I kiss her hand, and she is not wrong. When we show up at the hotel, we walk in, and it's a who's who in sports. I look over and see that even A-Rod and Jennifer Lopez are here. We walk in, and the room is massive, and pictures spanning Matthew's and Max's career are hanging everywhere.

"There she is," Zoe says. I look over and see that she is wearing almost the same color except her dress has a high slit on the side, showing you her long leg. She comes over and kisses Zara and then greets me with a hug.

I look around and see that Matthew and Max are standing almost in the middle with Allison and Karrie beside them. "Hey, there." I feel a slap on my shoulder and look up and see Cooper. "Isn't this something?"

I grab a glass of champagne from a passing waiter. "It's something."

"Matthew is fucking dying," he says quietly. "He thought this was going to be a small get-together. You should have seen his face when he walked in." Over the past month, I've gotten to know Matthew and Max really well. We even went golfing, and no one tried to kill me.

"If I can get everyone's attention," someone says, and

then a spotlight comes on. "Wow, that is bright," the man says, and I recognize him right away as Karrie's father, Doug. He owns the team along with a shitload of other media companies. "If everyone can take their seats," he says. The room slowly falls into place, and everyone finally takes their seat. He is standing on the stage in front of the fifty tables that are set up.

I follow Zara, and I see my parents already sitting at the big round table in front of the stage. I bend to kiss my mother and grab my dad's shoulder, and he just nods at me. Zara sits next to my mother, and my mother gushes over her as usual.

"On behalf of Cooney Communication, I want to thank you guys for coming out tonight to pay tribute to our captain and assistant captain as they hang up their skates." Everyone applauds them. "A very long time ago," he starts talking and then laughs when Matthew's face shows up on the screen beside the stage. "This little punk." He laughs. "I took a chance on this man who everyone crossed off their list."

I look at Matthew who looks at Karrie. She just smiles at him and kisses him. "I love you," she tells him.

"Not only did he come in and turn the team around, but he also became my son-in-law," Doug says, his voice full of pride. "On and off the ice, he puts one hundred percent dedication into everything. I've seen him scrap on the ice and end up with five stitches on his face, and the next day hold a tea party for his girls." Everyone laughs except Matthew who shakes his head. "I knew the time would come when this moment would happen, but I knew that the

Stingers wouldn't be what they are without him." He smiles while everyone claps. "It gives me great honor to announce today at his retirement party that the New York Stingers just signed him to be our new general manager." There are gasps and then clapping. "I believe he has a couple of announcements himself."

"Oh, dear lord," Zoe says. "I swear if she is pregnant again, I'm going to die." Karrie looks over at her and flips her the bird.

Matthew walks upon stage and shakes Doug's hand and then gives him a hug as they exchange words.

He steps up to the microphone. "Thank you so much for that introduction." He looks at Doug who just nods at him. "What he didn't say was that he was also at that tea party." Doug throws his head back and laughs along with everyone else.

"I don't even know where to begin with this," he says, and then he looks at Karrie. "Before accepting this position, I knew that I couldn't do it without the support of my wife and kids." Karrie nods at him. "I also knew that I couldn't do it without my partner in crime." Everyone looks at Max. "This"— and I swear he is going to say fucker, but he doesn't—"this guy. We didn't really start off on the right track." Max now throws his head back and laughs. "We entered the biggest pissing contest of all pissing contests." The crowd laughs, and Matthew leans closer to the microphone. "I won."

"He wishes he won," Max says.

"But I warmed up to him slowly and started trusting him on the ice and off the ice. Did you know he dated my sister right under my nose?" He points at Max who pulls Allison to him and kisses her. "She's still my sister." Oh, the crowd is roaring, and I swear these two can put on a comedy show. "Anyway, fast forward some years and throw in a couple of kids, and he's family, plain and simple, and that is what the Stinger organization stands for. Family." Everyone claps. I look over at Cooper who I swear beams with so much pride it's bursting out of him.

"So as the new GM of the Stingers, I knew that if I had to do this job and do it well, I needed him at my back. So I am happy to introduce you to the newest scouting agent for the New York Stingers." Everyone claps, and Max gets up and now walks on stage where they share a bro hug. "Do you want to say a few words?" Matthew asks him, and he just shakes his head no.

"Okay, so before we start this celebration, there is one last huge announcement," Matthew says, and everyone looks around the table to see if they know what they are talking about.

"I love you." I put my hand around Zara's shoulder, my thumb rubbing her bare arm. "With everything I am, I love you." She looks at me and tilts her head to the side.

"With the both of us retiring," Matthew says, "we knew that we needed two great players to fill those big skates we are leaving behind. And we knew that we had to go big or go home." He leans in to the mic. "So after much going back and forth, we finally agreed on the person who would fill one of those skates. Ladies and gentlemen, I am happy to say that earlier today, as my first order of GM the New York Stingers, we signed Evan Richards." I watch Zara's face as she turns to me, and I see the tears in her eyes, and she sobs.

"You did this for me?" she asks me, putting her hand to her mouth to try to stop the sobs.

"No, I did it for us." It's the last thing I can say to her because everyone at the table is standing up. I lean over and kiss her lips, and then I stand, going to my father and hugging him and then to my mother who is also sobbing. I walk to the stage, but Cooper stops me and smiles big.

"Welcome to the family, son," he says, hugging me, and I nod at him. I walk to the stage where Matthew and Max stand holding my new jersey.

"Don't think I didn't see you kissing my sister," Matthew says, and I shake my head. "It's going to be a good year," he says, shaking my hand. I stand there in the middle of them both holding up the jersey in my hand. Matthew finishes the speech, and I was giving him one more minute before walking off the stage. Zara was sitting with our mothers on her side as she silently cried, and it was killing me.

I shake Doug's hand and then make my way to Zara who gets up and throws herself in my arms. One of her hands goes to my cheek. "I'm sorry I didn't tell you." I smile at her and wipe away a tear with one of my thumbs. "I wanted to surprise you."

"You did all this for me?" she asks me, and I still shake my head.

"I did this for us," I tell her. "For me and for you and for Lilo and Stitch and our kids."

"Our kids?" she asks me, and I take the second biggest leap of faith today as I get down on one knee in the middle of everyone, my family and her family.

Zoe is the first one to gasp, and then all eyes are on me. "Zara Stone, check your Twitter account," I tell her, and she looks around.

"Someone get me a phone," she shouts. My sister steps forward wearing a smile and hands over her phone. No doubt planning what I told her to do. Zara looks down at the phone and sobs.

@ZaraStone will you be willing to change your name to @ZaraRichards.

"What started off as a simple tweet became the best thing to ever happen to me," I tell her and see that our mothers are hugging. "I don't just want you to be my girlfriend. I want you to be my wife, and I want you to be the mother of my children. I want to commit the rest of my life to making you happy." I grab the black box that I also picked up today after I signed the contract. "Will you be my wife?"

"Yes," she says, nodding her head. The whole crowd cheers, and when I look over, I see we are on the screens. She comes to me and grabs my face in her hands. "Yes, I'll marry you."

So there in the middle of five hundred people, she agrees to be my wife. I slip the five-carat princess cut rose gold diamond ring on her finger and seal it with a kiss and not just a little peck. I seal it so everyone knows she's mine.

"Dude, that is still my sister," Matthew says behind me, and we both laugh.

"This has to be the craziest thing that has ever happened to me," she says.

"Beautiful, this is just the beginning of our crazy!"

EPILOGUE

ZARA

"YOU NEED TO leave," I whisper when he finally collapses on top of me. "Everyone is going to be here soon, and it's bad luck for you to be here."

"It's bad luck for me not to start the day with you in my arms," he says into my neck, and I turn in his arms. "Why did we agree to this big ass wedding anyway?"

"Um, because your mother said she would kill you, and then my father seconded that motion." I remind him of the conversation we had at Christmastime after we moved into our own home.

When he accepted the offer with the team, the first thing he wanted was to buy us our own home. With the flooding at Zoe's place and her living with us, it became his mission. But he just didn't have one mission, he wanted to be close to my family. Now the only thing wrong with that is there were no houses for sale. Until one day there was, and it wasn't anywhere near what we were looking for, but he didn't care that this house had ten rooms, or that he would need a golf cart to make it from one side of the yard to the other.

I wanted to contribute to the house, but that got me a long side look from him, and no matter how much I complained about it to everyone, they just shrugged. "It's my duty to take care and provide for you," he kept saying.

My mother would offer advice, and it sucked. "Pick your battles." I didn't really know what she meant, but I knew that eventually I would have to find a battle to fight.

Zara's Closet was also the biggest talk of the town. After I dressed seven of the A-listers at the last Oscars, designers were beating down my door to work with me. I had more work than I had time, and even though I was in demand, I still made my own schedule. I traveled when I knew that Evan would be on the road, and when he was home, so was I. I knew that I didn't want us to be apart any more than we needed to be, so the decision was made for me. Or was it really?

"You need to go," I tell him, not letting go of him or even moving away from him. "If they find you in here—"

"Then they find me in here," he says, and I just smile and close my eyes, basking in his arms. I wish I could say that we didn't adapt well to living with each other. I wish I could tell you that the spark that you have at the beginning had dwindled down. I wish I could tell you that after over a year together, it was just same old, same old, but it wasn't. It's so much more. I have a connection with him that I didn't know I could have except with Zoe.

"Oh, my God." I hear Zoe shrieking from the doorway. "I thought we told you not to be here."

Instead of him feeling guilty, he just looks at her. "Don't you knock?"

"I knock when I know you are home," she tells him, folding her arms over her chest. "I don't knock when I'm sleeping right down the hall, and you aren't supposed to be here."

"I live here," he says to her, trying to hide his smile. Zoe and he have a special bond, a bond that was so important for me. A bond I didn't even know I wanted them to have. They both have my best interests at heart, they both team up when they know it's good for me, and they both really just love each other.

"I'm sure you could be without her for twenty-four hours, Evan." She shakes her head. "I'm not going to tell anyone you are here." She turns to walk out of the room. "But I won't deny it either." She closes the door.

"We should get up." I look over at the clock, seeing it's almost eight. "The hair and makeup people are going to be here at eight thirty."

"Fine," he finally says and rolls away from me, getting out of the bed and putting on his shorts that were right next to his side of the bed. And a soft knock on the door makes me look at him and smile.

"Come in," I say. I'm shocked when both of our mothers walk in the room. As soon as they see Evan, their smiles slide off their faces.

"I told you it's bad luck," his mother shouts at him. "I put your father in charge of you."

"Mom," he says, and my mother just rolls her lips. "I know

what you told me, but I'm not going to spend the night without Zara just because of an old wives' tale."

Jackie turns to my mother who just shrugs her shoulders. "I'm just happy he didn't throw her over his shoulder and elope."

"Will I ever live that down?" Allison says from the hallway.

"No," Karrie says from beside her, and they both walk into the room. "Isn't this a shocker?"

"Well, I see someone glowing this morning," Allison teases me, and I put my hands to my cheeks.

"Where is he?" I hear Matthew shout from downstairs and then hear him running up the steps. Evan tosses me his shirt to replace the cover. I slip it on, looking up at the mothers who look at each other and then see Allison and Karrie now trying not to laugh. "Dude, seriously, we left you at eleven, and you had strict orders to go to bed."

"And I did," Evan says. "I just did it in my own bed."

"Where is Zoe?" Matthew asks, and she walks into the room with a mimosa followed by Vivienne.

"I am right here," she says, walking to the bed and handing me the mimosa. "Why is this my fault?"

"You were supposed to make sure he didn't come in here," Matthew tells her, putting his hands on his hips.

"Well, it looks like someone shouldn't be wearing white today," Vivienne says, holding up her drink and smiling.

"Is he here?" I hear my father yelling, and then I look at Evan who I swear doesn't even bat an eyelash at having our whole family standing in our bedroom. "Son," my father says, poking his head into the room and then spotting my mother. He smiles at her and kisses her. "You can't be here."

"I can be here," Evan says. "One, I own the house, and two, she's here." He points at me. "And where she is, so am I."

"Well, I can't argue with that logic," my father says, and Matthew just nods.

"Now that we have that settled," Evan says, leaning down and kissing me. "I love you." He walks to the now crowd of people at the entrance to our bedroom. He kisses his mother and then mine on the cheek and then walks out without a shirt because I'm wearing it.

"You get up and wash yourself," Allison says. "We are going to be downstairs getting our drink on."

I shake my head as everyone but Zoe walks out of the room. "What do you need me to do?'

"Hold my hand." She nods at me, and I get out of the bed and walk to the bathroom, opening the little test and peeing on the stick. I walk out of the bathroom. "Three minutes," I tell her and go back to the bed. My hands shaking. "I should really drink something."

"Here is your virgin mimosa," she tells me. "It tastes gross, by the way."

"It's orange juice," I tell her.

"I know, but if you call it a mimosa, I'm expecting bubbly, and not getting it makes it gross." She doesn't say anything she just holds my hand. "Does he know you're late?"

"No." I shake my head. "I didn't even know until last night when I knocked over my tampons." Last night right before we left for the rehearsal dinner, I had a mini meltdown when I knocked over my tampons. I ran to my office and checked the calendar and realized I was nine days late. But I thought it was stress, so the first person I called was Zoe, and I begged her to get me a test.

"What in the hell are you guys still doing up here?" Allison asks and then stops midway into the room. "What happened?"

I try to hold it together and not let her see that I'm freaking out. "Nothing," I say and then put my hand to my mouth, blocking the sob.

"She's just really happy to be getting married," Zoe tries to say, but Allison doesn't move from her spot, and I don't have a chance to say anything because Evan comes into the room.

"I forgot …" he says and then stops when he sees me with tears running down my face. "What happened? What's wrong?" He looks at us, and he comes to me, kneeling in front of me. "Beautiful," he says and then he looks at Zoe, asking for help. I don't hear Karrie come back into the room nor do I hear our mothers.

"Did you change your mind?" he asks, grabbing my hands in his. "We don't have to get married." He brings my hands to his mouth. "We do not need to get married at all."

"That isn't why I'm crying," I tell him when I see the worry fill his face. I get up and hold out my hand to him. "Will you come with me?" He nods, and I look over at our mothers who are now holding hands with tears in their eyes. "The wedding is still happening," I tell them and walk into the huge ass bathroom. "Sit," I tell him, and he sits on the little seat I have in there.

"Beautiful," he says, his voice almost cracking. "I don't know how much longer I can take this."

I walk to the counter and pick up the test not looking

at it. "I'm late," I tell him in a whisper, and he looks at me confused. "My period." Two words making his eyes open. "I didn't know before last night, and well, I had a mini panic attack and forced Zoe to buy a test for me."

"Are you?" he asks. I walk to him, standing in the middle of his legs. His hands go to my hips as he looks up at me.

"I haven't looked yet," I tell him and hand him the test.

He turns the test over, and we both look down at the word that is on the middle of the test.

Pregnant

I look at the word, and then the tears fill my eyes. We never planned on getting pregnant. And I know that when I got sick last month, they told me that the pill would not work with the antibiotics so we were just a touch careful, not ever thinking it could happen right away. My hand goes to my stomach while he brings my stomach to his mouth.

"Beautiful," he whispers and kisses my belly, then pushes the shirt up and kisses it again. "I love you." My hands go to his hair, rubbing it softly, and he looks up at me.

"We are going to have a baby," he whispers to me, and I just nod at him, the tears flowing like a waterfall down my face. He puts his ear to my stomach. "I wonder if I can hear the heartbeat." Only he can make me cry and laugh at the same time.

"Are you guys going to be long in there?" I hear Zoe softly say from outside of the door.

"What do you want to tell them?" he asks me, and I just shrug my shoulders. "You know that Zoe is going to know." I nod at him. "Hell, she'll probably go through the pregnancy feeling your pain."

He gets up, taking my face in his hands and kissing me on the lips. "I love you with everything that I have, with every beat of my heat, and with every fiber of my soul."

"That better not be your vows," I joke with him, and now we hear men's voices also. "We have to get out there, or I think they are going to break down the door."

"What do you mean she was crying? Why was she crying?" I hear my dad, and his voice goes higher and higher.

I unlock the door and open it, and there in the middle of our master bedroom is everyone who means something to us. My father has my mother in his arms as he tries to comfort her. Patrick doing the same to Jackie but now with Candace standing beside them. Matthew and Max stand behind Karrie and Allison. Vivienne and Zoe both sit on the bed with Vivienne's arm around Zoe's shoulders.

I stand there beside the man who answered a crazy random Twitter date request, the man who brings me coffee, the man who holds my door open for me, the man who sends me flowers just because, the man who owns not half my heart but the whole thing. The man I know I want to grow old with, I want to have babies with, and I want to bitch about. He puts his arm around my shoulder and pulls me to him, kissing my forehead. I wrap my arm around his waist. "I know this is crazy," I start, and the tears and laughter come at the same time, "but we're having a baby."

Everyone gasps in shock. Zoe shoots to her feet and comes to me, hugging me. Everyone else comes to us all.

"Well, is she still going to wear the white dress?" Vivienne asks from the bed, taking a sip of my mimosa from before. "This is disgusting. It's just orange juice."

And just like that, the room burst into laughter, the only thing never changing is that Evan never leaves my side. Even when the hair and makeup people come, he doesn't leave. The only time he does leave is when I have to get into my wedding dress.

Thirty minutes later, I'm walking down the aisle on the arm of my father toward the man who I know is going to do everything in his power to take care of me. "I never thought I would see the day that I would be walking you down the aisle," my father whispers in my ear as we walk slowly smiling as we pass people he knows. "The first boy who said he liked you. Do you remember what you did to him?" I look over her and shake my head. "You kicked him in the balls."

"Oh right," I say, thinking back. "But in my defense, you actually told me to do that."

"Yeah." He laughs. "Don't ever tell your mother that."

We finally get down the aisle, and he stands his arm never letting me go. "Who gives this woman to be wed?"

"Her family does," he says, and then he looks over at Evan. "Welcome to the family, son." And then, just like that, he hands me over to the man who was always in my dreams.

MATTHEW

Three Months Later . . .

"The plane will be landing in five minutes, Mr. Grant," the flight attendant says before going to her seat, and I look out the window. Nothing but greenery, but what do you expect? It's Arizona. The plane touches down smoothly, and I unbuckle my seat belt and get up, pulling down the cuffs of my sleeves. I put my aviator glasses on and grab the leather backpack that Karrie got me when they finally announced I was the general manager for the New York Stingers last year. I have a whole season under my belt, and as much as it pains me to say, we fell short. There is no way to sugarcoat shit because it is what it is. It just wasn't our season. The pieces are definitely coming together, which is another reason I'm here in Arizona.

My latest trade. Some say it's general manager suicide, but I see it the other way. When the plane to the door opens, the stairs fall out, and I walk out with the warm heat hitting my face. It's already scorching, and it's only eleven. I walk down the four steps to the waiting black SUV parked there. The driver steps out of the car. "Mr. Grant?" He nods his head. "Pleasure to meet you," he says, opening the back door, and I get into the cool car. I take my phone out and send a text to Karrie, telling her I arrived. I'm not going to be here long, but by the time I get back home, it will be late.

I look out and see the palm trees as we drive down the highway. I check my email; with the season almost starting, it's time to get back into the thick of it, and this year, I'm going for the cup.

We pull into the parking lot of the Silver Spring Recovery Center, and the car stops under the awning. I get out of the car and look around. It almost looks like a hotel, but I know it's not.

I walk into the front door, and I'm greeted by the girl at the desk who smiles. "Welcome to Silver Spring Recovery Center, how may I help you today?"

"Hi there, my name is Matthew Grant, and I'm here to pick up Viktor Petrov," I tell her, and she nods her head.

"He was in the waiting area," she tells me and gets up from her desk. "If you will follow me," she says and leads me to a door she has to scan a card to open. We walk down a hallway that is all windows, and the sun is shining in. It really looks like a spa; she turns the corner and enters this huge room with four televisions on each wall all playing something different. A loveseat and two single seats are situated in front of each television. I look around to see a couple of people sitting in the room. A lone guy watches a sports channel, and I have no doubt who that is watching the show.

I walk over to him and look at him. Fuck, he must have hit the gym hard while he was in here. He for sure is about thirty pounds heavier, and fuck, if he isn't bigger than he was in May, and he actually looks healthy. He spots me and turns, and I see his hair is longer on top than normal. "Well, look at this. I get the VIP treatment." He smiles and gets up, holding his hand out to me.

"Figured I'd give you a lift home," I tell him, and he just nods. He picks up the bag that I just noticed on the floor beside him. "Have you been discharged?" I ask him, and he just nods. "Then let's hit the road. The plane is waiting."

He follows me out and says hello to the receptionist, giving her a little wink when he leaves, and the woman just sighs while he walks out of the door. The car ride to the plane is silent, and when he gets on the plane, he sits down in the chair in front of me. The attendant comes over and asks if we would like something to drink.

"Water, please," Viktor asks her. Even though I know he's

American and grew up in Russia, I expected him to have a Russian accent, but he doesn't; it's barely there. I order the same and wait for her to deliver the drink and for the plane to be in the air to start the meeting.

"I bet you're wondering why I signed you?" I ask him, and his dark blue eyes just stare at me.

"I know why you signed me," he says. "You'd be a fool not to sign me."

I laugh now. "You think very highly of yourself." He just shrugs. "But I can't ignore that when you're on the ball, you are on the ball."

"That's why you signed me," he says, taking a sip of his water.

"You're right, but I didn't sign you for the bullshit that you have been pulling for the past two years," I tell him, cutting to the chase. "Listen, I've been down. Fuck, my career was nonexistent when I went back home with my tail between my legs, but I got a chance." I watch him. "A very big chance and now I'm giving you yours."

He doesn't say anything, and I don't let him or give him room to say anything. "We are piss testing you weekly until I think it's good enough. If don't like the terms, you can leave now." He glares but doesn't say anything. "We have you staying in Max's loft for a month for you to get your stuff settled."

"I need to find a realtor," he says. "I have my stuff waiting to be shipped from LA."

"Already ahead of you there. My sister Zoe will meet with you tomorrow afternoon," I tell him. "She is the best there is, and if there is a house out there, she knows about it." He nods again, not saying a word. He doesn't say anything for the rest of the flight. He does eat, though; he eats everything they put in front of him.

When the wheels finally touch down, I look at him. "Welcome home, Viktor. Welcome to New York."

Appearing

www.ingramcontent.com/pod-product-compliance
Lightning Source LLC
Chambersburg PA
CBHW071347300726
48976CB00006B/1802